Jenny Colgan

sphere

SPHERE

First published in Great Britain in 2009 by Sphere

A CIP catalogue record for this book
is available from the British Library.

ISBN 978-1-84744-158-4

Typeset in Caslon by M Rules
Printed and bound in Great Britain by
Clays Ltd, St Ives plc

Papers used by Sphere are natural, renewable and recyclable
products made from wood grown in sustainable forests and certified
in accordance with the rules of the Forest Stewardship Council.

Mixed Sources
Product group from well-managed
forests and other controlled sources
www.fsc.org Cert no. SGS-COC-004081
© 1996 Forest Stewardship Council

FSC

Sphere
An imprint of
Little, Brown Book Group
100 Victoria Embankment
London EC4Y 0DY

An Hachette Livre UK Company
www.hachettelivre.co.uk

www.littlebrown.co.uk

To Jo and Al. Thanks for everything!

Acknowledgements

Thanks to my family, the board, the ever-supportive Feb mums, the École de Spectacle ghetto and especially my brilliant, gorgeous and patient Mr B, and the terrific wee Bs.

Part One

Now

Chapter One

Ever since I started working, I've always thought that everyone should get a day off the first time in the year that the sun shines. You know, the morning when you wake up and see blue in the corner of the window and smell spring in the air and your heart leaps. Don't you think everyone should just automatically get the day off to go out and enjoy it?

Obviously people might disagree on when this day actually occurs, and you'd maybe have to have an agreement about what temperature it had to be, and then everyone in Scotland would get really pissed off, and, well – it would probably be a bit difficult to administer, especially if the hospitals all suddenly shut down and things. OK. Maybe it's not the *best* idea I've ever had.

Right, how about everyone gets a 'sunshine' day a year and they choose when they take it, like some people get duvet days? Everyone just knows the day, don't they? You can tell on the street; it's weird, people smile at each other and stuff. Huh. So we're back to the problem of losing all the hospitals and policemen – and traffic wardens, so I'm not saying it would be an *out and out* disaster.

But, anyway. Today is a lovely day, and I am – we are – taking it off and going to the seaside!

Well, maybe not strictly *taking it off*. There are a few advantages to being a freelance photographer – mostly being able to work in your pyjamas, but on the downside, it does get annoying when people say, 'Hey, Sophie, do you go to work in your pyjamas *every* day?'

Anyway, it means you're always thinking about work, even on an official DAY OFF. But that's OK, because I've figured out a way to combine things. Which is why, right at this moment, I'm jumping up and down on the bed. Persuasive tactics.

'Come on! Come on! Let's go to the beach! And I'll do your pictures there!' He slowly opens one eye. 'Sophie. What on earth are you doing?'

'Look! Look out of the window!' I babble.

'How old are you, six?'

'What do you see that wasn't there before?'

'Uh, they've covered up the graffiti? The feral cats have all died?' So, we don't have the world's nicest view.

'Sunshine! There's sunshine! Let's go and take photos!'

'Can I have breakfast?'

'We could have an ice cream for breakfast!'

He thinks for a minute. 'Yeah, all right.'

*

It's hard not to get a little bit excited, walking against the flow of commuters as we leave for Southend with beach towels. Maybe I should go out with a beach towel all the time; I get as many envious looks as if I am carrying the latest Birkin, and it's all I can do not to bounce up and down on the dusty, mottled train carriage seats as I watch the grey buildings of London fade behind us, and the flat lands of Essex spread out ahead.

Apart from a few dog-walkers, the beach is deserted – and absolutely perfect. The air is a little fresher here, out of the city, but the sky is a soft scuddy blue, and the sun feels warm and life-giving, coming after such a long winter. I want to stretch out and luxuriate in it, like a cat. I turn my back to the sun so I can feel it through my clothes, and close my eyes.

'Ahhhhh,' I say.

He smiles. 'Happy?'

You know, it seems such an innocuous question, but it makes me pause. I look around at the dunes, at the old-fashioned hotels that still line the front, looking dilapidated this early in the season. I watch a dog run after a seagull, the dog clearly barking its head off but too far away to be heard.

Am I happy? It's been such a long time since I could answer this question in any kind of a positive way. It's hard to think about the kind of person I used to be.

I smile. 'Well,' I say, getting out my beloved Leica, 'yes. Although I'd be even happier if you can find somewhere open that sells fish and chips.'

5

He smiles. 'You are just so high maintenance.'

'But first,' I order, brandishing the camera, 'lots of you looking moody in the middle distance.'

I study him through my lens. He's not traditionally handsome, I suppose. Which suits me just fine, I'm not traditionally pretty. Pale, light skinned. I used to have long blonde hair I parted in the middle like Gwyneth Paltrow, until I met a drippy man at a party with *exactly the same hair*. Not only that, but he then dedicated a song to me on his acoustic guitar, which was mildly exciting until he opened his mouth and sounded like a twenty-four-wasp pile-up. The lyrics were something like 'Oh woman, you ripped my heart into little pieces of shit', which I wasn't very impressed about since he'd only just met me and everything. I cut my hair quite soon after that.

'Look solemn,' I instruct, which is difficult to say to a man who has a small piece of ice cream on his cheek – a leftover from our Magnum breakfast (white chocolate, of course. Dark chocolate is very much an after-dinner Magnum).

He sighs. 'Why?'

'Because you have to look like a great artist eagerly awaiting inspiration for his next masterpiece. I'm taking some shots for your new brochure.'

'Shh! Don't jinx us. Can't I just look like a cheerful artist eagerly awaiting his next cheque?'

'No-oh. That's a bad look.'

'What about a starving artist who doesn't know how he's going to pay the water bill?'

'Let me see it,' I instruct. 'Hmm. No. It's a bit disappointed-looking.'

'I was very, very disappointed by our water bill.'

'Shh! Look out to sea then.'

'Oh, yes, that'll be great. Then I'll look like I'm about to start sculpting those stripy lighthouses you buy at the seaside.'

I put the camera down. 'There's money in that! That could work!'

'No! We'll pay the water bill. Somehow.'

'I quite like those lighthouses,' I muse. Oh, yeah, that's the other downside to being a freelancer – always being skint.

'Stop! Stop! Please!'

'OK!' I say. 'Deranged! Passionate! Look just like that!'

'You do talk some binkety bollocks,' he complains, but keeps his head still as I shoot frame after frame. With the calm line of the sea behind him, and the sharp lines of his profile, I reckon they should come up rather well in black and white and if this mooted exhibition of his ever comes off, my pics can go in the programme.

Eventually I think I've got my shot and we've both earned our proper breakfast, so he heads off over the dunes.

I settle down on the sand to wait. OK, it's not luxurious Mediterranean weather, but that's kind of nice; there's a freshness off the sea, just in case you forget for one second you are in England. But apart from the waves, it's so quiet. I feel like we're the first people ever to discover this beach. I rest my chin on my hands and just stare out to sea.

Am I happy? Right here? Right now? Pff, it's a big question, with a big answer.

Chapter Two

When I was eleven, my mum died. It's all right, it wasn't your fault – or *was* it? No, I'm kidding, sorry. It's just people always look so upset. It's now over eighteen years ago, and I still hate having to tell people. They always look really stricken and shocked, and I end up saying, 'It's OK,' and somehow comforting them instead.

Up to then I was pretty normal, or at least I think I was. I was quite a shy girl whose main hobbies were beads, Barbie and playing schools. I suppose I lived in a big house but I honestly didn't notice that at the time. I thought everyone had a maid and their own dressing room. Anyway, as far as *that* goes, I would have traded the dressing room, every Barbie ever made and anything else I owned not to have the memory of the day the head teacher came into the classroom and, in an odd, strangled-sounding voice, asked if she could see me in her office.

Here is how I try to remember her. One night, I must have

9

been around seven, they were on their way out – they went out a lot, my mother loved balls and dancing and my father liked to indulge her. She was wearing my favourite dress – she had so many, but most she only wore once or twice. This one came out every year. It was a fuchsia-coloured silk (hey, it was the eighties) which she wore with her blonde hair curled up and a flower in it. My father would put the flower in. He would pretend it was a matter of utmost importance that only he could possibly get right, and would treat it like a serious operation, with lots of Kirby grips and hairspray. He would bend towards her, their profiles nearly touching, and carefully, fussily, arrange the orchid in her hair. Then they'd both turn to me, my mother's eyes sparkling with excitement as she bent down.

'Now,' my father would say. 'Sophia, you must decide. Is your mother acceptable to be seen in decent society?'

And I knew somehow that I had to keep my face very serious as if I was doing a proper inspection. My mother showed me her hair all over, and I'd check it carefully and say, 'Hmm . . .'

And Mummy would say, 'Please! Please tell me, Sophia, have I done enough to pass your inspection?'

And Daddy'd say, 'Yes, if we fail we will miss the party, and you know how your mother hates to miss parties!'

And my mother would make a sad face. After I'd waited as long as I could, I'd finally say, 'Weelll . . . I suppose you pass.'

'Hurrah!' And my mother'd kiss me, leaving sticky fuchsia lipstick on my cheek. My father made out that he was incredibly relieved and they'd promise to bring me back the best cakes from the party. Then my father would lend me his precious Leica and I would take their photograph.

We'd always had these little rituals; the fuchsia dress is the one I remember the most. Later in life I thought how odd it was for them to go to every single party with a little bag and steal the *petits fours*. But they did, because they loved me, and because we were a family, and I think that's when I first picked up my fondness for eating sweet things for breakfast.

After she went, of course, we fell apart. Even though I was eleven, it's a blur in my head. I hadn't realised how well and gently my mother had run the household until she left. Without Esperanza, who helped us, we'd have been eating cold beans out of a can within the week.

My parents' many friends were very sweet, of course, and crowded round and brought casseroles and asked me over to play with their children all the time. Except, weirdly, I always felt that I had to be on my super-best behaviour, otherwise the mothers invariably started to cry, and I hated upsetting everyone.

And after a bit of time had passed, even if I felt a little better and wanted to smile or join in with games, I could see the other girls and their mothers looking at me, as if to say, 'How can that girl play when her mum has died?' And that would make me feel guilty and sad all over again.

Daddy coped with it all by throwing himself into his work. He ran some sort of personal investment blah blah fund blah thing. He'd tried to explain, but I'd never really listened. He hurled himself at it, in fact, and very successfully too, which meant he was always away from home. He felt I needed more structure to my life, and the best opportunities, so he made the decision to send me away to boarding school.

Daddy really did think it was the best way, even though he cried so much saying goodbye to me I ended up patting *him* on the back. The maddest thing was that Kendalls was only about half a mile from where we lived in Chelsea. He didn't want to send me away, he just wanted me to be looked after in a safe environment, somewhere that didn't have memories of my mother spilling out from every face; from every dress, and gate and lamp post.

I did have a romantic idea about boarding school that I personally blame on Malory Towers, and my mother's favourite, *What Katy Did at School.* I wasn't averse to the idea at all. Whilst I wasn't exactly expecting anything to be fun, I thought midnight feasts, pony rides, and playing pranks on the teachers might be quite interesting. Plus, nobody had a mother while they were there, so I'd fit in.

Hmm. Boarding schools in books aren't exactly like real boarding schools. I should have known that, shouldn't I? Instead of lots of fun girls, there were lots of really pretty, quite fierce and frankly intimidating girls.

At first I was quite interesting – my tragic story attracted a lot of attention. As this flurry of interest died down, however, and it became apparent that I didn't yet have an expense account at Harvey Nics, I was left more and more on my own. Being a quiet girl had never mattered before as my parents were always there to listen to me, and I never felt lonely or out of place.

Here, however, I was as lonely and awkward as could be. Until the day I caught Carena Sutherland giving her hamster a pedicure. Did you know hamsters are allergic to nail polish? Me neither. I was just looking for a cupboard to hide in while I ate my lunch by myself. I had absolutely nothing to contribute to the other girl's conversations about diets, boys on television shows I hadn't seen, or music I hadn't listened to. If I'd been less bruised and awkward I'd perhaps have found it easier to meet people I clicked with. But I wasn't, and I didn't.

'*Shit!*' Carena was saying, looking at the clearly dead animal lying on its side.

'What's that?' I asked timidly.

'It's a very, very small orang-utan, what does it look like?' she scoffed, then turned towards me. I shrank backwards. Carena was by far the prettiest, most popular and most frightening girl in our class. Her parents worked away all the time and she said her nanny was going to let her go to nightclubs when she was thirteen. We kind of believed her.

'Don't tell anyone about this, right?' she said in a threatening voice. So I didn't, and I could see her eyeing me approvingly when Mr Carstairs spent twenty minutes grilling us all. I kept my mouth shut.

Two months later, she spoke to me again. My dad had just bought himself a Lamborghini. I have no idea what was going through his head. He must have just woken up one day and thought, Well, I've lost the love of my life – perhaps a big shiny red car will do. Or someone at work recommended it. Certainly he let Brad, his assistant at the time, go and pick it up for him and, on a whim, sent him to pick me up too.

The car made an incredibly loud roar coming up the street. It was bright red and looked absurdly flashy. All the girls came to look at it and then out stepped Brad. He was tall, handsome,

American, gay and extremely sweet to me. Dressed in a stripy shirt, hair perfectly gelled back and sporting big white teeth, he looked like the epitome of our twelve-year-old pin-ups.

'Hey, pretty lady,' he said. 'Want to come for a ride?'

In fact, he just dropped me at my dad's office and I waited an hour for my dad to get out of his meeting, then Daddy and I drove up the King's Road in near silence. Finally, at the top, Daddy turned to me.

'This is stupid, isn't it?' he said.

'Well . . .' I said.

'I thought buying this car would make me feel better.'

'Does it?'

'She'd have hated it, wouldn't she?'

'It's really, really tacky, Dad.'

'Yeah,' he said. 'I should have guessed when Brad liked it so much. Want to go and eat pizza?'

'OK.'

I don't remember ever seeing that car again. It was the first time I realised that my family was quite rich.

And the next day, Carena casually strode past me at break time, pretended to look surprised to see me, then said, 'Oh, Sophie, do you want to go to my house for lunch?'

Just like that. It was comparable, later, to the first time I was ever asked out by a boy (Marcus. Father farmed half of Shropshire. More comfortable talking to animals than girls. His kisses were like being licked by a large horse).

And from then on, we were friends, even when she found out Brad wasn't actually my extremely glamorous and somewhat paedophiliac boyfriend, but an employee of my dad's. She enjoyed my obvious admiration and I couldn't help it – she was dazzling. So sure of herself. My world was confusing and I wasn't sure of the rules, but Carena seemed to waltz through on an unstoppable cloud of self-belief that she would get everything she wanted and everything would stop for her. And it usually did.

We all smoked our first fags at Carena's; cadged our first vodka. Her other best friend was Philly, a scholarship girl, and Philly and I vied to be Carena's closest lieutenants. It was great not having to worry about what I was doing, because Carena always did. I started to adopt her 'don't care' attitude, her slightly supercilious look at the world. Perhaps I got a little mouthier, a little harder. I like to think I was too timid to have tipped over the edge into really bad behaviour – but then Gail happened.

One Saturday night, Carena was staying with me – I was thirteen – and Daddy came home from a business trip to Prague. He'd been doing a lot of flying recently. He came in late, and I could hear from upstairs that he had someone with him. They were laughing. My dad used to laugh all the time. Lately, not so much.

'Who's that?' asked Carena, putting on lipgloss in the large gilt mirror that hung next to the staircase and making a sexy face. We were making sexy faces quite a lot at the moment. They were probably not sexy so much as freakish, and scared a lot of our teachers.

'I don't know,' I said. My dad rarely brought anyone home except for his lawyer, Uncle Leonard (I didn't call him uncle any more, not since Carena had heard me and made fun of me).

The large door swung open.

'Sophia? Darling?' My dad's voice floated up the stairs. 'Are you home?'

I made a humphy noise of assent which I'd noticed Carena doing a lot recently.

Daddy came into the hall. He looked tired and he was putting on weight. But he had on a broad smile, and his eyes had crinkled up at the corners.

'Sophie, I'd like you to meet –' and almost with a flourish, he announced – 'Gail.'

Gail stepped forward with an anxious smile on her face. She was pretty and blonde, with an upturned nose and cute rabbity smile that at the moment looked extremely nervous.

'Sophie!' she said, her voice slightly too bright. 'I recognise you from your photos!'

I was so taken aback I could barely speak. It was totally obvious what was going on. He'd gone and got a girlfriend without telling me! I was genuinely knocked sideways. Carena made an gasping noise. I stared at her. My father was still looking up at me hopefully. On one side was Carena. Downstairs was my dad. And standing right in front of me was the biggest affront I could imagine. And she had lipstick on her teeth.

'Hello . . . Gail,' I said simply, without smiling or getting up. Gail's smile faltered immediately. And suddenly, this made me incredibly cross; what was she expecting, that I run down the stairs and give her a huge hug and beg her to be my new mummy?

My dad took Gail's elbow.

'Gross!' said Carena. I glanced at her, completely in shock. 'Come on,' she said. 'Let's go.'

For a moment I was torn. Then I turned and followed her.

'Who was *that*?' said Carina loudly as we reached my bedroom. The worst thing was having to admit that I didn't even know.

My dad called me in later that evening, after Gail had gone home.

'I'm sorry about that,' he said. 'It was spur of the moment. We were passing, and I thought . . .'

I stared at him. Thought what? That I'd like to meet . . . well, it had just never occurred to me that dad would find someone else. It had been only two years. He had me!

Daddy put out his arms. 'She's a lovely girl, Sophia. You want me to be happy, don't you?'

Of course I did, and I was too scared to tell him how I felt in case I upset him. But inside I was as furious and mixed up and jealous as I'd ever been in my entire life. Someone had taken my mum, but no one was having my dad!

Soon, my life was a weekly soap opera for my schoolmates as Gail tried her best to be friends with me. The ruder I was to Gail, the more popular I got at school. *EastEnders* had nothing on me.

She did try, she really did. There were 'family' outings, treats and special trips. I sulked through them all like only a thirteen-year-old girl can. If they had made passive-aggressive stropping about an Olympic sport, I'd have been a shoo-in, with

17

a good shot at heavy sighing, door-banging and the sour-faced triple jump.

So, of course, the inevitable happened.

It was one Friday afternoon, I'd gone home after school to pick up some clothes and money *en route* to spending the weekend at Carena's. I loved my dad's study. It always smelled differently to the rest of the house – my mother had never spent any time in there, so it didn't have the faint scent of her perfume (Miss Dior) which permeated the rest of the house and which I still can't smell without feeling that someone's just given me a swift punch to the back of the neck.

'Sweetheart, could you come in and have a word?' Dad said. I looked round, hoping he hadn't had my latest report. My huge excuse for bad marks was starting to look less impressive this far down the line.

He looked nervous. Well, good. Nervous was better than annoyed with me.

'Sophia . . .' He looked at his hands. 'Look, I was think-ing . . . I was thinking of asking Gail to marry me.'

Oh God. All my worst nightmares were coming true. I didn't even have the presence of mind to strop out, make a fuss or yell. I stood there, frozen, as my eyes filled with tears.

'Sophia, it's OK!' He reached out his arms as if to give me a cuddle, but I was stuck to the spot. Then he sighed.

'This isn't about your inheritance, is it?' he said gently. 'You know I'll always look after you.'

That thought had never even crossed my mind. Everyone at school had money. The topic just never came up.

I was petrified that I would lose my father. Oh, even for a

thirteen-year-old, I was self-obsessed. I just stood in that study and let the tears drip down my face, so he could see them.

And now, here I am on a beach, so much later, thinking, am I happy?

Anyway, let me just say that I definitely, definitely, *definitely* got my comeuppance. Let me tell you exactly what happened.

Part Two
Then

Chapter Three

We were at Toa, a trendy new restaurant in London. Carena, Philly and me cared a lot about what was hot. Philly had got a job doing PR for bars and restaurants, which was great because she got us into every party and restaurant going. We were all still friends, amazingly. Carena's air of casual superiority had meant she was still exciting to be with, and since my dad had got married he'd given me loads more freedom – easier than trying to get me to sit down and be polite to Gail.

Carena was still really gorgeous – incredibly thin, long legs and long blonde hair. She had a pout to rival Angelina Jolie's, and she had plucked her eyebrows into really high glossy arches which made her look surprised all the time. She said men liked a look of surprise because it's the expression they want you to have when they strip for the first time, like you're saying, 'Oh my God, I've never seen such a penis before!

What a huge and amazing surprise!' This was quite useful to know, but I wasn't sure I could manage it myself.

Philly kept a rigid eye on her figure by virtue of wearing two pairs of Spanx pants every single day, regardless of what was on the agenda. I swear she swam in them. She also talked a lot about having naturally straight hair, and how easy it was to look after, but I knew for a fact she went to the hairdressers every two days and her biggest phobia of all time was being caught in an unexpected rain shower.

Lunch always followed the same pattern: we would all look at whatever trendy new menu Philly was promoting that week and umm and ahh at it. Then we'd eye each other up and say, 'I think I'm going to have the foie gras hamburger,' and we'd nod knowledgeably and say, 'Yah, me too.' 'With chips,' someone would add, and we'd all nod vigorously and say, 'Yah, definitely, definitely chips.' Then the waiter would come round and at the last minute we'd say, 'Do you know what, I've suddenly changed my mind. I think I'll just have a green salad.'

The idea, I think, was to trick someone into getting the hamburger and chips, but we'd all known each other so long it never worked (except on Philly sometimes) so I'm not sure why we still bothered. We all pretended we might order pudding too. The waiters never even looked surprised; sometimes they didn't even carry a pencil to the table. D'uh.

Anyway, I had other things on my mind, and almost couldn't contain myself. Carena glanced at me.

'So,' she drawled, after glancing at the bread basket as if it was her arch-nemesis. 'How's your man?'

'Amazing!' I said. It was true. Ever since I'd met Rufus, I just couldn't play it cool. 'You know we were talking about going skiing, and maybe me meeting his grandmother, who has a seriously grand house, and then maybe a hunt ball—'

'OK, calm down,' said Carena with a smile, glancing at Philly. 'God, we thought you were going to be single for ever.'

So had I, I thought, but didn't say. I'd met Rufus at a party. Actually, it was a bit embarrassing, he'd been drunk and come up to me at the bar. I'd clocked him out of the corner of my eye and was wondering about him when he leant over and said, 'Do you mind terribly if I slap you on the arse?'

'Yes!' I'd said. 'I'd mind that a lot.'

'Shame,' he said. 'I'd really, really like to do that.'

'Tough luck,' I said, making sure I kept my bum well away from him. 'What about slapping your own arse?'

His face briefly brightened. He really was terribly drunk, but I still couldn't help noticing how handsome he was – his dark brown hair flopped over his long eyelashes and I could glimpse a flash of very white teeth.

'How about *you* slap my arse first then.'

'*No!* Go away.'

'Oh, don't say that, pretty lady! I'm Rufus.'

'Go away, Rufus.'

'It's because I'm drunk, isn't it?'

'Yes. Well, that and the arse-slapping thing.'

He turned to the barman. 'Pint of black coffee, please.'

And he winked at me. I gave him my number, but was completely surprised when he called three days later.

'I can't believe you even remembered me after all that booze,' I said.

'An arse like yours? Are you kidding?'

And that was my Rufus. My heart jumped every time I thought of him. He was a trust-fund baby, had a little green MG that I loved and we flitted about London having a whale of a time. He did indeed like spanking, but was so funny and cute and adorable that I forgave him and was really coming round to the idea that he might – just – be the one.

A couple of weeks ago we'd been sitting on his roof – it was a little precarious, but the view was gorgeous and it was a beautiful evening. We'd been drinking champagne and looking out across the park as the sun went down. It was perfect. I'd laid my head on his shoulder and he'd put his arm around me.

'Do you ever want more, Sophie?' he'd said.

'More than what?'

'More than just living the high life?'

I looked at him. 'But I thought you always said that fun was the thing to have?'

He took a slug from the champagne bottle. 'Oh, I'm sure you're right,' he said. 'I just feel sometimes our lives are so pointless. You take great photos, when you can be bothered – don't you want to do more of that?'

'I don't know, maybe I could. Well, what do you want to do?' I'd teased lightly. 'Go to medical school? Dig wells in Africa? Cure cancer?'

'I did bid at that charity auction the other week,' he mused. Then he seemed to dismiss this idea. 'We are having fun, aren't we? Life shouldn't be taken too seriously.'

He'd kissed me lightly on the hair as we finished the champagne, and I felt it was the most romantic evening of my life. We could share things . . . our dreams and fears; our hopes. I know Daddy worried I dated playboys, but Rufus really was different.

'You two *are* getting serious,' Philly said.

Normally I would have denied this totally, but it had been four months, and I couldn't deny I was really pleased with the way things were going.

'Well . . .' I said.

'You know, do you think he might *pop the question*?'

Philly was meant to be engaged to some banker and was completely obsessed with weddings even though he worked such crazy hours she never actually saw him. Carena was saving herself, she said, and to be sure, it wasn't for want of offers. But they had to be from the right type. I think she was holding out for a large house in the country.

'No!' I said. But I couldn't deny it had crossed my mind. He was so much fun, so flirty and cuddly and handsome. And rich, of course, that was useful too. It would be nice to live in his little Kensington crash pad rather than having to stay at home. Home was lovely and everything, but I wouldn't mind being away from my step-monster. Our relationship hadn't really improved much since I'd deliberately scowled through all one hundred and seventy wedding photos.

Philly leaned forward. 'Well, it is the gallery party tonight . . .'

The gallery party was one of the social highlights of the year, held outside in a London park. It was extremely romantic.

27

'Oh, you never know,' said Carena.

'It's only been four months,' I said, refusing to let them get my hopes up. 'Plus, I haven't even met his parents yet. I suppose they'll need to check me out to see if I'm suitable heiress potential.'

Carena raised her eyebrows. 'Is he quite that rich?'

'Oh, yes,' I said. 'His dad's in pharmaceuticals. Apparently the kidnapping insurance premiums would be higher than anything Rufus could bring in. That's why he doesn't work.'

'*Really?* I didn't realise . . . I mean he always dresses like such a scruff.'

'I like the way he dresses,' I said. In fact he lived in an old corduroy suit that his dad had given him. Shopping was too boring for Rufus.

'Now *that* is true love,' said Carena, polishing off the last of the champagne in her glass.

'Hello, Sophia, darling,' Daddy said as I passed him on the stairway.

'Hi, Daddy.'

Our relationship had changed when Gail came. It was still warm and loving. But it was as if he'd seen a side to me he hadn't realised was there before. For my part, I was sure she was always feeding him stories about me, which made me more awkward. Now we were over the teenage years and I had lots of freedom it was better, but it could still be tricky, especially since Gail thought I should work more, which was rich, because she'd given up working completely the day she'd married Daddy. And surely Rufus wouldn't want me to work anyway, except some charity stuff probably. That was a nice thought.

'Been at work today?'

I squirmed. It's not like I didn't have a job; technically I did. I was an assistant to Julius Mandinski, the fashion photographer. After I left school, with two not very impressive A levels (a bad return on his investment, my dad noted ruefully, though he certainly got his money's worth on my Kendalls attitude), I went to Oxford Brookes to study photography because I still had my father's Leica and loved taking photos. Secretly I really enjoyed it, but a lot of the girls from Kendalls were there and we were out every night at college balls, which seemed far more important at the time.

Julius had about fifty assistants. It didn't exactly pay much money and it was very unpredictable, because Julius would only work with the *crème de la crème* of models and on bizarre projects. So if it involved some nine foot Romanian sixteen-year-old cast upside down in a pool of resin draped in wild armadillos, Julius was your man. I usually just went in a couple of times a week to stand around and look moody whilst fetching vodka for the models. I hardly ever took a frame myself. It helped my dad feel I was doing something to justify my allowance. Carena didn't do anything at all.

'Yes, kind of. I caught up with the girls.'

'So, not actually *at* work then, kiddo?'

'No. I like your new tie, Daddy.'

But he didn't look in the mood to be fobbed off. He didn't look well, actually. Gail was always trying to get him to cut down on the brandy and rich food at the Savoy Grill, but he didn't really listen and I never backed her up on any subject as a matter of principle.

'You know, when I was your age—'

'You'd bought a company. I know, I know.'

'I mean, Gail showed me your grooming bills . . .'

Hmm, thanks, Gail, I thought resentfully.

'And, I mean, darling. You're spending more at your hairdresser's than I pay my juniors in a year.'

I shook out my long pale golden mane and gave a soulful look. 'But I thought you liked my hair, Daddy.'

'I do, sweetheart. But I just want you to find . . . you know, something more useful to do.'

'Julius Mandinski is one of the most successful fashion photographers in the country.'

Daddy looked a bit sad. 'Well, you know I don't understand any of that stuff.' Then he smiled. 'But I know you have a new boyfriend. You look secretive. When do I get to meet him?'

Now that, I hoped I could do. In fact, I was rather hoping Rufus might ask to see my father soon, with a view to asking him something . . .

'I'll bring him over,' I said, smiling. 'You'll like him.'

I hoped he would. My dad was self-made and could sometimes be a little funny about trustafarians, but *everyone* liked Rufus. Even Carena liked him, and she never liked anyone I went out with.

'Seeing him at this party tonight?'

'Yes!' I couldn't help but grin. I couldn't wait to see him.

Daddy eyed my bags. 'Wearing a new dress?'

Carena and I had done a little shopping, and I'd bought the most romantic dress I could find. There was a lot of sheer fabric, and it was quite long – not my usual type at all. 'That,' Carena had observed, 'looks like a very fiancée-esque dress.'

'Do you want the boys to like me?'

'I want everyone to like you. For you, not some dress, pumpkin.'

He kissed me lightly on the forehead. 'Don't drink too much vodka, OK?'

Gail was standing at the top of the stairs. 'Did you speak to her?' she hissed at my dad, who looked guilty.

'I just have to go make a phone call in the office,' he said, slinking away. Gail gave me a look.

'Hello, *Gail*,' I said, hoping Esperanza would have started running my bath; I like a good long soak before I go out in the evening. Gail sighed. 'Your father and I are worried about you.'

'Really,' I said. I knew what was coming.

'Your credit card bills . . . Sophie, I know you get quite a lot of leeway, but this is just ridiculous. You're taking the p— You're being a little ridiculous. And you really should be looking for a proper job.'

'Sorry, Gail, could we talk about this later?' I said. 'I'm in a bit of a rush.'

When it came to special treats, Daddy would always take me out by himself. For my twenty-fifth birthday he took me to lunch at Le Gavroche, and told me lots of stories about growing up in Nebraska. I'd heard them all many times before but I didn't mind in the slightest, it was just great to be with him.

At lunch, we toasted my mother as usual and I saw his eyes filling, but then at the last moment he leaned over and clasped my hand, and I saw that he was going to be fine.

'Gail does make me happy, you know,' he said, after a moment had passed. I didn't answer, but I did pat his hand, thinking it might make him feel better.

Afterwards, he took me to Asprey, where the staff knew him, and picked out the most gorgeous diamond necklace for me.

'You deserve diamonds,' he said. 'These are flawless, like you.'

'I'm not flawless,' I protested.

My dad made as if to glance around and theatrically lowered his voice. 'I know,' he whispered loudly. 'But I'm your dad, so I'm allowed to pretend that you are.'

He finished doing them up and we looked at my reflection in the mirror.

'What does "igloo" mean?' I said, noticing something written on the box.

'They're Canadian diamonds. Ethical. No one got hurt mining for them, no one got shot trading them. So they are good as well as beautiful.'

He stroked my cheek lightly. 'We'll take 'em,' he said to the clerk.

The diamonds caught the light brilliantly; they were so clear it was quite shocking.

'Straight to the safe,' he said, smiling. 'But just in case you ever felt the need to look extra-beautiful . . .'

I gave him a big hug. I knew I was spoiled, and lucky. After

these lunches I would always resolve to be a bit nicer to my
stepmother, because I loved my dad so much.

'I love them.'

'I love you.'

Chapter Four

Later that evening, I left the house for the party, heading down the steps to the cab. I wasn't to know it would be my last evening in this gilded world. I was wearing a lovely dress which shimmered in the late evening sunshine, a strappy pair of black Gina shoes and my hair was straight, soft and shone like butter. It was a warm evening, a time of day when London feels full of anticipation, I was young, rich, spoilt and in love, and I was on my way to the hottest party of the year. Everything was good.

The party was in Hyde Park. Huge sculptures had been erected throughout the grounds, and there were tents made of large swathes of material, lit by jetting flames. The waiters and waitresses were dressed in white togas and circulating with cocktails and small canapés, which I ignored, naturally. The setting sun reflected off the white draped linen and everything seemed bathed in bright pink light. It was quite beautiful.

There was no Rufus yet, and I couldn't see Carena either, so Philly and I helped ourselves to drinks and admired the acrobats tumbling across the lawn.

'Where's Rufus?' I asked immediately.

'Er, I'm not sure. Shall we mingle?' said Philly quickly.

I took another slug of my drink. Everywhere I looked there were couples laughing and looking deliberately glamorous together. There were photographers from magazines and thus a lot of hair tossing going on. I wondered if Rufus and I would get our picture taken . . . suddenly I was lost in a reverie about us announcing our marriage in *The Times*, maybe getting in a magazine – young society wedding of the year . . . I couldn't wait to see Rufus's country house, maybe we could have the wedding there . . .

Interrupting my daydream, my phone rang. Dad. Gail must have been on at him about my credit card bill again.

'Sophia, I need to speak to you now.'

I winced. The party was getting busier and I could see some more people I knew coming in. Talking to my parent on the phone wasn't the coolest way to greet them. 'Dad, I'm really busy right now.'

'We need to talk,' he said.

'Well, can it wait?' I said impatiently. The music and chatter was so loud it would be patently obvious to a four-year-old that I was at a party. There was a long silence at the end of the phone.

'Come home as soon as you can,' he said finally.

35

Feeling cross and sullen, I grabbed another drink and guzzled it, quicker than I normally would.

I turned away, stumbling through the party looking for my boyfriend. Philly had disappeared to network frantically so I felt grumpy and alone. Rufus had said he'd be here on time, yet here I was, in this pretty, flimsy dress, marching about like it was the first day of school all over again. I tried his phone, but it was switched off.

Finally, behind yet another flimsy sheet, right in the corner of the tent, I caught sight of him. He had his back to me. God, he was good-looking. His hair was dark and slicked back, and those white teeth. And the corduroy suit, of course.

There was obviously some kind of Moroccan theme back here, and there were cushions and candles strewn everywhere; across the grass and in cunning little nooks like this one. The drapery had changed from white linen to red velvet. One side was still open to the garden but we were almost completely hidden from view.

I turned off my phone, which had rang again with a call from Daddy – I didn't pick up – and started to head over. Rufus was talking to someone, I couldn't see who.

'Haven't you been a naughty girl?' he was saying, in those familiar, flirtatious tones.

'Oh, Rufus, do you think I need spanking?' came the reply.

I froze. It was Carena's voice. It couldn't be.

I stood there, absolutely rooted to the spot. I couldn't believe what was happening, right in front of my eyes. They were so close to one another ... Carena was wearing an absolutely fierce super-mini skirt. Next to it my romantic dress suddenly felt utterly ridiculous.

'Come here, you,' Rufus said. It's what he always said to me. But he wasn't saying it to me. As if watching a film, two people I didn't know at all, I watched as, in total slow motion, Carena moved her face up to meet his, and suddenly they were kissing.

The second they connected, I came back to myself. And I heard myself screaming.

'What the *fu*—!'

The worst of it was, that they didn't even leap apart. Rufus shook his head, looking like a confused dog. Carena looked at me with a pitying expression – one I'd seen so often at school but had never had directed at me before. It hurt.

'What the *hell* are you doing?' I screamed again, stopping the party in its tracks.

Suddenly, a load of flashbulbs went off in my face. The paparazzi may not know who I was, but this smelled like a story.

Carena turned round to me. 'I know this looks terrible,' she announced, unbelievably composed.

You think?

'But, Sophie – I think true love has struck us! And nothing could keep us apart.'

'Um, hmm,' said Rufus.

My brain tried to compute what I was seeing. They were hiding in a corner. He had his hand on her arse. It didn't look *exactly* like true love.

But I thought of what I'd told Carena that afternoon. About how this was the man, the life, the fun – everything I wanted. And all those years we'd been friends and I'd told her how wonderful she was, how cool and brave and fun. And finally I had something she'd wanted . . . and she'd taken it. Just taken it.

Philly rushed up, ludicrous in a maxi dress that made her look like she was shuffling about on her knees. 'Sorry, Carena, I tried to distract her . . .'

Oh God, so she knew all about it. When had they cooked up this little plan?

I stared at the three of them, aware my mouth was flapping like a jellyfish. I wanted to say something witty and devastating. Or, OK, I couldn't think of anything witty and devastating. Something rude and to the point. But I opened my mouth and no sound came out. Nothing at all. It was as if, at the same time as Rufus slashed my heart, he took my vocal chords along with it. I waited two seconds, just in case Rufus might turn and look at Carena, slap his forehead in despair and shout, 'Sophie, what was I *thinking*? This horrible slut put something in my drink and bamboozled me, but how could she when it's you I love? You I want to be with and look after and build a gorgeous life with for ever! Get away from me, you hag!'

I waited. He didn't. Carena glared at me, grasping the sleeves of his jacket. Rufus wasn't looking at anyone, in the manner of a dog just caught misbehaving under the table.

There was nothing else for it. I took off my six-hundred-pound shoes and threw them at them as hard as I could, then turned around and ran for it.

Sitting in the back of the taxi, my whole body was red hot. I could feel myself trembling. How could she? How could he?

My pretty dress felt like a silly joke. I burned up thinking about what I had said to the girls at lunch . . . about how, maybe one day, I thought we might be . . . I shook my head to try and get rid of the image. Then I remembered mentioning Rufus's big house. Was it possible? Had Carena suddenly realised that he was richer than she'd thought? No, surely not.

I thought about Carena – my best friend, who took me to my first Take That concert, and my first nightclub, gave me my first glass of champagne. What was she doing now? Was she still at the party complaining that I completely overreacted? Or was she embarrassed? Had she rushed out, feeling awful at kissing her friend's man? Somehow, grimly, I didn't think so. Oh God. Suddenly I thought I was going to be sick.

'You all right, love?' asked the cabbie, looking concerned.

I felt the tears well up. My sexy, funny Rufus – mine! My lovely boy! – distracted in three seconds by a short skirt and a surprised-looking face. To lose a friend and a boyfriend all at once. How could life be so cruel?

At first I didn't see the ambulance. I was half-blinded by tears, and the savage amount of alcohol I'd managed to knock back, so I didn't really pay attention until I saw it was right outside our house.

Blinking, I climbed out of the taxi. I glanced upwards. Standing by the large French windows, silhouetted in the gathering gloom, was my stepmother. She wasn't moving and she had her back to the window.

And the front door was open. It was never left unlocked. But none of this really registered as, deep in misery, I set off up the stairs.

The first thing I heard was crying. A soft sound that came from downstairs, which meant it was probably Esperanza. My brain couldn't compute: what did this mean?

From up above me came much more urgent noises – shouting, rough voices, things banging and moving around. Feeling like I was in a dream, I put my shaking hand on the banister.

At first I couldn't take in the scene in the drawing room. It looked like a film, or an episode of *Casualty*. Men and women wearing green and yellow neon jackets were everywhere, yelling and throwing things at each other. My stepmother was standing at the back of the room, by the windows. And there, lying on the floor, a ghastly shade of grey and not moving at all, was my father.

'Daddy!' I screamed. One or two of the paramedics looked up – those closest to my dad, the ones actually bent over him, *doing* stuff to him – didn't. A woman with a ponytail came over to me.

'Are you Sophia?' she said.

'It's Sophie, actually,' I said. Sophia was the name my parents called me. The woman looked at me strangely.

'Well, *Sophie*,' she said. 'I'm afraid your dad's had a very serious heart attack.'

Oh God, oh God. Was he going to die?

I knelt down on the floor, but the ponytailed woman gently pulled me back. 'It's best if you let our team work,' she said. 'We're doing all we can.'

I looked at my father's face. It was the most peculiar colour.

'Well do MORE,' I screamed. 'Fix him!'

'We're trying our best.'

'Well, try your best FASTER!'

There was a sudden silence in the room. I couldn't work out what it was; but there'd been lots of machines beeping and humming and making breathy noises. Suddenly I realised that they weren't making those noises any more.

A burly man with a shaved head who'd been bent over Daddy knelt back on his haunches. 'I'm sorry,' he said, looking at Gail and me. 'I'm really sorry. He's gone.'

From somewhere deep within me, I didn't even know where, I heard a great howl . . . 'Daddy! Daddy!'

The paramedics looked embarrassed. I reached him – Daddy – the body, I didn't know, and collapsed on top of him, hugging him with all my might. He still felt warm. But that was all. He didn't feel of anything else. He didn't smell of his normal smell – cigars, whisky if it was in the evening, cologne in the morning. He smelt of antiseptic wipes and, oddly, burning.

'Daddy,' I whimpered again, feeling the tears start to gather and run down my face. And I think the paramedics were as polite as they could be, and waited as long as they could before they had to pack up their things, wait for the undertaker, and leave.

Later, the house silent, Gail and I finally looked at each other. Years of animosity stood between us, like a huge rock. Suddenly I wanted to push it out the way, run to her, forget all the tantrums and the jealousies. I just wanted someone to hold me.

41

'Gail—'

She cut me off curtly. 'He called you. He wanted you. But you seemed to be too busy to pick up the phone.'

And she abruptly left the room.

Chapter Five

It's hard to describe the weeks after my father's death. I've never known pain like it. Nowadays I have taken that grief and locked it in a box, and buried it deep inside. Those weeks of swirling, half-awake nightmares, where I would wake up with a start and relive the whole thing again; the hazy, Percodan-fuelled days when I didn't even open the blackout curtains. It was a dark place, and I never want to go back there again.

Gail made all the arrangements, because I couldn't do anything at all. I couldn't eat, I couldn't leave the house. I needed so badly for someone to put their arms around me and tell me everything was going to be all right. I needed my boyfriend. I needed my friends. I had neither.

I called, once. Carena didn't pick up, although she must have recognised the number. Then I tried Philly, who after a few piss-weak expressions of sadness about my dad, put on a little girl's voice, and said, 'Are you really cross with Carena?'

'Am I what?' I said. Cross didn't really cut it. 'She's been . . . she's been a complete fucking . . .'

'You know she feels really terrible about it,' said Philly. 'And those Gina shoes really hurt.'

'Good,' I said grimly. 'I was hoping the diamante might take out someone's eye.'

'She says that it was a passion bigger than both of them . . . that she was just swept away . . .'

'You know what, I think I have more important things on my mind,' I said, bitterly.

'OK,' said Philly. 'Uh, what about the funeral . . .'

'Don't come,' I said. 'I don't want to see either of you.'

I really regretted that. It wasn't *my* funeral, though I'm sure Carena and Rufus would have found everything much more convenient if it had been. They should have been there though. Philly, who used to secretly eat all the muffins in our kitchen, and when my dad caught her at it one day he'd laughed hysterically and had a huge muffin basket sent to her house. Carena, who used to explain to him patiently why we needed to have our music so loud. They were part of my dad's life, too. At least he never met Rufus. And it meant, too, at the funeral, there was no one I knew, just hundreds of business-men.

'He was such a good man.'

'A terrific businessman.'

'Great to work with.'

All of that I'd expected, and I tried to swallow the ping

pong ball in my throat and thank them gracefully. But what I wasn't expecting from so many strangers were the things they said about me.

'He was so proud of you.'

'Says you've got a big job in photography.'

'He always said you worked really hard, that you were doing really well at college.'

Over and over again, people I scarcely recognised came up to tell me things my dad had told them about me. About how great I was, and how well I was doing and how happy I was.

Things that, when I thought about the uselessness of my life – parties, and lunches and messing about – just obviously weren't true.

Summer turned into autumn and I scarcely noticed. Then one morning Gail rapped sharply at my door.

'Sophie? Could you come downstairs please? We're in the study.'

Her voice sounded timid. I'd avoided her – avoided everyone – but I heard her come and go occasionally. I hadn't asked how she was; I was too selfish and caught up in my own grief.

Gail looked stiff and awkward in the study. Standing next to her was a tall, grey-haired man with small round spectacles and a pursed mouth. Next to him was my father's old lawyer, Leonard. He looked quiet and sad. He'd given me a big hug at Dad's funeral. I'd always liked him. He had four daughters and had known me since I was tiny. But it was clear from the way Gail was standing next to the tall chap that he was in charge now.

Sure enough, Gail immediately said, 'This is Mr Fortescue, my lawyer.'

I gave him a second glance. 'What about Leonard?'

'Leonard only worked for your dad. Mr Fortescue has been helping me out with a few things.'

I didn't like the sound of that very much. Leonard half-smiled at me, a little sadly.

'We just wanted to have a little talk with you. About arrangements and so on.'

Gail's eyes were fixed on a point about twenty centimetres above my head. She looked really uncomfortable. I didn't realise why I hadn't figured this out before – it hadn't really crossed my mind. But it was about Daddy's will. Of course. I briefly felt a cold hand clutch at my insides. Then ignored it; it wasn't as if I had to worry. 'I'll always look after you,' Daddy had said.

'Sophie,' she began, 'look. Now, your dad obviously wanted you to be well looked after . . .'

I nodded.

'Look, Sophie . . . I'm so sorry . . . this is going to come as a bit of a shock.'

'What?' The room suddenly swayed a little out of focus.

'There is an inheritance for you, of course there is. But here's the thing. Your dad . . . he put it in trust.'

'What does that mean?'

'Sophie, you know your dad was worried about you. He worried that you didn't really have a job.'

'I have a job!'

'Sorry, I know that. Well, maybe more of a proper career. He worried about your party lifestyle.'

I heaved a sigh. 'Was this him thinking this? Or you?'

Gail looked pained. 'I promise, Sophie, it has nothing to do with me. He was just doing what he thought was best. Nobody thought he would . . .' She suddenly bit her lip and turned her face away. 'We honestly didn't think that this . . . that we'd use this will. We thought we had years . . . for you to find a career path, for us to be together . . . for me to have a . . . anyway. Never mind about that.'

I could hardly take in what she was saying. Mr Fortescue patted her on the arm.

'And I know with everything . . . but did you even see the papers?'

I had. There had been a story, 'Cat Fight Spat with Party Brats' in one of the papers, with a very glamorous picture of Carena getting a shoe thrown at her. It made me out to be an unstable idiot.

'Well, let's not talk about that now. But it has convinced me that your father's will should stand.'

Then she stared very hard at the desk, like she didn't want to look at me any more.

'Sophie,' she said. 'It's in the will. You have to go and make your own living. For six months. Then we can review the situation. He loved you to bits, Sophie. But it didn't always do you much good, and he knew that.'

I staggered backwards, as if someone had thrown a punch. 'What?' I said. This didn't make any sense.

'Your dad . . . he was trying to make things better. You have to move out. Find your own way. It's only for six months!' she added, pleadingly.

'But you can't make me go,' I said. 'You can't throw me out of my own home. Daddy can't have meant that!'

The lawyers were shuffling their feet and looking embarrassed. Gail handed me the will and I read it there in black and white. 'For a period of not less than six months, the beneficiary will earn every aspect of her own living . . .'

Gail still looked embarrassed. 'You know what he was like with his ideas and schemes,' she said. 'He just felt you were wasting your life.'

'But I was just having a good time,' I said, truly shocked. OK, we went to parties and lunches and shopped a lot, but I thought he liked me doing those things. I thought every time he suggested I work harder on my career it was Gail being nasty to me.

'Can't I stay here?' I asked, feeling the tears spring up.

Gail shook her head. 'Apparently I could make you pay rent,' she said. 'Rent on your room in this area is eighteen hundred pounds a month. Before bills and food.'

I looked at her. 'But you don't have to do it, though, Gail? You're not going to throw me out of my own home after I've just been orphaned?'

There was a long pause, and I tried not to think of all the times I'd been horrid to her. She glanced at her lawyer again. 'Sophie, I'm sorry. I am. Really. But . . . I agree with your dad. You're twenty-five years old and still reliant on other people for everything. You won't grow up. You can't even use the washing machine or make yourself a cup of coffee. I think . . . I think it's what you need.'

I looked to Leonard for help, but he just smiled sadly at me and shook his head.

'Of course, you can take time to find yourself a place to stay, and go back to your old job . . .'

I didn't have much confidence that my old job was still there – I hadn't been to the studio for weeks. And seeing as it didn't pay any money how was that going to help me now?

I stumbled back upstairs in disbelief, then called down to Esperanza.

'Esperanza, could you please get me a non-fat soya latte?'

There was a long pause on the phone.

'Please?' I added again.

There was another pause. Then, 'I'm sorry, Miss Sophie. I was told not to do anything for you now.'

'What do you mean?'

'Your mother . . . she says no more coffee, no food, no cleaning in your rooms.'

'You *are* joking.'

Suddenly, I realised I couldn't talk my way out of this. It had started. It was really happening. And I had no one to blame but myself.

Chapter Six

Hunger drove me downstairs eventually. There was nothing in the huge pristine kitchen except for a newspaper folded up on top of the central island.

I took a look. It was a copy of *Loot*. Very deliberately folded open to the flat-hunting page. God. I picked it up gingerly. I thought ruefully about Carena's parents' house. They had a guest floor. Of course she didn't live there any more – she had a lovely apartment in South Ken – and the whole place was empty half the time. They wouldn't have minded . . . of course I couldn't. My friend had stabbed me right through. I couldn't forgive for real estate. I didn't even know if she would want me to. I tried not to think of her tearing around town. In my head I had horrible images of them, shrieking with laughter and kissing in exotic locations. Whilst I had . . . *Loot*.

Rooms to rent. All looking for 'friendly non-smokers'. I

didn't see any ads desiring someone 'quite grumpy in the mornings, very occasional social smoker'.

All the ads asked for six hundred quid a month, and for me to be 'tidy'. But I didn't know if I had six hundred quid. Oh God. My blood ran cold. My allowance. I'd never known life without an allowance. There was an envelope next to the paper. I picked it up. Inside was a cheque for a thousand pounds, signed by Gail. 'To get you started,' it said.

What would Daddy want me to do?

I knew, of course. Find a flat, do a good job, make a good show, then in six months' time I could come back and claim my inheritance. He'd have been delighted. I could do it. Of course I could do it, I wasn't stupid, and Gail and Leonard and everyone would be really impressed with me, and I'd be on my way to becoming the new Annie Leibovitz, and it'd be great. Wouldn't it, Dad? Maybe I could show them all, stop living my life as some expensive victim.

With hope jumping in my heart for the first time in weeks, I picked up the phone.

Oh God, but flat hunting is hell on a stick. Who thought it was a good idea to go and audition for a group of weird horrible strangers who keep a collection of their bogies on the bathroom mirror but somehow want you to prove to them that you're good enough to sleep in their airing cupboard, and by the way, would you mind doing all the cleaning in the nuddie?

That September Tuesday, filled with optimistic zeal, I'd started to call the numbers in the paper. I started with nice places I already knew – Notting Hill, Chelsea, Primrose Hill. Everything had gone.

The next day I tried again, but no luck. And the day after.

'How are you doing?' Gail asked when she saw me. She looked nervous, in case, I suppose, I bawled her out for ruining my life. She didn't realise that I was trying to be the new Sophie; stoic and upbeat and calm. Even though I had just been asked by a chap on the phone if I minded cats. I'd said no, until he explained he had *fourteen* cats.

'*Fine!*' I said, stoically.

'Good,' she said. 'I know it's difficult. When I first left home I lived with a fishmonger . . .'

I knew she was trying to be kind, but I couldn't listen to her story. At least she'd found a place to stay – she hadn't been thrown out by the person who was meant to be looking after her. She realised I wasn't really listening, because she changed track.

'Um,' she said, 'don't be alarmed, but there'll be men around the place over the next few days . . . just doing valuations.'

'You're selling up?' I said in a panic.

'No, of course not,' she said. 'I just need to get everything organised for the insurance. There's a lot of paperwork, Sophie. I've tried to spare you most of it. Look, there's no good way of saying this, but . . . you can't take anything off the premises.'

At first I didn't know what she was talking about. Then I realised, and blushed hotly. She thought I was going to steal things in the house and sell them to make money. Then I quickly realised this was a good idea and wished I'd thought about it before. Not that I'd have sold my jewellery. My necklaces and bracelets had come straight from my father. We'd chosen them together. They were special things, special moments. They were us, all I had left of him.

'What about things that are mine?' I said.

'Anything that comes under the house insurance policy can't be moved right now,' she said. That meant, I guessed, all my jewellery and bags. Then she looked up. 'But they'll be right here waiting for you, Sophie.'

I heaved a sigh. 'Can I take, you know, a change of underpants?'

'Of course, of course, it's just the insurance . . .'

'That's fine,' I said, cheerily, holding up the paper. 'Not everywhere I'm looking at has a dressing room and a walk-in wardrobe anyway.'

So I scoured websites, and called estate agents, and finally, just as I was considering joining that convent with really nice premises in Chelsea – it certainly wouldn't have made my love life any worse – I got a male voice on the phone. It sounded distracted.

'It's about the room,' I said, trying to sound cheery, but not annoyingly so, friendly but not nosy, and very, very tidy, with a reasonable, but not ridiculous, cat tolerance (just in case this was required), all in the space of four words.

'Oh yeah?'

He didn't immediately say, 'It's gone,' so this was an up.

'I don't smoke or anything . . . uh, and I'm quite easy to

live with.' As long as, I thought to myself, you don't do a straw poll of Gail and Esperanza, the two other people in my current house.

'So, can I come and see it?'

There was a pause, as I waited, all my nerves straining to see if I'd passed the telephone test or not.

'Yeah, all right.'

He gave me an address in Southwark. I'd never been down there.

'Can I come straight over?' I was trying not to betray my desperation, although I suppose a phrase like 'can I come straight over' doesn't exactly sound like someone who has millions of offers of great places to live and is weighing them up.

'Yeah, all right.'

OK, I was not such a puffed-up spoiled little madam that I'd never taken public transport, but I still felt an idiot at Sloane Square station, when I'd queued for about nine hours for my tube ticket, until someone told me there wasn't actually a tube station on the Old Kent Road, where I was headed, and that I had to go to Elephant and figure it out from there. Yeah! And *how much* did they want for a ticket? Surely a car service couldn't be more expensive than this.

At Elephant, where I emerged feeling quite proud of myself, I immediately found myself faced with a vast and completely incomprehensible roundabout. Was this the motorway? Immediately I realised that pretending I knew what I was doing here was completely futile. I was going to have to throw myself on someone's mercy. People were dashing by with shopping bags, children, bicycles, swooping down into underpasses or climbing stairs to random locations. There was a huge red building in one corner that looked terrifying, like some kind of children's prison, and traffic roaring past at about a thousand miles an hour.

'Excuse me?'

A young woman carrying loads of bags of heavy shopping pushed past me and didn't stop. Oh well. I tried someone else, an older-looking woman. 'I'm looking for the Old Kent Road?' She stared at me and unleashed a barrage of what sounded like Polish for 'Go away stupid girl and don't bother me with your ridiculous questions about roads I know nothing about.' Or something like that.

A gang of small boys on bicycles came up to me and eyed me curiously.

'Hey, lady!' they shouted. Oh great. That was all I needed; was I going to be mugged by a bunch of children. Weren't they all meant to be feral down here or something?

'You want the Old Kent Road?'

Help!

'She doesn't know where the Old Kent Road is,' one said in disbelief.

'NEH,' said another one. 'Let's send her to Brighton, innit?'

The one with the biggest bike, who was obviously the leader, hushed them with a look. 'Old Kent Road,' he said, indicating a wide traffic-filled road stretching miles into the distance, 'is that way.'

Then with what looked a bit like a nod, he took his little gang away. I felt oddly mollified, although the rain seemed to be falling a bit more heavily. I wished I hadn't worn my Sonia Rykiel soft suede boots, but I wanted to impress these people into letting me move in with them and I figured these boots impressed everyone. Normally.

Three quarters of an hour later I was very close to tears. The Old Kent Road is *enormous*. It should be called the Endless Fucking Old Kent Road that continually subdivides itself and refuses to stick to numbering rules, even if that would make it a bit tricky to fit on the *A-Z*.

I was looking for 896a. I was on 165, with many, many diversions, hypermarkets, motorway underpasses and general miseries en route. My suede boots were getting a white rim right across the top, and my feet were killing me. And probably by the time I got there the flat would have already been rented to a Bulgarian pianist or the Australian water polo team or something, or I'd have to sit down and answer (as had happened recently in Harlesden) questions on what bands I liked. Take That had not passed muster.

Every time I came to a row of houses I'd eye them up beadily. Quite often, it was true, to make sure somebody actually lived in them and that they weren't just waiting to be knocked down. As I passed one hovel after another I'd let out a sigh of relief, and hope there was going to be a nice row of white stucco houses coming up after the next Cash and Carry. There never was though.

After sixty-five thousand years, I realised this had to be it. My heart sank as I saw the wheelie bin half-blocking the gateway. A big green filthy wheelie bin with HANDS OFF graffit-tied on it in dripping white paint. I tried to push open the creaking iron gate that had rusted to immobility. I took a deep breath. Six months, I had to keep telling myself. Six months then back to my normal life, or what was left of it.

I gingerly reached out my finger, noticing as I did so that I was in need of a manicure. Fat chance. Bits of rust were flaking off the gate. I wondered if I needed a tetanus shot. As I stood there on the threshold of the scrubby little patch of front garden, I hovered for a moment. I'd seen some pretty grotty apartments on my travels, but this had to be the worst yet. I didn't even know where the hell I was.

'You can come in – we don't have a butler,' came an amused-sounding voice. I looked up to the top of the four crumbling steps that led to the peeling front door. I glanced up. A burly chap with the most ridiculous mop of black curly hair strewn over his eyes – like one of those big shaggy dogs you see around – was standing there looking curious.

'It just looks a little bit dangerous,' I said. 'The gate, I mean.'

The man didn't look in the least bit dangerous.

'Yeah, we know. Keeps the crack dealers and muggers from sitting in the garden. Uh, kidding,' he added hastily and not very convincingly when he saw my face. 'Is it you I spoke to on the phone? About the flat?'

'How did you know?' I asked, gingerly pushing the gate.

'I know, it's amazing,' he said, coming down to grab the gate – there was obviously a knack – and give it a solid twist.

57

'Almost everyone phoning up about it sounded exactly like you.'

I squinted. 'How do I sound then?'

As far as I knew I sounded like all my friends. The man stuck his bottom lip out then obviously thought better of whatever he was about to say.

'You sound great,' he said. We were now facing each other. 'I'm Eck.' He put out his hand. 'Short for Alec.'

'I wouldn't have thought you needed to shorten Alec,' I said, gingerly mounting the steps, and shaking his large outstretched paw.

'Oh, it's saved me literally minutes over the years,' he said. 'Come on up. Watch out for the—'

But I'd seen it already.

'Mattress,' I said. It was lying across the stairs.

'No, the mattress is quite useful after a heavy night,' said Eck. 'I was meaning more the springs popping out of the mattress.'

'Oh,' I said. 'Thanks. I guess.'

In my head, I sternly told myself that I must pretend that I was a princess in a story, being tested before my true form could be revealed and I could live happily ever after in South Kensington.

The communal front hall was a mishmash of post addressed to loads of different people; bicycles and bits of bicycles, and trainers that looked like they needed to be carted away by men wearing full-body chemical suits.

I followed Eck's broad back up some rickety stairs.

'How many flats are in the house?' I asked. It was about a quarter the size of ours, judging by the outside.

'Six,' he said. 'We've got the biggest one though.'

Six? *Six*? How many people lived in the building? A hundred?

On the first floor he stopped and pushed open the door.

'James! Cal! Wolverine!'

Wolverine?

I followed him through a narrow dark hall to a kitchen at the back, which had a rickety table propped up with a *Yellow Pages* and five mismatching chairs. Not the least effort had been made to tidy up for people coming round to visit. Or, terrifyingly, maybe it had. It was filthy. In the sink there were cereal bowls with smears round the rims. Teabags had been draped gracefully over the chipped Formica countertops. There was a distinct smell of something, but I couldn't quite get a grip on it. Lentils, I thought. Overlaid with toast.

Eck was obviously about to offer me tea but, giving the mug situation a quick glance over in a worried kind of a way, he just looked at me and said 'Um . . .'

'I'm fine,' I said quickly. 'Uh, if you were offering tea . . .'

Suddenly I remembered that I was meant to be impressing these people with my keenness to rent and suitability as a tenant. But looking around, the only suitability criteria I could imagine would be to have grey fur, sharp teeth and a long scaly tail.

There were scampering noises in the hall, then the others emerged, like they'd just got up. Maybe they had.

'Hello,' said the one Eck had indicated as James. I was surprised by how neat he looked, given his surroundings. I wondered if he was gay or in the military. 'Welcome. Is Eck

59

showing you around? He's a very good front man.' The military then.

'Well, we've done most of it,' said Eck, knocking my last remaining hope that somewhere there was a huge conservatory-cum-sitting room-cum roof terrace that I just hadn't been shown yet.

'Excellent!' said James. 'Tea?' Then he too glanced at the cup situation. 'Er.' He made the same helpless motion Eck had.

'No, thank you, I'm just fine.'

'Great. Excellent. A flatmate that doesn't drink too much tea . . .'

'That's definitely the kind of flatmate I am,' I said.

He looked at me closely now. I could tell he rather liked what he saw.

'Well, OK then.'

'Um, James,' said Eck, who looked to be the kind of *de facto* leader of the flat. 'Don't you want to ask her any other questions?'

James looked cornered. 'Uh, Eck, she's a *lady*.'

'So?'

James sighed and stuck out his bottom lip whilst he tried to think of a question to ask me that would prove my suitability as a tenant. Finally he came up with, 'Uh . . . do you believe in a strong military defence for the British Isles?'

We all looked at each other. Eck rolled his eyes.

'Yes,' I said brightly. 'Yes, I do. Submarines and all that.'

'Jolly good,' said James. 'Right. I'm off to play squash.'

'Yeah, OK, well thanks for all your help,' said Eck.

'I did my best.' James had lowered his voice so he was supposedly only talking to Eck, but I could hear every word. 'I mean, if I can't talk to girls at parties how am I supposed to talk to them in weird flat-sharing situations.'

'OK, OK, just go,' said Eck, flapping his hands at him.

'James is in the army,' he added once he'd gone.

'*Really*,' I said. 'Wow.'

I was not going to be drawn on the subject of James, in case he was Eck's brother or something.

Eck sat down on a rickety chair and indicated that I do the same. I'd really have rather not, but I didn't have a lot of choice.

'So, uh, Sophie. Why are you looking for a flat?' he asked.

Inner princess, I thought again. You are in a magic spell where you must prove yourself humble and then everything your heart desires will be yours.

I thought about what I'd buy when I had my own money. One of those little cottages in Chelsea perhaps – small, but really lovely, pink and cosy. I drifted off slightly. With a little back garden where I could grow herbs. I didn't know how you grew herbs, but how hard could it be?

Eck coughed expectantly. Obviously I wasn't going to tell the princess version, so I told the story I'd honed which I thought might explain things.

'I'm trying to get into photography,' I said, honestly. Getting my old job back with Jules was next on my list of 'hideous things I must do', straight after 'finding a flat'.

Eck looked at me a bit strangely. 'On the Old Kent Road?'

I hardly heard him, however, as I was transfixed by two men who'd just sidled in the door. The first was tall and saturnine, with dark floppy hair and razor-sharp cheekbones. He was extremely handsome. Not in the fresh-faced rosy-cheeked Windsor way of the boys I usually met, but rather in a let-me-tie-you-up-and-play-with-this-candle-wax kind of a way. I liked it.

The other was a small crouched figure with hairy hands and arms, and hair that looked like it had been thatched. Wolverine, I surmised. I switched my attention back to the first guy.

'It smells of wet blazers in here,' he said.

'Uh, that'll be me,' I said, rather clumsily. I managed to refrain from pointing out that my soggy DKNY soft cash-mere blazer still smelled better wet than their entire flat did dry.

The man looked at me a bit more closely.

'So, we're just asking Sophie here some questions,' said Eck. 'Want to join in?'

'Sure. Why do you want to move into this shit hole?' he asked, in a pleasant tone of voice.

'*Cal*,' said Eck. 'Can you be nice, please? You keep scar-ing people off.'

'Not much scares me,' I said, flirtily. Then I realised I was surprised at myself. Post Daddy and Rufus I hadn't really thought I'd ever be capable of flirting again.

'Really? Not even slugs?' said Cal, flicking on the kettle.

'Slugs!' agreed Wolverine, a hairy hand scrabbling in a bag of sugar cubes before grabbing some and stuffing them in his gob.

I glanced at Eck. 'You've got slugs?'

He rolled his eyes at Cal. 'Stop talking about slugs.'

'Um, that wasn't a no,' I pointed out. It was gradually becoming clear why this flat was still available. That Cal guy was hot though.

'We had *a* slug,' said Eck. 'OK, two slugs.'

'And when two slugs get together . . . a little music, a little wine, a bit of romance . . . many little slugs,' said Cal. 'Don't rent out the room, Eck.'

'James says it's fine.'

'James likes to sleep in a trench with sixteen other boys all masturbating into the same sock.'

Eck looked at me with a disappointed look on his face, as if he completely understood why I was about to run from the flat with my tail between my legs. He probably thought this was about the worst thing that had ever happened to me.

'D'you want to see the rest of the flat then?' he asked in a slightly defeated tone of voice.

'Sure,' I said brightly. All the boys looked surprised.

'Right. I'm going to tell her about the snake,' said Cal.

'Snake!' said Wolverine.

'There *really* isn't a snake,' said Eck, half-smiling. 'I promise.'

'You didn't mention a snake in the ad,' I said.

'There *isn't* a snake!' said Eck. 'Cal! Admit you were telling a lie.'

Cal rolled his eyes. 'There isn't a snake,' he said. '*Yet*. But I'm getting one. Probably. Tomorrow. Just to have lying about. Do you still want to move in?'

'Sure,' I said. 'I need a new python handbag.'

There was silence and I wondered if I'd gone too far. Then Eck laughed.

'OK! Look,' he said, turning to Cal. 'We don't have enough money to give Wolverine a room of his own for free. We just can't do it. We have to rent it out.'

I watched as Wolverine tipped the last of the sugar into his mouth.

'That'll give you worms,' said Eck.

'He's already got worms,' said Cal. 'Eck, *please* don't make me share with Wolverine any more.'

'If you can pay for it, you can have it,' said Eck. 'I'm sorry. That's what it boils down to.'

'Money,' said Cal. 'No one with any artistic integrity has any money.'

I wondered what Julius Mandinski would say to that. He was reported to own a huge penthouse in Shad Thames and a chalet in Gstaad. But Cal had already flounced out.

Eck led me out of the kitchen and along the dank landing. Various boyish smells emanated from different rooms, which I tried manfully to ignore.

'Here's the bathroom,' he said, pulling on a string without a handle, and setting off the world's loudest extractor fan. It clattered madly into life.

'It's a big noisy,' he howled unnecessarily over the din. 'Normally I just pee in the dark.'

I peered into the windowless room to see an orange suite, every available space was piled high with nearly empty bottles of shower gel and gummy razors.

'Is there an en suite?' I screamed back. He looked at me in consternation as I considered miming it, then decided against it, and we moved on. But the truth of it became increasingly clear.

'Is . . . is that the only bathroom?' I asked, trying to keep the tremor out of my voice. It couldn't be. It couldn't be. With one, two, three, four . . . well, three men and one feral *thing* living here . . . plus me . . . it couldn't be the only bathroom, could it?

Eck flashed me a quick half-smile. 'Yeah, we need to do shifts in the morning.'

'You do *what* in the morning?' I said, mishearing him. 'Oh. Oh.'

Finally we stopped at the end of the landing. Perhaps it wouldn't be as bad as the rest of the place. Maybe it would be a nice bright room that I could put a feminine stamp on and it would be like Katy's sick room in *What Katy Did*, a nice bright place for people to come and have a nice time and . . .

Eck opened the door. Oh.

I tried to get myself not to say it, but it just blurted out.

'This is . . . this is like a prison cell.'

'People keep saying that,' said Eck. 'Is it the metal sink?'

'Or the bars on the windows.'

'Well, yes, because it's at the front . . .'

'I see. Noisy, is it?'

A huge cement lorry rumbled past, followed by a car transporter. Both honked venomously for no apparent reason.

'Um . . .'

The room contained one single bed with a metal frame;

a cheap MDF bedside table; the metal sink (why? Why?) and one cheap MDF wardrobe with one door hanging askew. And some dust on the horrid fuchsia-coloured carpet. And that was it. That was absolutely all there was. It wasn't just the ugliest room I'd ever seen in my life (I *had* been to boarding school); it was the ugliest *thing* I'd ever seen in my life.

'Actually,' said Eck. 'We have had a couple of people who do want to rent it. You shouldn't listen to Cal.'

'Really?'

'Sure. Lots of people have never had a bedroom to themselves before.'

I thought of my lovely suite of rooms at home; my four-poster bed, my bath set in the centre of the bathroom, overflowing with Jo Malone suds. No crying. No crying. No crying. Six months, six months, six months. Princess, princess, princess. Be strong. And what were my alternatives?

'I'll take it, please,' I said, quickly and loudly, so that my voice wouldn't crack, and before I had the chance to change my mind. It was a step on the road. Despite the hideousness of it all, it was a step on the road. I felt a tiny flicker of satisfaction. It wouldn't be for long. Eck seemed nice. Cal didn't, but he certainly improved the view.

'Really?' said Eck. 'Great! Great! Let's go into the sitting room to sort things out.'

'Over tea?' I said.

He thought about it for a moment.

'There is going to have to be a time when you have your first cup of tea here,' he said finally.

'I know,' I said.

'If you just hold your nose to begin with, it's not so bad.'

'Unless you get a slug.'

'Yeah. God, I wish Cal hadn't mentioned the slugs. Could you forget about them?'

'Could you knock something off the rent?'

'Ah,' he said.

We headed back to the kitchen. It looked out over a car park where some kids who I thought should have been in school were desultorily kicking a ball around. I looked again at the mismatched chairs around the rickety table.

'That's pretty cool,' I said, still up for making a good impression. 'The vintage "salvaged" look.'

Eck looked a bit pained. 'Yeah,' he said. 'It is salvage. You've got to be fast to get to the skips round here.'

'Oh, yes, definitely,' I agreed.

Eck tried to push a copy of *Front* magazine, showing a pair of naked girls holding motorbike helmets over their boobs, behind a dirty-looking teapot. It only really drew attention to it. 'Well. Anyway.'

I crouched nervously on the stool as Eck did some paperworky things.

'Why do you live here, Eck?' I asked suddenly.

He looked up, surprised. 'Oh,' he said. 'Well, I'm a student. Obviously. Why else would I be at home at eleven in the morning?'

Everyone I knew was generally at home at eleven in the morning, I realised. It wasn't that unusual to me.

'I'm at the art college down the road. Goldsmiths.'

'Oh, are you an artist?'

There wasn't a single picture up on the walls anywhere, just a calendar hanging in the bathroom. For 2003. I thought artists lived in quaint garrets in Paris with large easels set up and the Eiffel Tower nice and visible through the balcony windows. Ooh, when I got my inheritance maybe I'd get somewhere like that and set it up as a photographic studio. I was almost veering off again when I realised Eck was still talking.

'I'd like to be. I work in metal.'

'Really? Can I see something you've done?'

Eck looked pleased, but awkward. 'Not at the moment. They're all at college. They're about nine metres long. I'm going through a bit of a spider phase.'

'Ah, a spider phase,' I said sagely, nodding my head, as if it was a well-recognised artist's path. Maybe it was. Not for the first time, I cursed myself for not paying more attention at school.

'Cal's at art college too. He's a sculptor as well.'

Ooh, this was looking up. Suddenly I saw us all at a glamorous opening (somewhat dressed up) with someone saying, 'And of course, the Old Kent Road school very much used Sophia Chesterton as a muse . . .'

'And Wolverine . . . he's just . . . I don't know where he came from actually. A lot of flats have someone like that, don't you find?'

I had not found. In my limited experience, someone you didn't know very well living in your house did nice things for you, like your laundry, or getting you a frappucino when you had a hangover.

Eck bent his head over his papers again and cleared his throat a little nervously. My dad always did say Limeys were funny talking about money.

'So. It's six hundred quid a month for the room. So I'll need that and the deposit, and did you bring references?'

I looked at him. What was he talking about, deposit?

'What do you mean, "deposit"?' I said.

'You do know,' said Eck, looking slightly embarrassed. 'You have to leave an amount of money with the landlord in case you break stuff or mess up the flat.'

Shit. Shit, I hadn't known that. Why hadn't I known that? Did everyone else know all this stuff? Did everyone get a handbook when they turned eighteen and I hadn't been paying attention that day?

'Uh,' I said. Then I just said what was on my mind.

'Eck, really – how could I break stuff or mess up this flat?' I said. 'I don't have a deposit. I've got six hundred pounds. For now. Then next month I'll have it again. Definitely.'

I tried to say 'definitely' with as much honest confidence as I could muster. If I could get a flat, I could get my old job back, couldn't I? Couldn't I?

But I wasn't lying about the money. That really was it. I couldn't put any more down. I just couldn't.

Eck looked really pained. Which was good. At least he wasn't going to hurl me out on the street. I felt my heart beating hard.

'I'm sorry,' he said, 'have you never rented a flat before?'

I shook my head, mutely. Eck excused himself, and

disappeared into the hallway. I hoped and hoped that this was a good sign, that he would be able to sort something out. Because if he couldn't . . .

I crept to the sitting room doorway, but I could just hear a discussion going on between Cal and Eck, with occasional grunting from Wolverine. I went back to my seat and closed my eyes. Just don't send me away, please. Because I really, and truly, had nowhere else to go.

After what seemed like an age, the boys filed through into the kitchen. Cal looked snotty, Eck embarrassed, Wolverine . . . well, hungry, probably.

'Here's the thing,' said Eck, staring at the floor, 'Cal thinks—'

'We all think,' interrupted Cal.

'. . . that one way we could get round the fact that you don't have enough money—'

'But Eck would like you to live here . . .' Cal's lip curled up. Eck stopped momentarily and shot Cal a dirty look.

'One way might be if you helped—'

'Oh, for goodness' sake, spit it out,' said Cal. 'Listen. If you want to stop me putting Wolverine in that room—'

'You won't,' said Eck. They shot looks at one another and I wondered how well they actually got on. Cal took over the conversation.

'You need to make up for not paying your share of the deposit.'

I couldn't quite concentrate, but it sounded like they were going to let me stay. That was a good thing, despite the state of the place.

'What do you mean?'

'Well, you can see the state of this place.'

I could.

'If you could look after it for us, we could forget the deposit.'

Nooo!

I looked at Eck. He shot me a hopeful glance.

'What do you mean, "look after it"?' I said, in case they meant, take nice long lovely baths here.

Eck rubbed the back of his neck. 'Well, you know. Do the hoovering. Scrubbing. Cleaning up mostly. We're usually too busy.'

Too busy? That wouldn't be the student life I remembered then.

'But we'd all chip in to pay your deposit so you could stay.' He looked awkward again. 'Will you have money coming in after that?'

'Of course,' I assured him.

There was a silence. For the last time, just in case I'd got it wrong I said, 'So you're saying I can stay if I clean?'

The boys glanced at each other, then Eck nodded. Oh great. So not only was I going to have to live in a germ sanctuary, I was going to have to clean it too.

'Isn't this a bit sexist?' I said.

'No,' said Cal. 'It's poor-ist.'

'Sorry,' said Eck. 'But we were trying to find a solution . . .'

I looked for my positive side again. It was fleeing for the exit, but I grasped it manfully.

'Absolutely,' I said. 'You're on!'

'Great,' said Eck, looking relieved. 'Cup of tea to celebrate?'

We looked at each other.

'I'll just go get my things, I think.'

'Yeah,' said Eck. 'OK.'

Chapter Seven

Of course, I didn't know what to pack. *Vogue* hadn't done an article on 'Capsule Wardrobes for Your New Shit Life'. If I was thinking logically, Wellington boots, three hundred jumpers and a hazmat suit.

I gazed at my wardrobe. It was arranged by colour so that shades segued into one another. I loved it. There was the raspberry Temperley silk dress I'd worn to Theo's twenty-first, which ended up in the fountain. In fact I couldn't have worn it more than once, but it had been a good, fun, dress and only about seven hundred quid, I seemed to recall. Christ. Maybe I could sell the dress? But I could see the heavy water stains the dry cleaner's hadn't been able to get out from here. Maybe not.

Oh, and that lovely pale green chiffon. I'd loved it to bits till a famous WAG had worn the exact same one ten days later and I'd had to abandon it for ever. So sad. Oh, bollocks, I was packing it anyway.

73

Gail eyed up my bags in the hall. She'd been fluttering around apologetically – but not apologetically enough to say, 'Do you know what, Sophie, I've changed my mind and in fact why don't we convert the basement into a crash pad for you and you stay there for six months and we'll say that that was probably what Daddy meant in his will.'

'It's just clothes,' I said, in case she thought I was stuffing oil paintings into the lining. 'And I had to put them in the Louis Vuittons, there aren't any other suitcases.'

'Good luck,' she said, smiling nervously. 'I couldn't wait to leave home. It was the most exciting day of my life.'

I stared at her.

'I realise this isn't the same.'

'It's not the same at all,' I said, miserably.

'But your dad thought you could do it,' said Gail. 'And, you know . . . I reckon you'll be stubborn enough to make a go of anything.'

This is probably about the nicest thought Gail's ever had about me.

'Yeah, thanks,' I said, a bit ungracefully, but I was really shocked. She moved towards me then, and I thought she might be about to give me a hug, but at the last minute something in both of us stopped it happening.

We could probably both have done with it though.

Now came the really hard part. I tiptoed downstairs and whispered her name.

'Esperanza?'

She came out of the kitchen, drying her hands and looking fearful.

'Miss?'

I twisted my hair awkwardly.

'Esperanza, you know I'm leaving.'

Her face gave nothing away. I couldn't tell if she was pleased or sad. Probably best not to know. I wondered how I would have felt if Esperanza had left one day and never come back? Would I even have noticed?

I felt really ashamed of myself.

'So, em. I wondered. Where I'm going . . . I'm going to need to do some cleaning. You know, look after things. And I wondered if you could help . . . show me what to do.'

At first she looked like she didn't quite believe it. Then her whole face crumpled – but with delight.

'Miss Sophie! You need me to show you what to do? You want my help?'

'Yes,' I said, finding myself blush.

'But of course Esperanza can help you! Come with me.'

And she grabbed me by the hand like I was four years old and dragged me into the kitchen. As she did so, I had a sudden sense memory of her hand on my arm. But as far as I could recall she'd never touched me before. Yet there was certainly something very familiar about her touch.

'When you were small,' she said, 'you used to love to help Esperanza. Always when I was working you would come down-stairs. "What doing, Espraza?" all day long. I had to give you your own duster and brush.'

That couldn't be true, could it?

'Then you went to school, and after that, pffff. You don't want to help Esperanza any more. You want to buy shoes.'

'I do like shoes,' I said, as Esperanza opened a large cupboard I'd never been into before. There were rows of cleaning materials lined up neatly – bleaches and sprays and powders, each with corresponding cloths and buckets.

We went through everything. It took hours, but it wasn't like I had anything else to do. How to clean mirrors without streaking them. How to remove limescale (when I thought of the flat on the Old Kent Road, my heart sank. The only way to remove their limescale would be a medium-range nuclear missile). How to empty the Hoover. By the end of it I was grubby and exhausted. We collapsed down to share a pot of builder's tea. Esperanza fussed over me and chatted and was so completely unlike herself I couldn't believe who I was talking to. She told me about her daughter in Guatemala – who was about my age, which, I realised, meant that all these years Esperanza was looking after our family, she hadn't been looking after her own. I couldn't believe I'd never really thought about that.

'She's teacher now,' said Esperanza proudly. 'I send home all my money from here and she goes to school and now she's teacher.'

I was genuinely impressed. Maybe if I'd gone and done something useful like be a teacher I wouldn't be here right now . . . Oh, who was I kidding? I didn't have anything like the patience and dedication. Plus, I thought ruefully, I'd spent my life dealing with kids anyway, everyone I knew had a mental age of about eight and a half.

I had to go. I'd packed my suitcases. I'd learned a couple of useful things. I wandered up one last time to look at my dad's room. There was no trace now, nothing left at all. I wondered how long it would be before Gail redecorated, and every last bit of him would be gone. I wondered what she was doing with all his Jermyn Street suits – he liked going to get tailored, used to take me with him. The tailors would give me lollipops and warn me sternly against playing with pins. I played with the pins anyway and my dad laughed, ruffled my hair and told me I had a taste for danger.

I hadn't. But it felt like I no longer had a choice.

'I think I'll see you soon,' I said to Esperanza. 'And . . . I know I've never . . .' Suddenly I found it hard to get the words out. 'I know I've never said it. Not properly,' I said. My bottom lip was wobbling a bit. 'But . . . thank you.'

Esperanza clasped me to her large bosom and gave me a huge hug.

'There you are,' she said. 'That's all you ever had to say.'

If I thought the Old Kent Road looked bad in morning light, it wasn't in the least bit improved by a dank, heavy overcast day.

I wondered if any of the boys were going to come out and help me up with my luggage. I gave them a good couple of minutes at the bottom of the path, but no dice. Maybe they weren't going to do anything until the cheque cleared. Or they'd been brought up in barns. That was certainly true of Wolverine, at least. So I lugged both the cases up myself, hurling them over the mattress, and heaved them to the end of the little dark corridor.

The room hadn't magically expanded, Tardis-like, since I'd been away. Neither was it filled with fresh welcoming flowers and a bottle of champagne.

I reckon flat sharing definitely needs an image overhaul. They should call it boutique living, something like that. Like a Manhattan hotel room – yes, this is a tiny cupboard with a view of a brick wall. But, hey, let us distract you by putting eleven pillows on the bed! Something like that. The broken, crappy wardrobe would take about three minidresses and no more. I pushed an entire suitcase under the bed immediately; it could support the broken springs.

The house was silent. Then I sat down on the bed and wondered what to do next. My nose prickled with the dust as I noticed a piece of paper on the floor that had obviously been pushed underneath the door.

Please, it said hopefully at the top,
clean toilet
and bathroom
and kitchen
and window's
I tutted to myself about the spare apostrophe
and floor's.
Thank you.

It didn't say how often they required these things done. Once a week? Daily? And did floors include the floors of their bedrooms? I decided immediately that it didn't. I had no intention of entering any of these trolls' rooms.

Esperanza had sent me away with a care package of her favourite cleaning products. Like a goodie bag, I supposed, only much, much shitter.

In lieu of a single thing to do or, I gulped, a single person in the world even knowing where I was – I supposed my mobile phone still worked, I didn't bother checking it any more. Everyone had stopped phoning. Actually, I wondered about that – Daddy had always just taken care of the bill. Maybe that would stop too. I checked the phone. Sure enough, it said, 'This number is not in service'. Shit. I'd never even got my own phone before. It had always come in through Daddy's office. I sat down on the bed. I wouldn't cry. I wouldn't cry. I wouldn't, wouldn't, wouldn't cry.

I pulled on a pair of Juicy sweatpants that I normally would never wear if I wasn't on my way to Pilates (little did I know then how much I was about to start living in them) and a C&C T-shirt. I would just have to treat it as my workout, that was all. Put some loud music on and pretend it was the hot new thing, like when everyone tried to pretend that pole dancing was a workout.

Kitchen first. I don't think I'd ever seen a more depressing room in my life. It was just so miserably dark and grim, with the cheapest, nastiest work surfaces, specially designed to trap germs and grot. Orange, brown and green tiles fought for space on the wall. The fridge looked like one of those fridges that could appear in newspapers with odd-looking women saying, 'I bought this fridge in 1952 and it's still working!' Or, it could have if it had been looked after or – I sniffed suspiciously – was actually working.

I found an egg-spattered radio – maybe Capital would have something perky to cheer me up.

'Welcome back to Indie Boys Radio,' intoned a voice. 'And now our Smiths' marathon continues with "Never Had No One Ever".'

I tried to find something else, but only came up against static, or hollering pirate stations broadcast from the tops of nearby tower blocks. It was a very old radio. But that was not going to matter! It was all about keeping a positive attitude. I just had to get through this, and the next couple of months, then I could go home – with my new, rock-hard biceps – come into my inheritance, and show everyone how amazingly well I was doing. I was thinking about setting up some kind of memorial charity for my father. For heart disease maybe – oh no, they already had quite a few of those. Well, I'd find something. Something in his name and I could hold a big fundraising party every year and all the mags would cover it and Daddy would have been so proud of me. It felt like an admirable aim to have. In fact, I thought, tying back my hair, I could almost see it now – me saying, 'I can understand the struggle people have to cure and heal; to work their way through every day. I've scrubbed floors. I've been down on my hands and knees . . .' Oh, no that didn't sound so good. How about, 'I've known the blood, sweat and tears . . .'

I was running my hand under the tap trying to fill a bucket, but it didn't seem to be getting any warmer. This wasn't the best of starts. All round the sink were piled bowls of cement-hard cereal. Why do people eat stuff that dries up like that? They must have insides like quarries.

I was just deciding who was going to draw the raffle – I liked Stephen Fry personally, but maybe Neil Morrissey at a push – when Cal pushed his way through into the kitchen, yawning wildly. He was wearing an unbuttoned striped pyjama top which should have made him look stupid but actually only enhanced the leanness of his torso – no hair – and a flat, narrow stomach. Most of the boys I knew were wide and barrel-chested; big, farmer's boys with years of rugby behind them. This scrawny, indie look, of a boy brought up on jam sand-wiches and glue sniffing, was new. I couldn't help but find it a bit sexy, especially with his black hair sticking up all over his head.

He looked surprised, then briefly pleased, to see me in his kitchen.

'Hello!' he said. 'I forgot all about you, Cinders.'

'I'm not Cinders,' I said, crossly.

'No,' he said. 'Not till you realise that you have to turn on the water heater for hot water. You'll be waiting to fill that bucket a long time.'

I said, 'Oh,' as if I'd known that all along, and turned on a strange-looking white machine which shuddered and juddered loudly and spouted out a thin line of scorching hot water that made me shriek slightly in a daft posh girl kind of a way. I tried to turn it into a cough.

'It's two o'clock,' I said. 'Were you in bed?'

Cal smiled broadly. 'No. This is what I wear to my top office job in the city. Any chance of a cup of tea?'

'The kettle isn't there any more.'

'Oh yeah, we were using it for tie-dye. Hang on.'

He stretched his long arms over me. He smelled sleepy – not bad, just warm and rumpled and a bit sexy. It was a good smell.

'Here we go,' he said, taking it down from a cupboard. He peered in it as he nudged me away from the sink. 'Could prob-ably do with a clean itself.'

81

The interior of the kettle was completely white, silted up with chalk, with red stripes in it.

'You think?'

'Maybe they're friendly bacteria?' said Cal doubtfully.

I set to it with the boiling water. Maybe we could just fill the teapot straight from that.

'It's great you're here,' said Cal and I felt myself soften up a bit. 'We really need someone to look after us. Like Snow White and the Seven Dwarfs.'

'No!' I said. 'That's not what it's like. It's just helping pay my way till I get my old job back.'

He looked at me lazily. 'You have a job?'

'Have you?'

'I'm a sculptor.' He shrugged. 'Michelangelo thought it was quite a cool calling actually.'

'Oh, really? Are you as good as Michelangelo?'

He smiled. 'No. No, Sophie, I'm not as good as Michelangelo. Can I still have a cup of tea?'

I smiled back at him and poured water in the kettle. Cal stretched sleepily like a big cat.

'Up all night?' I asked, saucily. To my amazement, I suddenly found I was tempted to run my fingernails down his chest. I looked at my nails. I hadn't had a manicure in goodness knows how long. Maybe he wouldn't mind.

'Hey, is there one for me?'

I interrupted my Cal's chest/my nails interface fantasy at the sound of a young voice with a heavy accent, possibly Spanish. There was a tiny, dark-haired girl with huge bosoms and a large bottom. In my circle we'd have considered her fat, but actually it was clear she was really very sexy. She had long messy black hair strewn over her face, and glossy olive skin, and black circles under her eyes which should have looked bad and which I'd have got sorted out at the dermatologist straight away but actually made her look sexy. She bit one of her huge pillowy lips.

'Hello.'

'Hello,' I said, a little stiffly. All my nail-based fantasies dropped into the sink with an 'uh-urr' type noise.

'This is Sophie, the cleaner,' said Cal. The girl raised her eyebrows slightly.

'I'm not "the cleaner",' I said. 'I live here. I've moved in. I'm helping out with the cleaning for a bit.'

'The bathroom is deesgusting,' said the girl. 'Deesgusting. The whole flat is deesgusting.'

'Well, I haven't started in there yet,' I said, feeling annoyed. It wasn't my fault that the place was a pig heap. The girl had immediately lost interest in me and wandered off, which was incredibly annoying, seeing as if she'd turned up at any of the parties I used to go to, nobody would have spoken to *her*.

'Here's the tea,' I said. Cal peered in the pot suspiciously. 'Do you normally only put one teabag in a pot of tea?' he said. 'Is that what you do where you come from?'

'No,' I said, reddening. OK, OK, OK. I hadn't wanted to admit it. But it was true. Between Esperanza, my preference for Starbucks and/or champagne, and the fact that we went out all the time ... OK. I'd never made tea before. I'd only seen it done on *EastEnders*. I never wanted to admit this to another living soul.

'You do it then,' I said. 'I've got bathrooms to clean apparently.'

The girl turned round. 'Ooh, your cleaner's quite stroppy.'

'I'm not the cleaner!' I said.

'Sorry,' she said, not looking sorry at all but wandering over to Cal. She snuggled under his shirt and – grrr – ran her nails down his chest.

'Can we go back to bed?'

'In the absence of tea,' said Cal. 'I say, yes, why not?'

He opened the wobbly fridge, pulled out a bottle of wine and the two of them disappeared, leaving me standing there with a teapot full of tepid brown water I didn't want to drink.

Four hours later I felt empty – like all the core of Sophie had been hollowed out and replaced with scouring powder and greyness. I'd given up on my nails long ago; they were gone, maybe for ever.

But the kitchen was *clean*, goddam it! Bucket after bucket of filthy water, crumbs, hairs, unidentifiable grungy bits, some pockets of smells that I couldn't believe were even legal, and it was getting there. The cabinets weren't brown, actually, they were beige, once I'd removed the patina of tomato soup. Still hideous, but not actually a contact hazard in themselves.

The floor turned out to be black and white diamond patterned lino, which reminded me of our black and white marble entrance hall in Chelsea, but I wasn't going to think about that. The main thing was that, though the oven wasn't exactly silver, it was no longer exactly black either, and had a lot fewer crispy black cheese boogers hanging off the side of it. I'd polished the tiles, scraped the drawer handles, washed and dried all crockery and cutlery (after first washing and drying all the tea towels, which looked like a tramp's underwear collection).

It was disgusting. It was revolting. I'd hated every second of it, without having to pretend I was even dimly aware (although thankfully they were *reasonably* quiet – I heard a couple of yelps, but was really doing my very best not to listen) that two flimsy walls away there was some skinny pale-bodied indie-boy sex going on, and I was incredibly curious, despite myself, to know what that was like. Rufus had been great fun, but, apart from the spanking, actually a bit of a wimp in bed.

But a cigarette-smoking sculptor . . . well, it gave me something to think about whilst I did the scrubbing.

When I stood back to look at my work, however, something changed. As I looked round I couldn't help it. I felt *pleased*. And a bit proud. It smelt nice and looked, if not good, at least borderline habitable. I'd taken something horrible and made it good. It wasn't like me at all. It wasn't bad.

Not that I was going to make a habit of it. And if the boys all poured in and threw beans all over the place, I certainly wasn't going to start over tomorrow. Not that I could anyway, I had to get a job so I could stop this cleaning nonsense as quickly as possible.

Just after six, Eck came bounding through the door, throwing his keys onto the side.

'Oh wow,' he said, stopping short. 'Look at this.'

I felt a bit of a grin rise up towards my face which I tried to dampen down again. What an absurd reaction to some soapy water.

'Wow,' he said again, running his fingers along the cabinets. 'I don't think I've ever seen . . .' He smiled at me. 'Well done, Sophie, it's brill.'

I smiled back. I couldn't help it, his enthusiasm was infectious.

'Welcome!' he said. 'Wow. If you keep making it nicer, they'll probably put the rent up.'

'Thank you,' I said, wishing I wasn't covered in utter filth. 'Had a hard day at the spider coalface?'

He grimaced. 'Don't ask. It's my last year, so I'm about to find out if the last three weren't a complete waste of time.'

'People love spiders though.'

He winced again. 'Oh God, stop, it's not funny. I should never have left accountancy.'

'An artist/accountant,' I said. 'It's very romantic.'

'That's what I thought,' said Eck. 'Till I got my first student loan through. Being good at sums doesn't really help.'

'I thought Bohemians didn't do sums.'

'Bohemians don't eat either. But I am starving.'

'I don't cook,' I said.

Eck laughed.

'What?'

'Just your face when you thought I might be asking you to cook.'

'Well, I don't.'

'That's OK, but you looked at me like I'd just handed you Cal's snake.'

'He doesn't really have a snake,' I said fiercely.

'No, he doesn't. And you don't really have to cook, so put the broom down.'

'What's up?'

It was James, bounding into the kitchen too; he seemed to have loads of energy, like a puppy. He was in his army gear and covered in mud and camouflage.

'Stay back!' shouted Eck. 'You can't come in.'

'Why not?' asked James. 'Enemy infiltration?'

'Yes,' said Eck. 'Your muddy boots and our spotless floor.'

James retreated and instead posted his head around the door.

'Wow,' he said. 'Sophie, what an amazing woman you are.'

Great. I'm always waiting for someone to call me an amazing woman and when it comes it's for my bloomin' domestic goddess skills.

'I'll go have a shower,' said James. 'Can't wait to see what you've done in the bath . . . Oh.'

'I'll get to that tomorrow,' I said. 'I'm not superwoman.'

'Yes, you are,' said Eck. Then he coughed and looked embarrassed. 'Um. Anyway.' He looked around. 'So, no cooking . . .'

'Fish and chips,' came hollering from James's direction. It sounded like he was hitting his boots together and letting the mud fall all over the floor in the hallway. 'Let's get fish and chips. I've been on manoeuvres and we can't mess up the kitchen.'

'So you're just going to eat fish and chips every night for the rest of your life?'

James's head reappeared. 'I've heard worse plans. You want some?'

Well, this was a day of firsts. Actually, I had had fish and chips before, apparently, I just couldn't remember them. Because my dad was American, he'd insisted we all try England's national dish at least once. It seemed, even for a man used to the Herculean amounts of grease used in US cuisine, it was still too much. Since then I'd rather collapse in a faint than eat fried food (in fact, I had; Carena and I once went through a period of skipping lunch and getting stuck into the cocktails too early), and was quite happy to have let it all pass me by.

Now, however, I realised I was absolutely ravenous.

'Sure,' I said. I had twelve pounds left – would that cover it? I hoped so.

'What about Cal and his baggage?' said Eck. I was pleased to hear that.

'Are they *still* at it?' said James. 'Christ. Either they're starving or they're dead, so we'd better check. And it's not fair to leave Wolverine outside all day.'

James came back in fifteen minutes with a huge, steaming, fragrant blue bag. Ketchup, salt and vinegar were lined up and liberally sprinkled over the hot crackling fish and the tasty chips. It was completely and utterly delicious. Not only that, but I washed it down with a beer. I mentally apologised to my thighs and to my holistic nutritionist Fluffo Magenta (who I hated seeing anyway, she only wanted me to eat more stuff you pick in the woods) and wondered how many calories I'd burned scrubbing underneath the cooker. Loads, probably. And on my list of current worries it was way, way down there. So I tucked in merrily.

Cal emerged alone from his bedroom.

'Don't tell me – you've nobbed her to death,' said James, cheerfully.

'She's gone home,' said Cal. 'Finally. Fantastic, it can be really difficult getting them out of the house.'

'You have trouble getting girls to leave this house?' I said, unable to keep the scepticism out of my voice.

'Well, you're still here,' said Cal, popping open a beer and taking a long draught. 'Save those pickled onions for Wolverine, he's sulking.'

The four of us sat round the rickety table; James told us about his sergeant commander, who had a face like a Muppet and was always finding it difficult to scream commands without getting the piss taken out of him by people saying, 'Gee, Kermie' or singing the 'Mahna Mahna' song.

Eck talked about trying to liberate a large amount of scrap metal from a junk heap, only to come up against a terrifying gang of teenage scrap merchants, hell-bent on plundering his booty.

'They were like pirates,' he said. 'Little mini-bitey pirates. With flick knives.'

'Were you terrified and turned round and ran away?' asked Cal.

'Of course!' said Eck, shooting me his lovely smile. 'I'm an artist and thus meant to be soft and I don't care about admitting it. There must be easier ways to steal sheet metal.'

'Have you tried the roof of the art college?'

Eck rolled his eyes. 'Durr! Of course!'

Then Cal turned his attention to me.

'So, Miss Mop. Tell us about you. What do you do then?'

Keep calm, I told myself. Keep calm. They don't need to know I'm coming into millions of pounds in a few months, it would only make everything weird. Plus they'd want to know everything and it wasn't a story I felt ready to tell yet. Not to strangers, and as for my friends . . . well. The less said about them the better.

'I'm into photography,' I said, mouth crammed full of ketchup-covered chip. 'I work for Julius Mandinski.'

I thought if they were arty they might have heard of him, but there wasn't a flicker of recognition. And, as I hadn't been into the studio for weeks and no one had bothered to ring or find out how I was or anything, I probably wasn't working there any more anyway.

'Who's he? Some posh twat that takes pictures of women's arses being bitten by crocodiles then sells them to idiots?' said Cal, managing to make even chip eating look like a slightly more elegant activity than I'd ever imagined it could be before.

I took a breath to start a healthy defence of Julius, but it was true, crocodile arse-bitage was never entirely out of the question. I told them about the time he tried to bring a wolf into the studio for a shoot and six Polish teenagers had gone totally ape shit. They laughed gratifyingly.

'So, come on then. Why are you here?' said Cal. 'Seriously. Slumming it for research? Fun?'

Eck gave Cal a look. 'Shh.'

'Can't I ask a question?' said Cal.

'Well, I'm here,' said James in his well-modulated tones.

'You're here because you don't mind sleeping in a forest with twigs up your jacksie,' said Cal. 'Four walls are quite scary for you. If we had any furniture, you'd bolt. So, come on, Cinders. You're clearly posh. What was it? Trust fund row? Been buying too much Louis Vuitton?'

I *knew* those bastards had watched me drag my luggage in.

'Or are you doing research for some Britflick? Are you going to go back and report to all your friends what amazing squalor you found in SOUTH London? And you'll all laugh your heads off and order in more Cristal?'

'Leave it, Cal,' said Eck, manfully. 'You're being a nosy, chippy bastard.'

I could feel myself going pink. I *never* blush.

'I just have a reasonable interest in my fellow man – or woman,' said Cal. 'That's the domain of the artist, you know.'

'Or the domain of, you know, the arse,' said Eck. But James and Cal were still looking at me expectantly.

'It's all fake,' I said finally. 'And my grandmother sent me to elocution lessons. She's a terrible snob. We're from . . .' I cast around in my head. 'Er, Hackney.'

The others nodded, except for Cal, who narrowed his eyes at me.

'Whereabouts in Hackney?'

'You wouldn't know it.'

'I might.'

'Actually, we're so poor our road didn't have a name.'

'Is that right? So you're not bourgeois scum then?'

'That's terrible,' said James. 'You know, the army is a good way out of poverty too.'

'That's your answer to everything,' said Cal. 'Not everyone wants to catch ringworm on the Brecon Beacons, you know.'

'It would do you a bit of good,' said James, slightly riled. 'Get you out of doing nothing but sleeping, shagging and drinking beer.'

'It's true,' said Cal. 'I do so *hate* my life.'

He gave me another shrewd look. He really was a nosy bastard.

'Didn't you have any friends you could stay with?'

I shrugged and tried to make myself look harder than I felt.

'I wanted to get away. Get in touch with my creative photographic soul. Wouldn't want to get in anyone's way.'

Eck grinned at me. 'I'm sure you won't be,' he said.

'Ooh, look at you,' said Cal, sneering at Eck. Ugh, he really was unpleasant.

'Sorry, princess,' said Cal to me. 'I'm a right old bastard sometimes.'

'Sometimes?' scoffed Eck, clearly pissed off.

The weird thing was, though, that despite the intrusive questions, I actually had a good time that evening. An actual good time. The conversation changed to other things, like James's manoeuvres, and Cal and Eck kept taking the piss out of each other, and Wolverine came in and removed the pickled onions with a grunt and there was just a nice, relaxed atmosphere that I couldn't remember since . . . since, well, for a while.

If I went out to eat with the girls, there was always hundreds of people, and lots of shouting and showing off, and competitive non-eating, and that wasn't always that much fun either. This – just sitting round a table with a bunch of people, chatting over the day – well, it felt new, and it felt quite nice.

So I was in quite a good mood when I took myself off to Cell Block H, only slightly ruined by having to use the loo, which was by some way the grubbiest I'd ever seen, and was clearly going to make tomorrow even muckier than today. Then I lay in bed, in that strange room that I couldn't imagine would ever feel like home; listening to the boys still playing music, rolling spliffs and talking, the huge lorries thundering down the Old Kent Road on their way to Dover, the rude boys in their low-slung Citroens banging out bass all the way up the road, and the regular screams of police sirens.

I was so exhausted, though, that even that couldn't keep me awake. But in my dream, my dad was trying to call, but the phone wouldn't ring. It just made the sound of sirens.

Chapter Eight

Cleaning. Not for everyone. Boy, oh boy. There are some people in this world who like nothing better than to line up the contents of their drawers in alphabetical order. Why couldn't I have been one of those? Five hours in that tiny windowless bathroom – for all the noise the extractor fan gave out, there was no way I was getting enough oxygen in. I wondered if I was actually going to die, and if so, what would do for me first: bacterial disease or bleach fumes? Bit by bit things started to improve. Looking at the thirteen toothbrushes, in various states of hideousness, I decided the best thing to do was just to throw them all way and let the boys start afresh. Surely it was cleaner not to brush your teeth at all than to pick some dead hedgehog at random?

I also ventured out of doors to pick up a new toilet brush, the one there being a shade of brown I didn't want to contemplate. Where does one buy a toilet brush? I was sure I'd seen something at Cath Kidston, but I couldn't quite remember.

I wouldn't like to say this part of London was grim but, oh God, it was *so* grim. It was like they'd wallpapered the whole place in grey and old fast-food wrappers. The traffic was horrid and relentless, it took half an hour to cross the road. There were lots of weird discount shops I hadn't seen before. Normally I get excited by the sight of shops I've never seen before, but these turned out to sell old potatoes out of boxes like in old films of communist Russia. It would have made me shiver, until I noticed that they did champagne for six pounds a bottle. That could definitely come in handy some time, when I had a job again and could buy stuff, rather than exist on dry Weetabix from the back of the newly cleaned larder.

I bought a few bits and pieces that I thought were cleaning products – the words were in Cyrillic, but they looked like they'd do the job – and went back to queen drudgery.

If I'd thought the kitchen odds and ends were gross, I hadn't seen anything yet. Hair – SO MUCH HAIR. I remembered reading somewhere that hair was the most germ-ridden substance in the human body. And it was everywhere! From a bunch of filthy strangers I didn't know! I just closed my eyes and pretended I was in CSI and investigating a murder as a very clever highly trained forensic specialist. It was very unlike me to fantasise about having a job. I was amazed how much it helped. I'm sure this wasn't what Daddy would have had in mind for me. He probably meant for me to get a job in a shop, share a mansion flat in a block. Or work in a nursery, like Princess Diana.

The toilet bowl was even worse. There was no way around this. Here I was. Not so long ago I'd been striding up the red carpet to the Fashion Rocks summer party, just behind Tamara Mellon and within spitting distance of Mischa Barton. What were Tamara and Mischa doing right now? E.g. did they have their head stuck down a stranger's toilet bowl whilst scratching off poo with a toilet brush bought from the ninety-nine-pence shop? Perhaps they did. But somehow, I doubted it.

Crouching, I overheard Eck and Cal in the hall. They seemed to be having quite an intense conversation.

'Just ask her,' Cal was saying. 'What can possibly go wrong?'

'Well, she says no and we all have to live here for the next five years,' said Eck. 'Neh. Don't think I will.'

'Where are your balls, man?' said Cal.

'Where's your brain?' retorted Eck rudely. 'This could be a very bad idea.'

There was a pause.

'She's pretty hot though,' said Cal.

My heart started to pound. Could it be . . . could they be talking about me? They obviously didn't know I was in here. Did Cal think I was hot? I squatted by the toilet bowl. God, my hair needed washing.

'Try her room,' said Cal.

It was me! Ooh! Oh my God! I couldn't help feeling excited. But what was Eck going to do? Someone was going to ask me out! See, Rufus the Rat! I wasn't just someone else's old sewage . . . ugh, never think about old sewage whilst crouching by some stranger's toilet bowl.

'No,' said Eck.

Oh, so, maybe not then.

'Come on, don't be a coward.'

'It's OK for you, you distract women by pointing to something and whipping her knickers off with the other hand,' said Eck. Ooh, that sounded like fun. 'I just like to think I'm a bit more—'

'Of a coward?' said Cal.

'No!'

'Chook . . . chook. Choook, chook, chook . . .'

'Stop making chicken noises, it's stupid.'

'Bork . . . bork, bork, bork, bork.'

'What's that, a chicken being sick?'

'It's a party, Eck, not a marriage proposal.'

Eck sighed. This was wildly exciting – being talked about in a way that, for once, didn't include the phrase, '*Such a shame*'.

Then he took a deep breath and I heard his tread down the corridor. Oh my God! He was going towards my room! I heard a knock, then there was a long pause.

'Not in!' he said finally. 'Great! Fancy going out and getting a bacon sandwich?'

'All right, Casanova,' said Cal.

'I'll just have a slash,' said Eck.

I stiffened. Oh God! A quick glance around confirmed that there was nowhere to hide, unless the shower curtain was loamy enough to disguise me completely. I could shout out that I was in here, but then they'd assume I'd been ensconced having a poo for about an hour, which wasn't really the image I was seeking to convey. Maybe I'd just have to pretend I was so caught up in my life's work – cleaning their shit off a toilet, obviously – that I couldn't possibly have heard a word.

The door creaked open. Eck entered, flies already down, one hand fishing in his trousers. He couldn't have been more surprised to see me if I'd been a dog doing a handstand.

'Urgg,' he said, snatching his hands away from his fly. I averted my eyes, but it was plain he didn't know whether to zip it up – thus drawing further attention to the area – or just leave it alone, with possible visible consequences. I studied my mop bucket as hard as I could.

'Uh, hello!' I said, in a voice that came out in a much higher pitch than I'd intended. 'I didn't hear you come in.'

'Didn't you?' said Eck, in a voice that betrayed so much relief I wouldn't have been surprised if pee had started gushing out right then. 'Oh, good.'

He stood there for another second. I could hear a giggle behind the door. Obviously Cal had figured out where I was.

'Bacon sandwich, Eck?' he shouted. 'Or do you want to go dancing?'

Eck's face burned a bright red.

'Was that someone shouting?' I said helpfully. 'I couldn't really hear.'

Eck still seemed frozen to the spot.

'Do you want me to get out while you have a pee?' I said kindly. He nodded, looking in some pain. I smiled sympathetically and headed outside, still wearing my rubber gloves.

Cal was leaning against the kitchen doorframe, looking louche and superior. What is it about unbelievably confident men? Even ugly ones (which Cal definitely wasn't) just exude a sense of sexiness, just by giving off the impression they know what they're doing. I suppose there's something quite primitive about it – the idea that when they finally got you into bed, nobody at any point would be saying, 'Gosh, sorry – this bit goes where again?' Anyway, it definitely works.

'Ooh,' he said. 'Like the rubber gloves. Planning a special evening?'

'Just trying not to get boy germs,' I said. 'Difficult round here.'

The toilet flushed, loudly.

'So how are you getting on with our Eck then?' said Cal, an amused look on his face. 'Nice guy, don't you think? Are nice guys your cup of tea, princess? Not by looking at you.'

'You can't tell anything by looking at me,' I said.

'Really? Not that you went to private school, wore a boater, can ride a pony, know your way around a yacht and like dancing in ludicrous shoes? All in Hackney, of course.'

'Yeah, yeah, yeah,' I said, but I felt a chill in my heart. If Cal found out the truth, would they chuck me out? Treble the rent? Go to the papers?

'Those are dreadful dancing bunions you have,' said Cal, staring at my feet. From the bathroom came the sound of some fairly frantic hand washing.

'Listen.' He lowered his voice. 'We were thinking of having a bit of a party. I think Eck would quite like you to be there. Fancy it?'

'Are you going to be there?' I said, before I could stop myself.

'Well, you are the naughty thing, aren't you?' he said. 'Everyone's going to be there.'

Suddenly there came a yowl from the bathroom. We both turned round towards the door.

99

'*Argh!* Fuck, fuck, fuck, fuck, fuck, fuck.'

Cal and I looked at one another.

'What's up?' shouted Cal.

'It burns! It burns!'

There was the sound of the shower being turned on and someone jumping into it, fully clothed. Shrieking.

'What have you been doing in there?' said Cal to me, unfairly I thought seeing as I wasn't the one who'd just set myself on fire.

'Nothing!' I said sulkily, pulling out the strange foreign cleanser I was still clutching in my rubber-gloved hands. 'Cleaning up for you, remember?'

Cal grabbed the bottle and held it tentatively between two fingers.

'Shit,' he said, letting his breath out slowly. 'Do you know what this is?'

'Cleaning product?' I said. 'They come in bright packaging and smell funny.'

'This is oven cleaner,' said Cal. 'The stuff you leave overnight that you can't touch with bare flesh. Have you been swilling it down the toilet?'

I shrugged. 'Seemed to be doing the job.'

'Splashback,' said Cal. 'Oh God.'

'It burns!' came weakly through the door.

'How would you know?' I said sulkily, feeling cross for being in the wrong. 'I can't imagine you've ever cleaned anything.'

'And you have?' said Cal, looking amused.

'Yes,' I said. Well, Esperanza had showed me something. I hadn't maybe quite matched the brand name.

He handed me back the bottle. 'Take this away from me, I feel like a cigarette and don't want to actually explode.'

The noise from the bathroom had degenerated into whimpering.

'I'm going out,' said Cal nonchalantly. 'Only call an ambulance if you have to. Wolverine!'

Wolverine scampered out of the bedroom.

'Bye then.'

'Stop, don't leave me . . .' I said.

But it was too late.

Twenty minutes later, Eck emerged from the loo, looking rather pale and shaken.

'Um, are you all right?' I said tentatively. I didn't want to rush to admit liability. Plus, I'd made tea. This time I'd left the bags in far too long. The cups were dark brown and it tasted like pure muck.

'Well, I saved it,' he said, looking frightened.

'Well, that's great news!' I tried to be cheery. 'Perhaps . . . I made a *little* mistake with the cleaner . . . but I'm going to fix that right away.'

'You probably should,' said Eck. 'The toilet's smoking.'

I waited for him to mention something about a party, but he didn't. He didn't drink the tea I'd made him either. Or sit down.

'Do you want to sit down?' I said.

'Not yet,' he said gingerly.

'I'm sorry,' I said.

'You really are from a different planet, aren't you?' he said, shaking his head.

'Oh, I don't know about that,' I said. 'I'm just like anybody else.'

I really was desperate to know if he was going to ask me out or not. My ego really needed this.

'I mean, I love dancing and things, just like normal people.'

'I don't think I'm ever going to dance again,' said Eck, looking pained. So, I was going to have to take this as a no, then.

'Like George Michael,' I said wisely. 'Until he got his sexuality sorted out, and now he dances all the time.'

I sighed to myself. Maybe they were having a party here but I wasn't even invited to it. Maybe I'd have to sit in my room all night holding the coats. The idea of an upcoming social event, something to look forward to with a nice-looking boy – either of them, really – had really cheered me up and I'd felt almost happy. Right up to the point where I burned off Eck's penis.

Eck looked up, a slight sagginess visible under his chocolate brown eyes.

'Sophie . . .' he said. 'Do you think we should have a flat party?'

Ooh! I thought, as I swilled forty-seven litres of water down the cistern. After I'd done that the thing was pristine; it wasn't actually that bad a way to clean a toilet, as long as you didn't then use it for a couple of days. A party! Dancing! Booze! The only sticky moment had come when Eck had asked me, with quite a hopeful look in his eye, if I'd like to invite some of my friends. It was hard to explain that, a) I was a bit disappointed as I'd hoped the whole idea of having a party was to sneakily get a chance to ask me out, b) all my friends had inexplicably appeared to side with the woman who stole my boyfriend and didn't like me any more, c) even if that hadn't been the case, they wouldn't come here, and d) if they did, they'd probably be really sneery and unpleasant about everything, as would I have been a few months before.

I moved on to the bath, more carefully this time. Good God, though, who'd been the last person to use it, Fungus the Bogeyman? Should I stick my fingers down the plughole like Esperanza had suggested . . . my eyes crept to the deadly oven poison. No, Sophie. No.

Chapter Nine

Cleaning the flat was obviously brilliant fun and everything – if by brilliant fun you mean horrible boring dirtiness that didn't pay me any money – but it still didn't solve my original problem. I needed my job back, and pretty damn fast. I hoped Julius would understand the principle of compassionate leave, but I wasn't holding out much hope. There were roughly 165,000 girls in London who'd like to work for practically nothing for a famous *avant-garde* photographer who gave amazingly druggy parties in his super-hip loft and only slept with twins.

I dialled my old work number. 'Hello?' said a smooth, sleepy-sounding voice. Weirdly, I think it sounded a bit like me.

'Hi there, it's Sophie Chesterton!'

There was a long pause. A loooonnngg pause. Not by any stretch of the imagination the type of pause that is just taking in a deep lungful of breath so they can scream, 'WELCOME

BACK! WE MISSED YOU SO MUCH!' down the phone at you.

'Sophie,' said the voice, finally, smoothly. I recognised it as Ladushka, a terrifyingly elegant woman who did something unspecified with galleries. 'What can I do for you?'

I aimed for cheerful perkiness, but it might have come out as strained desperation.

'Well, I was just calling to tell Jules I'll be back in to work tomorrow, and I'll want to chat to him about, you know, my conditions and things . . .' My voice trailed off. There was another, not very encouraging pause.

'Sophie, Jules thought you'd left.'

'I didn't leave! My father died!'

'Well, yes, but . . . it's been weeks, and it was only ever an internship anyway, so . . .'

'It was my job! You can't fire me from my job because my father died!'

'No, Sophie, it was an internship, with a small sum attached . . . I mean, you didn't think that was a salary, did you?'

It was certainly more of a salary than I was getting now.

'I was sorry to hear about your father,' said Ladushka, her voice softening. Which meant I could tell that she knew the battle was over and that she'd made her position quite clear. 'You must miss him terribly.'

Not so I was going to own up to her.

'Eh, could I just speak to Jules?'

'I'm terribly sorry, he's in Reykjavik shooting girls swimming under the ice for Italian *Vogue*.'

I'd hit an impasse.

'No mobile signal up there,' Ladushka added quickly, just in case I hadn't finally, irrevocably got the message.

'I see,' I said.

And I did see. Easy come, easy go.

I confided in Eck. I had to confide in someone and he was the only person handy.

'I've lost my job,' I said.

'Oh no!' he said. 'Did they ask you to clean the loos?'

'What do you do when you lose a job?' I said, realising I sounded a bit pathetic.

Eck raised his eyebrows. 'Well, you get another one. Or if you're desperate you could sign on.'

'Really? Do people still do that?' I said, wondering if I put a headscarf on nobody could ever recognise me.

Eck eyed me over his paper and toast.

'Not very many your age with four working limbs,' he said.

'Is that meant to make me feel guilty?'

'No. Do you feel guilty?'

Just about everything, all the time, I didn't say. I just sat there.

'Do you want to look at the jobs in my paper?'

He handed it over. There was quite a lot of jobs on offer for someone with my qualifications, i.e. not much. But they all seemed to involve something called hostessing or exotic dancing.

'You need to buy a better quality paper,' I said.

'It pleases me to think I read the same paper as exotic dancers,' said Eck. 'Don't worry, Sophie. You'll get a job. You could waitress, or you're getting quite good at cleaning . . .'

I'd taken to the surfaces of everything with a tin of polish. I'd gone a bit overboard – OK, you could get slightly high walking in the house. And I'd used one of my old pairs of Agent Provocateur pants as a duster. They didn't fit me any more for some reason.

'Nope,' I said, standing up. 'No more cleaning. I'm a photographer. That's what I am. That's what I've always wanted to be. I'm dedicated, and I'm going to do it.'

'Yay! Good for you!' said Eck, saluting me with his toast. I grinned back at him, then stopped suddenly and hoped I had enough money left for camera film.

The dedicated photographer trudged around every studio in London in the end. That's OK, flat hunting had made me quite good at trudging, and it gave me something to do during the day, apart from watch out for dropped pound coins on the street. I couldn't rely on the boys sharing their fish and chips forever.

I wished my portfolio were bigger. God, after Daddy put in my own dark room and everything. That made me feel all squirmy and guilty. I took a lot of shots en route though; of a sudden piece of beauty amongst the graffiti, and rubbish on the bypass; a wildly optimistic daffodil pushing up through concrete, or a grubby child, eyes wide, pointing at a fire engine.

The West End had nothing for me. They had photography assistants up to their eyeballs, which coincidentally was where the legs of those photography assistants came up to too. East London wasn't much help either. So finally I ended up even further south from where I started out; down the bottom of the endless Old Kent Road, in New Cross. I'd just taken the address from *Yellow Pages*.

In the end it was less a studio, more a big garage that some-one had knocked a large north-facing window into. Inside, one corner had big, red velvet drapes pinned up. The rest was the usual photographer's mess of empty coffee cups and cabling, as well as a large selection of slightly dubious-looking clothing. Suddenly I wasn't sure about this at all. It looked definitely a bit on the seedy side.

'Hello!' yelled a voice from behind the curtain.

'Hello,' I said, trotting out my spiel. 'I'm looking for a job? I've been working with Julius Mandinski, and I'm looking for a bigger challenge.'

A burly figure stepped out from behind the curtain.

'Oh yeah?'

It was Julius.

'Julius!' I said. He looked at me, and I could tell he was trying to remember my name.

'It's Sophie, remember? Your assistant? I thought you were in Reykjavik.'

'Uh, yeah,' said Julius. He looked a hundred per cent not very happy to see me. 'What the hell are you doing here?'

'Well, what are *you* doing here?'

Suddenly I heard a squawk from the door behind me.

'Well, I'm not going to be big sister, right, so you might as well just get over yourself, Kelly.'

'I would do,' came a voice that sounded like it possessed extremely long fingernails, 'if you weren't looking like such a hideous old bag. Maybe we could be, like mother and daughter, yeah?'

'Oh Christ,' said Julius, looking worried and glancing at his watch. Two little minxes pushed open the door. Neither of them could have been taller than five foot two. Both had really cheap blonde synthetic hair extensions down their backs, obvious fake logoed bags (I recognised them but would never have bought them) and very pale lipgloss. They could easily have been sisters.

'Hello, Grace. Hello, Kelly,' said Julius. I glanced at them in disbelief. He knew these girls? The only girls he ever worked with were over six foot and under six stone.

'JULIUS!' they both started up at once. 'I'm not going to be the big sister.'

'She's an old trout,' said Grace, whose eyebrows were possibly more arched than Kelly's, though it was a close run thing. 'One, she's twenty-one anyway, two, she's had too much sunbed, and three, all the kids have dragged her tits down to the ground anyway.'

'They have not!' said Kelly, affronted, 'And I'm smaller! I should be little sister!'

I looked at Julius and he shot a look at me.

'I don't understand,' I said.

Julius rolled his eyes. 'You trust-fund honeys never do. There's no money in fashion photography, darling. The fees are so low it hardly covers the models' waxing bills. This is what pays for the flash pad.' He waved his hand at the lowly studio. 'Bit o' glamour, bit o' catalogue.'

He turned away from me. My mouth dropped open.

'Now, can we just get the tops off, girls, and get started?' he said.

'No,' said Grace. 'Not till she confesses that she looks older than me.'

'No way,' said Kelly. 'Bitch.'

'Now, come on, girls. This is for the *Sport*; you've got to look like you love each other.'

'Neh,' said Kelly.

'I've got another two girls in an hour,' said Julius to me desperately. 'I've really got to get this done.'

I put on my poshest voice. I don't know why, it helps me sound louder and like I really mean things.

'God, girls, you both look gorgeous,' I said, putting on a ludicrous 'fashion' accent. 'You both look like twins to me. Why don't you play it like twins and let me see how it goes – I want to take a few Polaroids.' And I took out my little camera.

Both the girls' eyes widened with excitement. Well, I hadn't *said* I was anyone important, had I? Kelly shrugged off her pink fake-fur gilet.

'Which one's the oldest twin?' asked Grace.

'You know,' I said to Julius out of the corner of my mouth, 'I'm also pretty good at cleaning up.'

'I don't need—'

I kept my best card till last. 'And keeping my mouth shut.'

Julius heaved a big sigh. 'Then I guess you've started, love,' said Julius.

I stopped off at the off-licence and bought some cans of something with Greek lettering on that I figured must be beer to take home in celebration.

'You never thought I'd do it,' I said to Eck when I told him I had a proper job in photography.

'I absolutely did,' he said and raised his can to me then drank it.

'Jesus Christ, what the hell is this?'

'I don't know,' I said. I'd never bought beer before.

Cal sniffed it. 'Is it . . . is it fizzy ouzo?'

Eck stared at me incredulously. 'Were you raised in a barn? On the moon? A moon barn?'

'Here's a hypothetical question,' mused Cal annoyingly. 'I wonder what it would be like to have never had to buy your own beer before.' And he shot me a suspicious look.

We were eating lemon chicken out of a silver-foil tin. This wasn't the light tempura I was used to in smart Japanese restaurants. It was thick and heavy, smothered in batter, with a viscous sauce that clung to your teeth and made them ache. It was delicious.

'So where exactly are you working?' said Cal.

'It's a photographic studio. I'm in photography. Ergo, this is the job for me,' I said.

'What kind of photography though? Babies? Fruit? Cats?'

'Uh, more . . . catalogue.'

'Catalogue? Like underwear? Like, Page Three?' said James excitedly.

I shrugged. 'Maybe.'

For the first time, I had stunned them into silence. I felt quite proud of myself. Until James said, 'Lovely jugglies! Ooh-err! Fantastic!'

'So posh – so down with the Page Three mob,' said Cal thoughtfully. 'You are a wonder, Cinders. Though they do always say the posh birds are the dirtiest.'

I ignored him. 'I'm not actually *doing* anything like that,' I said. 'I'm an assistant. I get coffee and fix lights and hopefully I'll work up to doing stuff for myself.'

'Do you have to, you know. Spray the girls to make them wet or anything,' said James, as if this was a completely normal topic of conversation and he was only being polite.

'No!' I said. This wasn't strictly true. That very afternoon there had been a bit of T-shirt soppage. Kelly had been very unhappy.

'Well, this is stupid, isn't it?' she'd said. ' It's going to give me goosebumps. Blokes will be popping their corks over a chicken.'

Hot water, however, didn't have quite the same effect in terms of making the nipples pop out, so cold it was. I'd started to learn on the job already.

'It's all entirely respectable,' I said, mimicking what I'd heard Julius tell Kelly's mother when she rang up to check on her. 'All the great artists liked to picture beautiful women.'

'With their knockers flailing in the wind. I heartily approve, Cinders,' said Cal. 'Do you never feel like joining in?'

'Absolutely not.'

'They wouldn't have you,' said James. 'Not enough embon-point . . .'

'You really are a bit of a soft porn expert, aren't you, James?' said Cal. 'Not enough bromide in the tea?'

'Do they really still put mucky pictures up in lockers?' I asked, interested.

'The enlisted men put pictures up in their lockers,' said James. 'I'm an officer. But I do *inspect* the lockers.'

'Who's your favourite?' I said. 'Maybe I can, you know, get her autograph.'

'With a big "x" on the paper,' said Cal.

James gulped. 'Really?'

'You start washing up your own coffee mug,' I said, 'and with this party coming up ... you never know what might happen.'

And that night all the boys did their own washing up. Even Wolverine licked out his bowl.

Two weeks later I was walking down the road in the rain. I'd had a stupid dream that Daddy was downstairs in the kitchen, teasing Esperanza and trying to sneak an extra croissant for breakfast before Gail smacked his wrists.

The flat was looking much better. I'd taken down the kitchen curtains and washed them. Unfortunately I washed them with one of my pairs of knickers so they were now a hot pink, but I figured it gave them a party atmosphere.

Cal, after what I liked to imagine as his hugely flirtatious chats with me, seemed very engrossed in this new girl who'd been over a couple of times. I'd realised the Spanish girl was a one-off when a parade of lovelies had marched through the door, but this one had made it back twice now – a record. He'd better not be falling in love with her, I thought mutinously. Not when I was right here. Interestingly, the girls he came home with seemed to have nothing in common, apart from the fact that they were all spectacularly beautiful. I didn't know how good a sculptor he was, but he certainly had an eye for the female form. The current girl was petite and

Chinese, with fine features, perfect skin and nice manners. The old me would have probably given her stink-eye. The new me was absolutely, definitely *not* someone who even looked at other people's boyfriends, so instead I made her tea and told her she looked good in Cal's old shirts. Which, annoyingly, she did. Bum. Two cute boys in the flat and I was getting nowhere.

And I got my first real pay cheque! OK, that wasn't quite the thrill I was hoping for. It would barely cover brunch at The Wolseley and wouldn't have lasted five minutes in Sephora. It was a paltry, disgusting amount, most of which I'd immediately had to hand over to Eck. But it was all I had, for now.

I hadn't called Gail. I didn't want it misinterpreted as begging. And, secretly, deep down, I wanted her to be impressed with me when I returned with a proper job, a proper life. Well, a somewhat hand-to-mouth life, to be honest, and probably not the healthiest, we realised, the third night we spent necking the filthy fizzy ouzo (actually after the first four tins it wasn't that bad), but nonetheless it was mine. I had sent Esperanza a postcard, though, now I knew she'd be thinking about me and worrying. I wanted her to know I was all right.

Hurray, hurray, hurray! I thought when I got paid. At least this meant one really good thing: no more cleaning! I was going to warn the boys sternly that if they mucked this place up again I was going to come in their rooms at night and kick them sharply in the shins, but from now on we were going to share . . . then Eck apologetically asked me for my contribution to the electricity, heating, gas and water. Water? Really? The stuff that comes out the sky? I said, and Eck said yes, and I said

114

with a sigh, OK, let me just go fill a pail with that very expensive water and start mopping floors with it, and he said, all right then. And then when I got down the hall he called after me, 'Thank you.' Which cheered me up. A little.

So I was slightly in my own little world walking down the rainy street, when I heard a car pull over behind me. I was used to being shouted at on the street now, whether by builders, drunks, schoolchildren or just bog-standard crazy people. It was the life of the Old Kent Road. Builders shouted at girls; old ladies shouted at bus drivers; motorists and van drivers shouted at each other; cabbies shouted at cyclists; schoolkids shouted at kids from other schools; and a few people shouted at themselves. At first I'd found it a bit lairy and off-putting. Now I didn't even notice, or if I did, thought it gave quite a nice sense of community. Nobody shouted at their neighbours where I lived; you didn't know them, and they were off in Dubai anyway.

So I didn't really notice when someone kept shouting my name; I was wondering if there'd be any free newspapers left on the bus, and whether I could get Wolverine to stop sharpening his nails on the sofa, and, at the back of my mind, probably, a little bit, thinking about my dad. So the voice was quite exasperated by the time I heard, 'SOPHIE!' I stopped short and turned around.

'Oh. My. God,' came a voice. The car, a silver BMW, slithered to a halt on a double red line, causing much shouting and beeping from the vehicles behind.

Utterly immune to all of that, Philly and Carena stepped out of the car.

115

'Your maid told us!' said Philly. 'But we didn't believe it! Old Kent Road!'

I knew I shouldn't have sent Esperanza that postcard.

'I mean, OH MY GOD.'

Yeah, yeah. Philly's parents were from Surbiton; she wasn't exactly the novice to squalor she liked to pretend.

Carena was more circumspect, slowly raising her huge Chanel glasses from the tilt of her tiny nose. She was wearing a pair of incredibly tight, jet black jeans that somehow didn't look tarty at all, and a black floaty printed Chloe top. She looked sensational. I realised that I was still wearing my old Juicy tracksuit bottoms. Well, it was only because I was going to work . . . well, really, it was because none of my jeans would button up any more, and the weather wasn't good enough for dresses. And I hadn't had my legs waxed in weeks. I suppose I could shave them myself, but I was a bit scared and the cheap shop's razors looked lethal.

Plus, who cared? I'd have dressed up for Cal, but he always had his head buried in some bird's cleavage. Eck might give me the odd yearning glance, if I wasn't imaging things, but he still had some bleach-related residual anxiety. And as for the studio, well, surrounded by that many images of scantily clad womanhood, I was quite happy to have my trackie bottoms on all the time. Something that completely disguised the shape of my rump made me feel more secure. All of these thoughts ran through my head because my heart was pounding a mile a minute.

A huge tow truck came up behind the BMW and started honking loudly. Carena turned round and gave it a serious stare, but the truck driver was unfazed and was shouting, 'Get your fucking scrawny arse out of my fucking lane, you fucking bunch of fucking cunts.'

Philly gazed at me, her eyes wide, as if this was the biggest fun she could imagine.

Carena stopped in front of me and lowered her huge eyes. I stared at her. Everything I wanted to say, everything I wanted to ask . . . but before I could start, she jumped in.

'Sophie,' she said. 'I've spoken to my therapist and he says I must make a full and frank apology, and that you must accept my apology and make amends if you are to find your own happiness.'

This took me back so much I couldn't think straight. What was I supposed to say to that? Uh, thanks, someone else's idiot therapist that I've never met?

I thought about all the conversations I'd had with Carena in my head, where she would be genuinely prostrate with sadness, because she'd ruined her life and her friend's life with her horrible selfishness. I wanted her to be struck with the horror of what she'd done, and utterly miserable. I didn't want her to look like she was running errands for her therapist.

Also in my imaginary meetings I'd always, always looked rather amazing and Carena had been looking lumpy and wearing sweatpants.

Strangely, it was Carena who'd hurt me far more than Rufus could. She'd known me for longer, after all. She knew what he meant to me, she knew where my insecurities were, and she had, Jolene style, taken him just because she could. Whereas my lovely, lazy boy had obviously never really been mine to begin with. I gave my heart an experimental prod. Was it possible I was over him?

'Get in the car! Get in!' yelped Philly. 'We're all going to get knifed.'

Seeing as the honking of the truck was getting deafening, and we were all standing there getting rained on, I didn't seem to have much alternative.

Still without saying anything, I got into the car.

The smell of fresh leather was intoxicating; I realised it really had been a while. In fact, I hadn't travelled in a car at all since I moved south of the river. It was damp buses all the way.

'Where are you headed?' said Philly.

'New Cross,' I said before I could help myself. Then I cursed. I should have stuck to name, rank, serial number.

'What are you doing in New Cross? Have you got a J – O – B?' said Philly. Previously she'd been the only one of us who'd had anything like a proper job and really resented us for it. She sounded absolutely thrilled.

'Yes, I've got a job,' I said stiffly. 'I have a job. I work now. People work. Work happens. Et cetera.'

Philly found somewhere to park the car and I reluctantly took them to my local greasy spoon for a coffee. There weren't any Starbucks round here. But you could get a cup of tea and a sausage sandwich for a pound-seventy.

''Allo, *cara*!' shouted the friendly guy behind the counter when we walked in. He was always nice to me and complimented my blonde hair.

'I see you know everyone there is to know, as ever,' said Philly. Was she trying to be nice or horrid? It was hard to tell.

We got our teas – Carena asked for just hot water, then sat running a very clean finger suspiciously round the rim of the mug instead of drinking it. We took a corner table. The smoking ban may be pretty well instituted everywhere else, but here there were suspicious smells and butts. Maybe they were just left over from the last time it was cleaned. They were very good sausage sandwiches though.

'Well?' I said finally.

Carena put on an appropriately sad face. She looked like a naughty nun.

'I just . . . I'm so sorry, Sophie. We just got so carried away.'

'You don't get carried away,' I said. 'You always know exactly what you're doing.'

'I didn't . . . I mean, you hadn't been together that long.'

'You knew very well how much I liked him. After all the twats I had to put up with, I'd finally met a nice guy, so you took him.'

'Well, he was obviously there for the taking,' said Carena, looking stung.

'I'm sure he still is,' I said. 'Hope you have him on a short leash. Or did you get bored with him and throw him out?'

She didn't answer that. Oh God. So much worse had happened. I thought about how much I'd missed having my friends at the funeral. My choice was clearly quite simple. Either swallow my bitterness and have someone to talk to, or hate them forever. Or, of course, pretend to forgive them but still secretly hate them forever. And have someone to talk to. Maybe that one.

'It's OK,' I said finally. 'He was a total loser anyway.'

'Well . . .' Carena announced dramatically at exactly the same moment, 'We're getting MARRIED!!!'

Philly screamed excitedly next to her.

I turned over the timescale in my head. What had it been, weeks? Months, I supposed. I had really started to lose track of time. God.

'Now, don't scream, Philly,' said Carena. 'I'm sorry, Sophie. The excitement just overcame me for a moment there.'

'Really,' I said.

'I realise this must come as a shock to you.'

Uh, d'uh. My insides were telling me I wasn't as half over him as I'd hoped. Oh God, oh God, oh God. He *had* been ready to propose. Just not to me!

'Well, I've had other things on my mind,' I said stiffly.

Carena and Philly immediately assumed the 'Sad Face' I remembered so well from my childhood.

'I was sorry to hear about your dad,' said Carena, although she sounded a lot more convincing about this than she had about Rufus. 'I really was. I wish . . . I would have come to the funeral.'

'Well, you didn't,' I said briskly. I couldn't talk about that now.

There was a long pause at the table. A long pause. I wanted to wait till I felt I'd made my point, but it was getting ridiculous. And I was going to be incredibly late for work.

'So you've tamed Rufus!' I said finally. 'Amazing, well done you!'

'And they said it couldn't be done,' said Carena, her colour returning.

'Without faking a pregnancy,' I said. 'I'm kidding, OK.'

I made a superhuman effort to swallow all my gall. I might be talking to Carena again, but I'd never be one of her little lapdogs.

'If you like, you can tell me all about it.'

Carena glanced at Philly. 'Shall we?'

'Oh, do,' said Philly. 'It's genius. I can't believe it worked.'

'I *know*,' said Carena.

I picked up my teaspoon. It was, literally, quite greasy.

'Well, you've heard of that book called *The Rules*?' started Philly.

'From, like years and years ago?' I said. 'Like the nineties or something? And you're just meant to never answer the phone.'

'Oh, it's a bit more than that,' said Carena.

'This is genius,' said Philly. 'Let's see . . . a man is desperate to sleep with you. What do you do?'

I thought about Rufus in the bedroom then banished it from my head. It hadn't been his finest arena, to be sure.

'I do not know,' I answered truthfully.

'You don't sleep with him!' said Philly.

'You haven't slept with him?' I said, looking at Carena, who looked like the cat who'd got the cream. 'But you slept with half the Klosters Olympic team.'

Her face fell. 'We all have a past, Sophie.'

'You really haven't slept with him? But remember the yacht crew in Antigua?'

'I don't really miss you that much as a friend,' grumbled Carena.

'Does he think you're a *virgin*?'

121

'He really is desperate,' said Philly.

'Let me see,' I said.

Faux-reluctantly, Carena lifted her elegantly manicured hand from underneath the rickety Formica table. It didn't look like it belonged there, but sure enough, on her fourth finger was a huge, huge, huge diamond.

'Shit.' I whistled. 'He really *is* desperate.'

And I wondered if this was the right time to tell her that after the spanking he was a tad . . .

Ah, she'd find out soon enough.

'So we wanted to see you were OK,' said Philly, leaning over and fixing me with a limpid gaze designed to express sincerity and caring. 'After everything that's happened . . .'

'Yeah, yeah, yeah,' I said, stirring my tea. I'd started taking sugar – the boys always made it really sweet – and without noticing dropped a couple of cubes in my glass. The girls simultaneously winced.

'What on *earth* are you doing?' said Carena. 'Sugar! It's . . . sugar . . . it's . . .'

'Delicious,' I said. 'Want some?'

'You've changed,' said Philly.

'Yes,' I said. 'I have.'

Philly leaned forwards. 'You know, there's one thing I wanted to suggest,' she said.

'Oh yes?'

'Have you thought about the Priory?' she said. She and Carena glanced at each other.

'What are you talking about?' I said. 'I don't need the Priory. I need a job that pays more than minimum wage!'

'Do you think you're in denial?' said Philly, looking point-edly at my tea.

'Do you think I'm addicted to *sugar*?' I asked.

She shrugged. 'You know, people go in for all sorts of rea-sons,' said Carena. 'Exhaustion, stress – your father's death may be making you depressed.'

I knew it. They've always wanted to get inside the Priory in case there's anyone famous in there.

'You think?' I said. 'You think my father's sudden death might be making me sad?'

'Maybe you feel guilty about it,' said Philly.

That took the wind out of my sails a bit. Without knowing she'd hit the nail completely on the head. Of course I felt guilty. If I'd answered my phone . . . If I'd been at home . . . If I'd gone to be with him . . . If I'd looked after him before . . . If I'd been the kind of daughter he deserved, after working hard all his life. Of course I felt fucking guilty.

'I feel *sad*,' I said emphatically. 'That's exactly how I should feel. I don't need to give someone lots of money I don't have to recognise the fact that I'm sad. I'd need a mental hospital if I *wasn't* sad.'

'Of course,' said Philly. 'But, you know. The Priory is prac-tically a luxury hotel. The perfect retreat to bring your body and soul back together.'

'Why don't you go then?' I said. 'Oh, no . . . you said you need a soul.'

Then it struck me. 'Are you doing their PR by any chance?'

'Um, maybe.' Philly forgot herself for a moment, then put her serious face back on.

Right, that's enough. I stood up.

'I think you need to throw off your sadness,' said Carena. 'Buy a beautiful new dress. Go dancing. Lose some weight.'

Well, there's nothing like being told to lose some weight to help you throw off your sadness.

'You're not listening, are you?' I said. 'I don't have any money. I'm living on nothing. That's why I've got a job. Why do you even think I'm down here?'

Carena looked around. 'Oh, I thought you'd picked up a funky five-thousand-square-foot warehouse somewhere. Have they frozen your allowance whilst they work out the lawyer's fees?'

'Well, kind of,' I said. 'I don't get it for six months. Well, four months now. I had to go and get a real job and things.'

Carena's eyes widened. 'You're kidding?' she said. 'A job? No allowance?'

'Nope.'

'Oh my God. I can't imagine.'

Philly rolled her eyes. 'Oh, you know, some people *do* live without trust funds.' She paused. 'Not me, obviously, couldn't do without mine . . .'

'It's not that bad,' I said. Here was genuine sympathy at last.

'Tell Gail to just bloody well sort it out!' said Carena. 'Or borrow my lawyer and sue her to hell and back.'

'Thanks,' I said. 'That's a genuinely kind offer. But it's probably easier just to wait.'

'Oh, you poor thing,' said Philly. 'What's it like being poor? Tell us all about it.'

And she sat forward, perfectly painted mouth slightly open, desperate for squalid details. Carena too. Her gaze had caught my bra strap. I don't know how you wash bras – you don't put them in the machine, do you? I needed to call Esperanza again. So I'd just been letting them get a bit grubby.

'What's your flat like?' said Philly, prompting me. And I was about to tell her.

Maybe make light of it, tell a few jokes . . . or just dissolve into tears and admit it was awful, everything was shit and please, please, could they like me again and could I stay in Carena's guest suite? I felt I'd done my best to be strong about everything that had happened but now, I was sure if I abased myself enough and begged they would let me back in. OK, they'd patronise me for a bit, try to lend me clothes and things, but eventually it would all be forgotten and the remaining months would pass and I'd get at my money and all would be forgiven and forgotten and I could go back to normal. All I needed to do was eat a bit of humble pie now . . . tell them how dreadful everything was . . . tell them how unhappy I was and throw myself on their mercy. How hard could it be? Then everything could go back to normal . . .

I opened my mouth to start my tale of woe when the café bell tinged for people coming in.

'Hey!' said the man behind the counter. 'So good to see my favourite boys today.'

'Good to see you too, Avi,' said a familiar, drawling voice. 'Why, hello. Is that Cinders? On one of her posh lunches out? Sex in the Shitty?'

It was Cal, with Wolverine in tow.

Cal immediately clocked the talent at the table – Carena of course, blonde and gorgeous, Philly, putting the effort in – and his expression turned wolfish.

'So what's all this then?'

I suddenly felt really gratified that I was living with a hot guy. Nobody had to know how.

'Oh, hello, mucky pup,' I said, as if I was so unbelievably casual about seeing him I'd hardly noticed he was there. 'This is my flatmate, Cal. Carena and Philly were just having to head off, I think.'

'No, we're fine,' said Philly hurriedly. 'Not all of us have to go to work in the morning.'

'Quite right too,' said Cal, smiling and showing his lovely teeth. 'I wondered where Sophie had been hiding her friends. No wonder she was trying to keep them out of our way.'

I muttered something.

'Would you like to sit and join us?' asked Philly.

'Would love to, darling, but we're having tea on the run.' He winked at her. 'The kiln waits for no man. But Sophie's invited you to our party on Saturday, right?'

'*You're* having a party?' said Philly to me. This obviously didn't quite dwell with her image of me as a depression-laden Priory case. Wolverine had moved closer to her and seemed to be trying to sniff her neck.

'Oh, it's just for a few friends,' I said, feeling embarrassed, but quite pleased at the same time.

'And you weren't going to invite us?'

I arched an eyebrow and she retreated.

'You should both come,' said Cal sincerely, 'beautiful

women are always welcome.' Carena batted her huge eyelashes at him. Hey, don't start this again, I thought crossly.

'Hey, Sophs,' Cal said suddenly. 'Are you done here? Come outside, I want to ask you something.'

My heart beat a bit faster. Ooh. And this was a perfect time to make an exit. Suddenly I didn't feel the urge to confess everything and beg to come back at all. Suddenly, having mysterious gorgeous bad boys drag me out of coffee shops didn't seem like such a bad way to live, particularly compared to someone else's charity.

'Excuse me,' I said. 'It was lovely to see you guys. Thanks for checking up on me!'

Phillly eyed me like I'd just gotten away with something. 'I still really think you should come to the Priory with us.'

'The Priory?' said Cal. 'What on earth are you talking about? She's not going to the Priory! We need her here with us!'

He didn't add, 'Because she scours out the loo and washes our stinkables,' and I was eternally grateful.

'I'll see you,' I said. Then, my heart feeling lighter than it had in absolutely ages, I bounced up from the table and marched out the door, Wolverine following at my heels like a bodyguard.

Oh, wow, that felt good.

'Thanks,' I said to Cal.

'Who were those terrifying things?' he asked. 'You looked like a dog that was about to get beaten round the head.'

'They're my friends,' I said. 'Or, at least, they used to be.'

127

Cal gave me a long look. 'What on earth happened to you?' he said.

'Nothing,' I said shortly. Then, 'Why did you invite them to the party?'

'I said they looked frightening,' said Cal. 'I didn't say they didn't look hot. Especially the blonde girl; yowza.'

Talk about giving out mixed signals. 'What did you want to talk about?' I said a touch sulkily. He obviously wasn't about to beg me to go out with him if he was mentioning Carena.

'Oh, yeah,' said Cal. 'Now this party's really shaping up, I wanted to ask you – could you bring some girls along?'

'Like those girls you just asked?' I said.

'Oh, no, that was just reflex,' said Cal. 'No, some *girls*. You know. Like the girls you work with girls. Dolly birds. Hot pop popsies.'

'Glamour models.'

'Yes, well, whatever they like to be called. Like you said. Can you bring some? There's lots of lonely boys out there.'

'Not you, then,' I said.

'No, of course not me. But look at Wolverine.'

Wolverine gave out a little howl.

'And even Eck. The ladies like him, but he's always getting his worried look on and scaring them off. Even James spends too much time crawling through mud.'

'So you want me to procure some totty?' I said.

'Uh, yes. That's it. Totty procurement patrol. Think you're up to it?'

'I think you're a disgusting, sexist disgrace to pigs,' I said, my perky mood evaporating instantly. 'Why don't you just hire a bunch of hookers?'

Cal looked genuinely wounded. 'Oh, come on Tinsel tits. It's just for fun.'

'Well maybe not all girls want fun. Or like being talked about like that.'

Cal rolled his eyes. 'Sorry, sorry. I should have known you were going lezzer from the trackie bottoms.'

'I'm not going lezzer,' I said, making a mental note to change my trousers. 'And even if I was it would be none of your business. I just don't like you talking like that.'

Cal raised his eyebrows and turned to go. 'OK. Well, if you ever meet any girls who look like they might enjoy, you know, parties, and fun, it'd be nice if you could ask them because we know lots of guys, and sometimes guys and girls quite enjoy mixing together in social situations. But if this offends your high moral principles, don't.'

And he gave me a look and headed off.

I was fuming. Horrible sexist pig! Arsehole!

At the junction he turned back, and my traitorous heart leapt a little.

'Oh!'

'What?' I said crossly.

'And we need more kitchen cleaner!'

I stomped into the studio ninety minutes late. Julius was standing there pointedly squatting at the foot of a well-endowed brunette, pretending to fix a light but looking up her skirt a bit. She was chewing gum loudly and looking unimpressed.

'Is this part of it, right? 'Cause my geography teacher used to do this all the time. Drop a pencil, and—'

'No!' said Julius, puffing a bit and straightening up. 'Oh, hello,' he said to me. 'Decided to grace us with your presence, have you? What happened, are you moonlighting for *Harpers and Queen*?'

'No,' I said. 'That's you. I'm really sorry. I got delayed.'

'Well, this isn't Mayfair,' said Julius. 'I'm not running this place as a loss-leader, OK? I didn't hire you to hang around and look glamorous.' He eyed me up and down. 'Didn't you used to look glamorous?'

'Never mind about that now,' I said, going over to the new girl. She really did look young.

'Hello,' I said. 'Are you new?'

The girl shrugged. 'Yeah.' She looked up at me suddenly. 'It's like my first modelling job, innit! Isn't there, like champagne and stuff?'

'If you're Kate Moss,' grunted Julius, moving some more lights back. 'And you, darlin', are no Kate Moss.'

'Well, I've got tits for a start,' said the girl, whose name was apparently Delilah. She was eighteen years old, and didn't seem to be as phased by getting her breasts out for the first time in front of complete strangers, as I might have been.

'I can get you some tea,' I offered.

'Neh,' she said. 'I've decided I'm going to start as I mean to go on. Champagne or nuffink.'

Julius and I looked at each other.

'Nothing then,' we chorused.

Delilah scowled. 'OK then. Tea.'

Actually, she proved to be pretty good. What the papers want is, obviously, a pair of massive jugs, which she certainly had, but they also like a pretty face and a nice smile, as if to say, 'Don't worry, dirty old man, I'm loving this! It's great!' Delilah, for all her sullen attitude (and fair enough, she'd been hanging about in a draughty studio whilst Julius grubbed around her for an hour waiting for me), could turn it on when she had to, and it was looking to be a good session. The 'twins', who'd become extremely popular, were coming in at lunchtime, to shoot again. They were through to the last thousand for a new reality show and, despite being sworn to secrecy, were wildly excited about it.

Delilah watched them, wide-eyed as they bustled in. Kelly was wearing a flamingo pink boa round her neck and a pink PVC mini. Grace was wearing the same, but in baby blue.

'I can't believe you took the pink again,' Grace was complaining as they clip-clopped in. 'You always do that.'

'I do *not*,' said Kelly. 'It's not my fault pink suits my complexion whereas yours is more . . . bluey grey.'

Grace sniffed. 'Well, it makes you look tarty.'

'You're just annoyed because nobody wolf-whistled at you.'

'There were hundreds of wolf whistles! All the way down!'

'Yeah – for the bird in the pink, innit. Face it.'

Delilah jumped up off the sunbed we'd planted next to a big plastic palm tree to make it look as if she was sunning herself topless on a desert island.

'The twins!' she said in a breathless tone of voice, like you might say 'Madonna!'. 'Can I have your autograph?'

The twins looked unbelievably pleased (as well they

might, I thought, while feeling secretly pleased it had been my idea to twin them up in the first place) and Kelly stepped up.

'I sign first,' she said. 'As head twin.'

'As fattest twin,' said Grace, 'you can sign first.'

'So, now you're models, right,' said Delilah, adding, 'This is my first day.'

'Well, put your top on then,' suggested Kelly. 'No point showing off the goods when you're not getting paid.'

Julius raised his eyebrows as if to imply he couldn't care less, but he let the camera drop.

'Do you get to go to lots of celebrity parties and things?' said Delilah. 'That's what I want to do. Go to, like good parties and that.'

'Oh yes,' said Grace. 'It's brilliant. Last week we were paid, right, a hundred pounds each to go to Whispers in Crawley. And we got up on stage and everything! And there was a football player there!'

'Ooh, who?'

'Tilnsley McGuire. Wolverhampton junior thirds!' said Grace.

'Everyone has to start somewhere,' said Kelly.

Oh God. How I longed to tell them about the time we went to Elton John's White Tie and Tiara ball (actually it was quite boring, we spent the whole evening slagging off other people's plastic surgery), or the opening of Shoreditch House, or the Cartier launch where Rio Ferdinand carried Carena out over his shoulder, tickling her mercilessly. God, I missed being rich sometimes.

I realised I had a stain from a sausage sandwich on my trousers (today's? yesterdays?). Would they believe me? Probably not.

'That sounds brilliant,' said Delilah.

That's how I found myself doing it. I couldn't help myself, these girls seemed to think I was just some kind of invisible ancient creature, only there to service their needs for tea.

'I've got a party you can come to,' I said. 'Lots of trendy artist types.'

Grace's little forehead furrowed like a wrinkled tomato. 'Artists?' she said.

'Yeah,' I said, 'and musicians. People in bands and things.'

Well, I assumed as much. People at art school were always in bands, weren't they?

The girls still looked doubtful.

'There's free booze.' Even as I said it I was wondering if this were true.

'Where is it?' said Kelly, strapping on a pair of the thigh-high boots they were wearing for today's shoot.

'Hey! I want the pink ones!' shouted Grace.

'No fuckin' way!'

'Yes fuckin' way, it's my turn.'

Julius covered his hand with his eyes.

'It's not fair!'

'Julius!'

'JULIUS!'

'Hey,' I said. 'Why don't you wear one colour each. It'll look like you share everything – *very* sexy.'

The girls jumped up and down and squealed with delight at this idea.

Julius half opened a red-rimmed eye at me. 'Fanks,' he said.

Chapter Ten

In my old life, arranging a party meant hiring a party planner and a designer florist. It meant little canapés, and inventing brand-new cocktails, and quite often a string quartet. I took after my mother: I loved parties.

Our party wasn't much like that. Eck came home with seventy-two balloons, so we blew those up, then the boys hung the long ones with two round ones on either side so they looked like penises. 'How old are you?' I asked them, and they explained to me that it didn't matter how old you were, boys always found balloons shaped like penises funny and would when they were eighty and I wondered if that were true of the boys I used to know and concluded that it probably was. And James came home with some jelly, and some vodka from the local no-brand supermarket that smelled pretty much exactly like the oven cleaner. But that was about the extent of our preparations.

'Did you send out invitations?' I'd made the mistake of asking. All the boys stared at me in complete disbelief.

'Is that what they do in *Hackney*?' asked Cal.

I shrugged. 'No! I just wondered.'

And that was it. I was nervous. Would anyone come? Would anyone talk to me? Maybe they would come, chat me up, take me out, get into my knickers then go and marry my best friend. Oh, no, hang on, that had already happened. I groaned again. It was like pushing on a mouth ulcer with my tongue; it hurt, but I couldn't seem to leave it alone. Nope, I had to move on. I was going to be at a party with a houseful of boys. The odds had to be in my favour.

And it was just as well the bathroom was clean, because it was well and truly hogged come Saturday. I couldn't believe how vain they all were. I reflected, slightly sadly, that obviously none of them were considering pulling me, because I saw them kicking about in their grundies all day long and it didn't bother them in the slightest.

'Hang on,' I said, queuing up outside and banging on the door. 'Until I came along you were living in three feet of soil.'

James opened the door. He was gelling his usually soldier-neat hair up in spikes, which looked phenomenally dated, but I didn't want to say anything in case it had come back in again whilst I wasn't looking, seeing as I'd kind of let my *Vogue* subscription lapse.

'Exactly!' he said. 'Now you've given us somewhere nice to bring ladies back! So our odds are *much* better. Thanks!'

'It doesn't seem to bother Cal,' I said. I wasn't really looking forward to my time in the bathroom, especially since I'd shone up the mirror. It had, I now realised, been better a little murky. My hair had an inch of dirty-looking roots; my legs were hairy; my eyes had big dark circles under them from having to get up every morning; my hands had a rash from the cleaning products; my skin looked dingy from missing regular facials and I'd put on nearly a stone having neglected my previously efficient regime of never eating solids unless I totally couldn't help it. Could I pull it off? My slinky black vintage Azzedine Alaia no longer fitted, and I wasn't 100 per cent sure about the zip on the Stella McCartney, which had never really suited me anyway. But I had a delicate, shimmery red chiffon dress, which was just the right side of go-go girlish (or, at least, I hoped it was, particularly now my stomach protruded over my hip bones), and some seriously dangerous-looking shoes. I just wanted to show people – well, Cal, if I was being brutally frank – that I didn't actually spend *all* my time crawling along the floor on my hands and knees picking up feathers. (I had demanded to know why there were feathers all over the house. Nobody would answer me, which meant they'd been at the conceptual art and absinthe again.) Nope, I was going to wow this party.

Eck came up to me in the corridor. 'Hey,' he said. 'If you were choosing a shirt . . . for a bloke . . .'

'Uh-huh?'

He held up two, one a pale green, one with little blue flowers on it.

'Oh right. I thought it was a hypothetical question.'

'OK. Please would you choose a shirt for a bloke.'

'A bloke? What kind of a bloke?'

'A devastatingly debonair and creative one with the strength of ten men and the heart of a lion.'

'Oh,' I said. 'I don't know any like that.'

'OK. Me then.'

'The flowers,' I said. 'Definitely.'

'You don't think it's a bit fruity?'

'Eck, you're at *art college*. It's too late to be worrying about all that. Anyway, women love a man in pastel colours. It shows you're in touch with your feminine side but comfortable in your masculine side.'

'That does sound fruity. James!'

'Don't ask James, for crying out loud! He's wearing a boot-lace tie. Look. Fruity is quite good. You'll be Just Gay Enough.'

'Look, I don't want to be prejudiced or anything, but I haven't been to a party for ages. Being gay enough is really not what I'm trying to get across.'

I smiled. 'Are you on the pull?'

Suddenly the mood shifted and there was tension in the air.

He looked at me, with a serious look suddenly. 'Are you?'

There was a long pause as a look passed between us, ruined only by the loud sound of the flush going off, and rattling through our completely antiquated plumbing.

'Get out the bathroom, James!' I hollered. 'That's an order.'

'Oh, OK,' he said, appearing at the door. James responded well to orders. The spell was broken.

'Hey, look, some feathers!' said Eck, pointing down the corridor. As I turned to follow his finger, he slipped into the bathroom ahead of me.

*

Peering in the tiny mirror in my bedroom I realised I hadn't even bothered putting mascara on for weeks. That was amazing; I'd never been able to go down the street for a copy of *Grazia* without a full lipgloss session in my life.

In fact, as I examined my face, I realised it was worse than I'd ever thought. My eyes were horribly bloodshot from cheap beer and, I had to admit, some nights of crying; my skin looked like it had been hiding under heavy clouds – I wondered if north London got more sunshine than south London. Maybe that's why it was so much more expensive. My hair was a total mess. It had always been my crowning glory, long and pale gold. Recently I'd just been washing it under the tap and leaving it. It didn't look, as I'd on some level been hoping, like sun-kissed easy-going Sienna Miller beach hair. It looked like a witchy mess. Seeing it properly – all frizz and dark roots – for the first time in weeks nearly made me cry. They didn't talk about this in the grief manual.

So, well, all those eighty-quid blow drys had been worth it after all. This was a disaster. I was going to look like a completely hopeless old hag in a too-tight nice frock. It wasn't going to work at all. I stifled a small sob, but there was a huge lump in my throat. I couldn't go to the party. I just couldn't. I'd just stay in here and they could throw the coats on me. The more the better. Hide me away.

Sniffing, I pulled up the ever-tightening waistband on my sweatpants when I heard the phone ring. My new phone, that is. My lovely silver one was gone. I'd managed to get hold of the cheapest pay-as-you-go model they did. It was pink. I had a sneaking suspicion it was actually for children.

The built-in ring tone was 'Glamorous' by Fergie. It wasn't glamorous.

The number wasn't one I recognised. No. Why would it be. Probably a misdial.

'Hello?' I said, trying to keep any evidence of sobbing out of my voice.

''Ello!' came the voice back. 'Is that Sophie?'

'Yes.'

'Thank fuck. It's Delilah.'

'Oh, hello,' I said. That's all I needed to hear from right now, some gorgeous eighteen year-old with massive knockers who would look fabulous – well, trashy-fabulous, which I suspected would do – in a bin bag.

'What am I going to wear to this bloody party then? Is it posh or what?'

'Anything you like,' I said. 'You'll look great, I'm sure.'

'But aren't they like students or something? What do students wear?'

'Just wear a nice dress,' I said. 'You'll be fine. You'll be better than fine. You'll be unbelievably popular.'

'Oh, I know that,' she said dismissively. 'I just want to fit in.'

There was a pause. She obviously wanted me to ask her over. I didn't think that was a good idea right now. No, definitely not, seeing as I was actually going to hide under the bed for five hours. No. No she couldn't come over.

'Can I come over?' she asked.

'Oh, all right,' I said. Then I sighed.

'What is it?'

'I don't really want to go,' I said.

'Why not?'

I paused. 'I'm having a bad hair day,' I said. 'Very bad.'

'Oh, you should have said! I'll be right over!'

'Uh, no, it's all right . . .'

'Neh, I did two years at beauty school, didn't I? Hairdressing and everything. I'll bring my bag.'

'No, really, it's—'

'And I'll bring a bunch of clothes and you can tell me what to wear. OK? Get some voddy in and tell me where you live.'

I think maybe having spectacular knockers can give your confidence a real boost.

Twenty minutes later I was having a cup of tea and listening to the boys compete with each other as to what the party music was going to be. James had some military marches going. I had the horrible thought that he probably had sex in time with them.

Cal had some kind of weird esoteric stuff blaring out which sounded like someone hitting a tin dog on some aluminium piping, and Eck was playing The Killers. I wished I had some Madonna to even things out a bit. There was already a large pile of empty beer cans in the kitchen and a huge whiff of hair gel hanging around the place – gosh, they *were* taking this seriously.

'Hello!' Delilah bellowed cheerfully. She appeared to be carrying more kit than I'd moved in with. 'Christ, look at you. We've got our work cut out.'

'OK, OK,' I said. She was wearing spray-on tight jeans with a pink fluffy top.

'Are the jeans OK?' she said anxiously. 'I can't change them now, I'd need metal-cutting equipment.'

Delilah clomped up the stairs. She didn't seem the least bit bothered by the big damp stains on the ancient wallpaper, or the fact that the only pictures on the wall were of motorbikes ripped out of magazines.

'Got any voddy?'

'No,' I said, apologetically. 'But we can steal the boy's beer. Or there's some filthy—'

Delilah wrinkled her nose. 'It makes you fat, beer. And it doesn't get you pissed fast enough. Here . . .' And she handed over what appeared to be a bottle of wine originating from more than one country.

'Great,' I said, genuinely pleased to see it. If I really was going to have to go to this thing, the wine was going to prove very helpful.

Delilah turned round to face me and her brow furrowed. 'What's up wiv your hair? Why don't you get your roots fixed and that?'

I didn't know how to tell her that I was scared of every hairdresser who wasn't Stefano, and that I couldn't afford to get my hair done.

'OK,' said Delilah, pulling a large pair of GHDs out of her bag. 'I hope nobody is arriving early, because this is going to take a while.'

She turned me round so I couldn't glance at myself in the mirror as she began her transformation. Two large glasses of wine and a lot of pulling and tugging later, Delilah let me have a look at the end result.

My first inclination was to laugh. I looked nothing like myself at all. My long blonde hair had gone; it was now styled in a kind of big beehive, coiled around itself in a way that made my head look gigantic (but did hide my roots). I had bright green eyeshadow that followed the shape of my lids, and lashes thick with black mascara, and my lips were a bright coral pink. I looked like a slinky backing singer for a Sixties band. It was a bit peculiar, but, 'I like it,' I said. And I did. I didn't look like me at all – I'd always aimed for low key, sleek, expensive. All of that was gone. I looked a bit hard and up for a laugh, but in a fun way.

''Course you do,' said Delilah. 'You owe me a pint. What are you wearing?'

I opened up the half-swinging cupboard door and showed her the contents. Her eyes went wide immediately.

'Shit!' she said. 'Is this stuff all real?'

I shrugged. 'Yeah.'

'What did you do, steal it to order?'

'No!'

'Were you, like, a posh man's mistress and he bought you loads of presents and that?'

'No!'

'So where did you get it?'

I decided to merely distract her. 'Do you want to try something on?'

'Yeah!'

I stuck her in the little Pucci minidress. Even though she had a little pot belly – and, obviously, those flailing knockers – she looked utterly fabulous in it. In fact, the bosoms busting out of the top gave it an additional appeal.

'Can I wear it?' she asked breathlessly.

'I think you're going to have to,' I said. 'Anyway, I can't get in it.'

Stupidly, I suddenly felt the gap between being eighteen and being twenty-five, and I didn't like it. I glanced at my new look again. No, I was fine.

'Put this on,' said Delilah, giving me the Alice Temperley frock that I'd thrown in – it was meant to make me look pale and floaty and romantic. Mixed with the crazy hair and the dramatic make-up, though, it looked cool, edgy and very, very art school.

'We are super-hot,' breathed Delilah in all seriousness. Downstairs the doorbell started ringing and I could hear a lot of voices shouting and bottles and cans being opened. Cal's music had won. I felt excited. 'Shall we go?'

Well, upstairs in my bedroom I had thought I looked a bit odd, but I soon realised my outfit was absolutely nothing compared with what this lot were wearing.

The girls (I could mostly distinguish between the sexes) were all pin thin (it was with a soggy sense of horror that I realised I was among the oldest and fattest there), and wore mismatching tights on either leg, bin bags, punk hairdos, wedding dresses, psychedelic dungarees or combinations of all of the above. They looked like they'd all descended from another planet, or at least a particularly cool area of Tokyo. They had beehives too (hurrah!) or dreadlocks or Mohicans and their hair was lots of different colours. Weirdly, I noticed, although obviously they were all trying to be highly individual and everything, they all looked a lot like each other. Almost as one, they turned to eye up Delilah and me, standing there in our party dresses, with a distinct air of suspicion, not helped at all when the twins came screaming up the stairs. They were wearing PVC miniskirts, both in pink, so someone had obviously refused to back down.

'*Deli!*' they screamed. '*Sophs!*'

'All the girls look *really weird* here,' yelled Kelly, not lowering her tone despite the pallid vampires pouting at us.

'And the boys look weird too,' added Grace. 'But quite sexy.'

I was relieved. Well, I didn't want to be responsible for inviting people to, like, the worst party ever.

'This is, like, the worst party ever,' came a familiar voice from the corridor. Oh God. That sounded like Philly. I'd hoped they wouldn't come, and deliberately hadn't contacted them. I'd forgotten Esperanza had told them my address.

'Let's go on through,' I muttered to Delilah and the twins. The silent art student vampires watched us as we moved towards the kitchen.

'Yummy yum,' said Cal looking at us as we entered. He was mixing 'punch' in a washing-up bowl. I knew what had been in that washing-up bowl and vowed to avoid it at all costs. He was wearing a white shirt, tight black jeans, a black jacket and black Converse.

'What's this crap you're playing?' said Delilah. 'Can't you put on some decent music?'

'Well, nice to meet you too,' said Cal.

'Yeah,' said Kelly. 'We can do our Pussycat Dolls routine.'

'I'm being Nicole,' said Grace.

145

Suddenly, I badly wanted to see their Pussycat Dolls routine. From the look on Cal's face, so did he.

'Cinders! It's a miracle,' said Cal, looking me up and down again. 'What have you done with your lovely hair? But, you know. Fantastic.'

I twirled for him and he winked at me wolfishly.

Cal was eyeing me up like a horse buyer at a county fair. I felt nervous under his gaze. Then Eck came in with some of his friends.

'Nice shirt,' I said. He looked like he might be blushing slightly.

'Thanks,' he said. 'You look . . . different.'

'Good different?' I said in an encouraging tone.

'Uh, yeah . . .' he looked around. 'Have you got a drink? Would you like another?'

He smiled hopefully at me and I felt a sudden rush of excitement. It had been such a long time since I'd been chatted up properly, by someone who didn't automatically assume that I would immediately cop off with them as soon as they showed me the keys to their Porsche. Of course Eck didn't have a Porsche. Or a Ford. Or a pushbike. But nonetheless, it was interesting.

'Yes, please,' I said cheerfully, holding up my glass. Cal raised his eyebrows at me and I waggled them back. A girl could flirt. At least, I used to be able to, and surely this skill hadn't been lost for ever?

'What the *hell* is this place?'

I heard the voice suddenly on the stairs. Even though I'd

146

registered Philly's presence already, hearing Carena still made me stop, and panic. She had come. I hadn't actually thought she would. Never in a million years. At short notice? On a Saturday night? Impossible.

'You wanted to come here, darling,' came a familiar, deep, amused-sounding voice in response. I froze even more. It was Rufus.

'What's the matter with you?' said Cal curiously. '*Tatler* just turned up to take your photo?'

'No,' I said. Eck returned from the fridge with some wine, and I gulped mine so quickly I scarcely thanked him. I was nervous and had too much energy to know what to do with myself.

'You agreed to come,' I heard Carena hiss back, obviously she was used to houses with slightly more solid walls than ours.

'I thought it was a party and might make a change from wedding meetings about crockery,' Rufus sounded like he was complaining.

'Well, it is a party, isn't it?'

I wished there was another exit to the kitchen that didn't involve throwing myself out of the window. I didn't want to see Rufus . . . but oh, I did. I'd always wondered if he'd ring, once he heard about my dad. Maybe he'd feel so mortified and tortured with grief he'd realise he'd made the biggest mistake of his life . . . instead, of course, he'd been out pricing wedding rings with Carena. He can't possibly have given me another thought.

'Who wants to dance?' I announced quickly. The music was still gruesome, but I had to get rid of this nervous energy. And what the hell was Carena playing at, bringing him. OK, I'd said I was over him but that didn't mean I meant it. Did she really have to rub it in? I thought about what I knew about Carena. Yes. I suppose she did.

Another thought struck me. They were going to spill the beans – reveal my identity to the boys. I didn't want to have to cope with all the questions and the interest and how they'd look at me differently if they knew I was going to be rich. I quite enjoyed (apart from the cleaning) my anonymity here. I didn't have to keep up with anyone, look right, eat right, get invited to the right places. It was pretty mucky, but surprisingly relaxing.

'I will,' said Eck, but Cal caught my eye just at the wrong moment. I didn't have much time.

'OK,' I said to Cal.

'You next, yeah?' I added to Eck as I dragged Cal towards our living room.

'Uh, I didn't really want to dance anyway,' Eck was mumbling, turning back to his mates with an embarrassed-looking expression.

I ducked my head to the facing wall and held Cal's jacket over my face. Fortunately there were about a thousand people in the hall, and Carena had her nose up in the air, so we managed to squeeze past undetected.

The music was throbbingly loud in the living room, but, weird as it was, I found I no longer minded. Tentatively at first I moved my arms into the air and let my body sway in time. God, I do love to dance. That doesn't necessarily mean I'm very good at it, but I do love doing it. There's an old cliché that says 'dance like no one's watching', but I don't believe in that. I think you should dance like everyone in the world is watching you and you're Madonna at Wembley Arena. So, art student girls – get out of my way!

As I warmed up, I could feel Cal starting to respond. He was a surprisingly good mover – oh, OK, I wasn't that surprised. Nobody as confident as Cal was a truly bad dancer. But he was slinkier than I'd thought, sexier than ever as we started moving closer and closer. His mouth made a little moue of approval as he watched me twirl about. Good. Ideally I didn't want him to watch me critically and then go 'Woah, horsie'.

I shimmied closer. He did likewise, till suddenly our chests were nearly touching and we were holding eye contact for longer and longer. I felt I could dive into his dark eyes; the desire to touch his lean pale chest was becoming overwhelming. I forgot about Carena and Rufus. Even Daddy. I forgot about anything except the grind of the music and the heat of the floor and the very small distance between us. Now our movements were completely synchronised, moving more and more slowly in rhythm with one another till it felt inevitable to . . .

'God, I nearly didn't recognise you,' came the voice. 'Till I saw those arms waving about madly of course. What on *earth* have you done with your hair?'

'Hello, Carena,' I said, standing back from Cal. My plan to be an elegant strong woman on the surface took a real battering when I saw who was standing beside her.

Rufus looked as handsome as ever, maybe more so. I felt

my heart flip. He looked a little embarrassed. But under the circumstances, not as much as he should have done.

'Hi, Rufus.'

'Uh, hi, Sophie.'

I thought he was looking away in shame, until I noticed his gaze wobble away to where the twins had started on the most absurd mock-lesbian dancing I'd ever seen in my life. Which didn't seem to bother Rufus or ninety per cent of the other men in the room, who were suddenly transfixed. Rufus clearly still just wanted to have fun.

'Uh?' I said.

'Oh, yeah,' he mumbled. He couldn't meet my eyes, even when he tried. I noticed Carena's long fingernails tighten on his arm, although she was pretending to be looking elsewhere.

'So . . . life going well?' I said.

'Uh, yeah . . .' He looked about to ask me the same question, but must have realised, from the hallway décor alone, that that would be pointless. 'Look, I'm sorry things went . . . well you know. We had fun, didn't we?'

I think it's then I felt something that I couldn't immediately identify. It felt weird. I realised what it was: I actually felt a bit sorry for Rufus. Which might sound strange for me to say. But for Rufus, everything was fun. And the second it wasn't, you had to find something else to take its place. Nothing was constant, nothing was worth working for. I realised it was a bit rich for me to be thinking this when a few weeks ago I really hadn't done a day's work in my life, but there it was. I spotted his eyes flick to Grace and Kelly again – in search of more 'fun', I think, and for the first time I felt some of the ice leave my heart.

'We did,' I said. Which was true.

Carena stopped pretending to look round, and, sensing it was safe to be herself again, raised her eyebrows.

'You *live* here?'

'Yes,' I said. 'South is the new Nice.'

'Right,' she said. 'Well, happy flat warming.'

She really was tiny. Her waist looked like a child's. Had I ever been that small?

'You look really slim,' I said. I liked the idea of not feeling bitter any more and wondered if giving her a compliment might help. 'Really, skeletal. Near death.'

She beamed. 'Thanks! Well, anyway, it's hardly like Daddy or Rufus would let me go off the peg, but I want to stay at sample size just in case.'

I shook my head at her in confusion. 'What?'

'For my wedding dress. You know. Sorry, is that insensitive to bring that up again?'

I glanced at Rufus, who was drooling like a big friendly dog while watching Grace and Kelly.

'You know what?' I said suddenly, finally meaning it. 'Don't worry about it.'

Philly came up out of nowhere and kissed me affectionately. I was quite touched before I realised she had hopped in and was now standing between Cal and me. She started gyrating in front of him.

'Dancing?' she said.

I hoped Cal would say something chivalrous, like how he was dancing and that he would turn to me and say, 'But *she* is my partner.'

151

But he didn't. He smiled cheerfully at me, moved a little to the side, and he and Philly started dancing. I turned to watch. God, he was a good dancer. Philly was giving it her best hip shimmy but unless I was very much mistaken he wasn't dancing anything like as close with her as he had with me.

'Oh, Sophie, what *are* you like at holding on to a man?' said Carena, as if this was hilarious.

'Now, Rufus, go and get me a drink. Champers if they have it. Do you have it? No? No?'

I rolled my eyes. 'No,' I said.

'Gwah?' said Rufus. The twins had stepped their lesbian dancing up a bit and were now pretending to tongue each other. Rufus had actual dribble coming out of the side of his mouth.

'Get me a *drink*, darling.'

Rufus blinked himself back into the present. 'I want to stay in here.'

The twins had sidled right up to him. I did hope they didn't nick his wallet.

Carena glared at him and, slinking slightly, Rufus moved away from Kelly and followed Carena out of the room, like a dog who'd done something naughty on the kitchen floor. Just before she moved out of earshot, though, she turned round one last time to me.

'Oh, is Gail all right?' she said, her face suddenly full of mock concern.

'Why?' I said, my senses immediately on red alert.

'Because I heard she's moving out. Just wondered what was up?'

Carena's tone was saccharine sweet but her words struck me as if I'd been stabbed. Moving out? Of my house?

'What do you mean?' I said. 'Where's she going?'

'I don't know,' said Carena. 'I just heard people talking about it in Mirabelle.'

I could feel my heart pound loudly.

'I'm sure it's nothing,' she said.

But I didn't think it was nothing. If a frenemy like Carena came all the way to the Old Kent Road to casually drop it into conversation, there was a strong chance it actually meant quite a lot.

I sat back down in the kitchen, all the booze I'd had earlier – and the news – making my head spin. I tried to call both Gail and the house but wasn't getting an answer from either place. This made me feel worse than ever.

'What's up?' said Eck. I looked at him, his face was genuinely concerned. But I didn't know what to say – my house and possibly my inheritance, which I hadn't told any of them about in a wish to stay reasonably normal – were possibly gone. Or Gail has vanished with everything or Carena was just trying to wind me up because she's my arch-nemesis, or, a million different things . . . my head couldn't settle.

'Nothing,' I said. 'Money problems. Possibly.'

Even as I said that I felt my heart pound.

'Oh, the fun kind,' he said.

'Are you on a student loan?' I asked. He nodded.

'What's it like?'

He looked at me. 'Are you serious? Haven't you been to college?'

I toyed between an outright lie and the outright truth, neither of which seemed particularly useful at the moment. Yes, I had been to college. But I hadn't had to live on a student loan.

'Can I have another drink?'

'Sure,' Eck said, and he headed off in search of more wine.

'Hey,' came a sinuous voice to my left. 'Why did you bring all that totty to the party when it insists on just dancing with each other or complaining that there's no champagne?'

I blinked, struck out of my vacant reverie. Cal looked nine foot tall looming above me. I made my mind up. My life was an incredible mess, possibly. I had to sort out about a million things, not least my evil ex-friends. But for now there was only one thing I could think of to clear my head and make me not think. And it wasn't another glass of wine.

I stood up, wobbling a little. 'Could we go upstairs for a bit?' I said. It came out breathily, almost as a gasp.

'Are you all right?' he said, looking a bit concerned.

'I've just had some bad news,' I said.

'What's up? Prince William marrying somebody else, Cinders?'

'No.'

I didn't want to tell the whole sorry story. I didn't want to talk about it. I didn't want to think about it. I didn't want to think about anything at all.

'Could we just get out of here?'

Cal glanced around. 'You mean, move to the undiscovered west wing?'

'What about your room?' I said.

He stopped teasing me and looked straight at me then. 'Are you sure?'

I took his arm. I wasn't sure of anything, I just had to get out of there and try and stop all these questions running round my head. 'Yes,' I said.

I followed him as he swept towards the kitchen door, the noise of the party outside ominously loud. Just as we got there I heard a voice say my name and turned round. It was Eck. He was standing there, holding my drink and looking perturbed.

'Sophie. Are you OK?'

Cal gave him a quick, annoyed glance.

'I'm fine,' I said, trying to sound like I knew what I was doing.

'Are you sure?' he said.

Cal's lips twitched in annoyance and he continued on. Eck's expression looked pained.

Cal's bedroom must have been the largest in the house, at the front. The bare wooden floorboards in here didn't look quite as bad as they did on the stairs. On every available surface were bits and pieces of twisted metal and clay.

'Is this what you're working on?' I said.

Cal grunted. 'Something along those lincs.'

Then he threw himself back onto his bed. I sat down on a stuffed armchair in the corner of the room. It made me feel oddly formal.

'I found that on a skip,' he said.

'Where's your snake?' I asked, suddenly nervous.

'There's really no snake,' said Cal, laughing. 'You do have

to get over believing that. OK. I gave it five pounds and told it to take itself to the cinema tonight so it didn't spoil the party.'

'What's it going to see, *The Adder Boleyn Girl*?'

'Actually, it's got more art house tastes. I think it's seeing *Snaking the Waves*.'

I smiled and relaxed, even as I felt Cal's eyes upon me.

'You're a mystery woman, Cinders,' said Cal, softly. 'I don't know what to make of you, I really don't.'

Even the sound of his voice sent shivers down my spine. Enough talking. His dark eyes were completely inscrutable. But for now, seeking oblivion, seeking something new, something to make me feel good, feel better, I didn't care. This was what I wanted. I gave him a look that conveyed exactly that. The noise of the party was loud below us, but I didn't give a toss.

Cal sighed. 'I knew having a female flatmate was going to mean big trouble,' he said. Then he got up, his wiry height blocking out the light from the lamp, strode across the room and suddenly, brutally, kissed me.

Chapter Eleven

It was just like I'd hoped it would be. Fierce. Not particularly gentle. God it felt good to be with a man who knew exactly what he was about and what he wanted; even if – maybe especially if – he'd honed his skills through an insane amount of practice with different girls. Nonetheless it didn't feel as if he was going through the motions; Philly once slept with an ex-boy-band member and said he was completely lazy, as if he was doing it because he felt obliged to share himself with the world, just because so many women fancied him. Oh, and he was unbelievably, insultingly concerned about the condom going on properly, implying she was riddled with disease and desperate to steal his spunk at the same time. (Not completely unwise on his part when dealing with Philly though.)

I took in the smell and sense of Cal's long, lean body. He wasn't muscly, but skinny and smooth. Weirdly, he wasn't entirely unlike a very sexy snake himself. I finally fell into an exhausted sleep around five, watching the shadows brighten across his concave cheeks, his eyelashes nearly brushing the cheekbones. It was the first dreamless sleep I'd had in weeks.

Of course, and I'd known he would all along, when I woke up in the morning, he had gone. Vanished. At least he'd had the manners not to disappear the second it was over, and go and see if there were any more pickings to be had at the party. He'd hardly got warmed up, I reflected, by the time I'd hauled him upstairs.

I brushed away my disappointment. I'd known this would happen, of course. This was what boys did to me. Rufus had done it, and Cal would do it too. And I'd wanted a quick fix. And it had worked, for a while, even if I wasn't particularly proud of myself. I'd used him far more than he'd used me. Still.

Oh God. I suddenly realised I was going to have to do the walk of shame in my own bloody flat. Surely not. I glanced over at the window. No, we were three storeys off the ground. Climbing out wasn't an option.

I looked around. The room looked a lot less romantic in the harsh light of the morning. There were no curtains on the windows. How could people live like that? Had it genuinely just never crossed his mind to get some curtains? I guessed not. I suppose when all your concentration was focused on sculpting and shagging, maybe you somehow skipped the other stuff.

Well, I had to do something. I was desperate for the toilet for starters. I looked around for clothes. Oh God, of course there was only the dress I'd been wearing the night before. I could grab one of his shirts, but, one, it would look totally, embarrassingly presumptuous and, two, I'd seen too many girls arrive shyly in our kitchen having done exactly that. I didn't want him to think for a moment that I was one of those, desperately hanging around for too long; calling long after he'd stopped answering. I mean, we had to see each other. I didn't want him to get the wrong idea. Plus, I wasn't sure I'd look better than them in it.

Holding my dress around me, trying to get it to cover everything, I put my foot on the cold floorboards. They squeaked immediately. Bugger this cheap and decrepit and tacky house and everything in it. As I went vertical, I could feel my head starting to spin. Normally I reckoned I didn't get hangovers but now I wondered if it was because I'd been more used to drinking nice, clean, expensive champagne, and not the gut rot I'd partaken of last night with such gusto. Now my head felt like a cement mixer and my stomach was full of acid and an emotion I really didn't like. Shame.

Really, it probably wasn't the best idea to crap on your own doorstep, no matter how sexy the doorstep . . . well, that analogy wasn't working terribly well. Despite a distinctly dizzy, sicky, yuck sensation and a taste in my mouth to suggest that at some point I'd dug a tunnel in the woods with my teeth, swallowing all the worms along the way, I was just going to have to get on with it.

Taking a deep breath, I launched myself through the door.

159

Nobody in the corridor, good. Oh, whoops, I had overlooked that there was someone in the corridor – Wolverine, stretched out and having a nap. Carefully, I tiptoed past and made it to the stairwell. Then I tiptoed down the stairs, creaking on each one. Halfway down I decided I didn't care and made a flying leap down the rest towards my bedroom door, my dress floating out behind me. 'Yaaaargh!' I yelled, as I came face to face with Eck, and he came face to face with me. And one of my boobs, which was hanging straight out.

Normally I'd have expected a friendly quip or something, but he merely glanced at me, said, 'Hi, Sophie,' in a very flat voice and skirted past me to head up the stairs. I backed myself against the wall.

'Hi, Eck,' I said quietly. He had been flirting with me. And then I just waltzed off with his flatmate. It must have felt like a kick in the teeth. But Eck . . . I couldn't just have copped off with him. At least I knew Cal was a thick-skinned crocodile who got through women like packets of crisps. I'd never even seen Eck with a girl. Who knows what a one night stand would mean to him? Still, I hadn't wanted to make him feel bad. Not for anything. At the very least I'd hoped we were friends.

'Got a bit drunk last night,' I said, staring at my feet.

'Really?' he said. 'You didn't seem that far gone to me.'

'No, no,' I said. 'I was. I can hardly remember a thing. My head is about to fall off. I feel . . . really stupid.'

Which I did, standing butt naked on a freezing cold stairwell explaining to one flatmate why I'd just shagged another flatmate.

Eck looked a bit mollified. 'Oh, I wouldn't worry about it. A lot of girls . . .' He seemed about to say more then stopped himself. 'I mean, don't be too hard on yourself.'

And that made me feel guiltier than ever.

Reaching the safety of my bedroom, I threw on a pair of jeans and two jumpers and stared in the tiny mirror. Last night's make-up had congealed all the way down my face. My cheeks had green stains on them. I looked a terrible, terrible, horrifying fright. Which didn't really matter, as I was now going to stay in my bedroom for ever.

Oh God. Let me see. I supposed I should be as businesslike and as unfussed as possible. I remembered Meiko, a gloriously pretty Japanese girl with whom Cal had enjoyed a particularly athletic weekend. She left him little origami gifts at the front door every day for a fortnight. He had to know I wasn't one of those.

So, mind set, I limped nervously into the kitchen. Whereupon my resolve crumbled instantly. Cal's long lean pale body was leaning against the fridge, and he appeared to be in the middle of recounting some hilarious anecdote to James, which stopped the second I emerged, leaving me instantly suspicious that they'd been talking about me.

'What ho!' hollered James, all but confirming my suspicions.

'Morning,' I said, as breezily as I could manage, which wasn't very.

'MOR – ning,' said James in a cheeky, wink wink, how's-your-father type tone. How he ever got here from the 1950s I'd never know.

'Hey,' said Cal.

I tried to analyse his 'hey'. Was it a 'Hey, how *you* doin'?' sexy kind of hey? Or a 'Hey, who are you again, never mind I'm not that fussed' kind of a hey? Or was it a 'I am literally completely shagged out and did things to you last night that can see you in prison in several Southern American states and thus will keep conversation to a minimum until we've at least had the chance to have a cup of coffee together' hey?

'Hey,' I said back. I looked hopelessly at the kettle. Everyone paused for a while.

'Uh. Tea?' I said. The others nodded.

We hovered in silence as the kettle boiled. It took nine-and-three-quarter hours.

'So,' said James finally. 'Uh, what are you two up to today? Uh, maybe don't answer that!'

Cal looked awkward. 'Uh, well, I have to . . . uh, do a few things.'

Oh, for crying out loud. Actually, Cal, I got the message when you slunk out of the room without waking me. But, you know, *thanks*.

'Me too!' I announced. I certainly did. Call my lawyer for a start. I may be feeling like a disinterred zombie, but this was something I couldn't put off for one second. Lawyers don't mind working on Sundays anyway; if they go near a church the water starts to burn them.

Cal looked incredibly sheepish suddenly, almost shifty. I stood up again, tea in my very shaky hand.

'Em, Sophie . . .' he started. Oh God, here it came. The talk. Next he would say, 'Can I have a quick word?' And then he would politely say that he didn't really think it was a good idea blah, blah, blah, and I'd agree, obviously, but it would still be annoying because he got it in first.

'I'd love to chat, Cal, but I'm really dead busy . . . could you drop me an email or something?'

This was a trick response; he didn't have my email address, living as we do in the same house, and I didn't have a computer any more. He looked startled and momentarily confused.

'Well, best get on,' I said, in a silly voice that made me sound like a cheerful lady vicar.

Cal opened his mouth, then closed it again. Then said, quite meekly, 'Uh, OK . . . speak later.'

'Sure thing,' I said breezily.

I know I am a selfish person. My stepmother always liked to mention it, Carena used to say it if I ever asked to borrow her lipgloss, and my dad even wrote it up in my will for the world to read.

So I decided just for once to use it to my advantage, and I stole all the hot water, every last drop. I stayed in the shower till I felt the layers of sweat and sex and dancing and grime finally wash off. In this house, however hard I tried, I never felt truly clean. There was too much limescale deep in the bones of the pipes; too much old newspaper stuffed in gaps in the walls. Plus, I'm not that good a cleaner.

Once outside, I phoned Gail again. And the house. Nothing. Where were they? What were they doing? Where was Esperanza? If Gail was going somewhere bigger – had cashed in my dad's shares or something – why wouldn't she let me know? If she was stealing stuff – well, that didn't make sense. I may have been mean to Gail, but I know my dad loved her. Why? Why?

I decide to go see Uncle Leonard, my dad's old lawyer. He could advise me. He was my dad's best friend. He could tell me what to do. Though why hadn't he rung me already? No, I couldn't think like that. I imagined it in my head. I'd go in and tell him all my worries and fears that the worst had happened, and he'd calm me down and say, 'Well, there's nothing going on, Sophie. Your stepmother has bought a lovely penthouse in Malibu and decided to vacate the house ready for when you come home. It was meant to be a surprise. We made a mistake; it wasn't six months in the will, it was six weeks your dad meant. We're so sorry. Please come back.'

And I'll say, 'Great, that's fine, accidents happen. Could you help me find a great interior decorator for the house?' and he'll say, 'Absolutely, that's just what your father would have wanted. He'd have been so proud of you.'

'Ugh, look, that slut's got chin rash!' comes a harsh teenage voice behind me. 'Chin rash!'

And I will never, ever take the bus again.

St John's Street is really lovely, where Leonard lives. His house is brown brick with some closed up windows, and it's narrow and rickety like it's auditioning to be in a Dickens' adaptation. I knocked hard and hoped they were in.

Nothing happened for ages, and I was wondering what on

earth to do next when the door creaked open. It was Leonard. He'd clearly been having a nap; instead of wearing his immaculate three-piece with fob watch, he was wearing an old shirt and trousers with a dressing gown over the top. His hair was all tufted up at the back of his head like fluff, rather than smoothed down impeccably with rather too much wax as it usually was. He was trying to poke on a small pair of spectacles and focus on me at the same time.

'Hello?' I said.

'Who are you?' said Leonard, not at all in his normal kindly voice. 'Westminster Abbey is that way.'

'Leonard . . . Leonard, it's me.'

Leonard squinted and finally got his glasses on properly.

'*Sophie?*' he said, sounding shocked. My hangover must have been worse than I thought. And my roots problem. 'What on earth happened to you? Were you kidnapped? I haven't heard from you in months.'

'Uh, no,' I said. 'Uh, Leonard, I need to know about Daddy . . . I need to know about his will and what's happening.'

Leonard's face fell. This wasn't good. Leonard's face should not fall at this point. It should light up and he should say something like, 'Well, I should jolly well hope so too,' and light a big fat cigar. Or something like that.

'You'd better come in,' Leonard said.

Leonard's wife June made tea and I sat down on an uncomfortably slippery, leather-buttoned armchair in their lovely library.

'Now, Sophie,' he started, looking nervous. He'd gone upstairs and put a checked shirt and a green cashmere jumper on, but he still didn't look right without the fob watch.

'Firstly, as you know, your stepmother hired Mr Fortescue. It appears, ah, that she thought she would benefit from someone . . . more dynamic.'

'Mmm-hmm,' I said. 'But you must know what's going on . . . I heard a rumour that Gail's not living in the house any more, and I can't get anyone on the telephone.'

Leonard looked grave. 'I heard that rumour too. Mind you, I wouldn't believe everything you hear . . . I mean, I heard you were living in a squat down the Old Kent Road.'

I didn't say anything.

Leonard squinted at me. 'You're not, are you?'

I shrugged, as if actually living in a dive on the Old Kent Road was actually wryly interesting and colourful.

Leonard took off his glasses and wiped them on his sleeve. Then he let out a great sigh.

'Why didn't you come to us?' said Leonard. 'I've known you since you were a little girl. We'd have taken you in. June misses having young people round the house since the girls have grown. Why didn't you, Sophie? Didn't you want to come here?'

I felt terrible. The truth was, in my shallow, nasty spoiled way, I'd always just thought of Leonard as being like hired staff, not much up on Esperanza. Carena and I never played with his stolid, thick-eyebrowed daughters. It had just never occurred to me.

Both his daughters were lawyers now, like their dad,

earning tons of money, no doubt, and both married and having babies. I'd had invites to their weddings but hadn't even bothered to reply. And here was Leonard offering to take me in. Frankly, it was a chance I didn't deserve. I lowered my head.

'Thank you but I'm fine, Leonard, honestly.'

'You don't look fine,' he said. 'Is that a skin disease?'

No, it was chin rash. Well, I hoped it was chin rash. There was a small chance it might actually be scabies I supposed, given the night I'd had.

'It's nothing,' I said. He didn't look convinced.

'So,' I said. 'Please. Tell me everything. Even if it is gossip.'

Leonard still looked pained.

'I understand. You have client/attorney privilege, right?' I said.

Leonard snorted. 'I do wish people would stop watching American television. I'm not an attorney, I'm a lawyer, and no, privilege ends with death.'

'Oh. OK,' I said, resolving to stay quiet.

'I have to tell you,' said Leonard. 'Your dad's affairs . . . I mean, nobody expected him to die so young.'

An overweight overstressed over-drinking cigar-smoking workaholic man in his fifties. For the millionth time I felt that acid pang in my stomach. Why hadn't I done something? Why didn't I look after him? Mum couldn't be there to do it. It was my job.

'Uh-huh,' I said, clutching my hands together and trying not to cry.

167

'There, there,' said June, coming in with Earl Grey tea and some sandwiches. She patted me gently on the shoulder. 'It must be so raw still.'

Of course her kindness made it all worse – it had been so long since anyone had been kind – and I felt myself starting to snivel. I couldn't cry again, I couldn't.

Leonard looked pained at what he had to say.

'Sophie, dear, your father made some very high-risk investments . . . leveraged a lot of debt from one company to another.'

I didn't quite understand what he was saying, but it didn't sound very good.

'You know, that was his personal investment fund . . . he built it up from nothing. His position had changed quite rapidly with the central banking crisis, and things were very much in flux at the time of his death . . .'

'What you're saying is,' I forced the words out. I had to be clear. 'It's quite possible that there isn't any money at all.'

'It's more than possible,' said Leonard, his cheeks pink. 'I think it's likely, Sophie. The debt had been moving up and up, and I do think . . . I mean, a couple more years and he'd have been back in the black again, for sure, if he could have ridden the wave . . . Sophie, I'm so, so sorry.'

I choked back the tears. 'But he'd have looked after me, though? He always looked after me.'

Leonard took off his glasses and wiped them on his sleeve. 'Of course he did, Sophie. But . . .' he trailed off.

'But my money . . . my money . . . surely it's ring-fenced somehow? *Surely?*'

I couldn't believe what he was saying or what it might possibly mean.

Leonard shook his head. 'I don't think so, Sophie . . . banks employ very clever people to find money. Anything there at all . . . it will just all go into debt repayment. They're very strict. Unless he'd handed it over to you years ago.'

I shook my head, nearly speechless. 'The house, the cars, my inheritance, all of it?'

'Everything. It'll just go to a faceless bank.'

I started to shake. Everything gone. Everything. The holidays. The flights. The nightlife. The paintings. Everything. All of it. My entire life.

And I couldn't help thinking; if I had got back in time; if I'd saved my dad, we'd have come up again. He'd have recovered, made the money back. Sorted things out. But now . . .

'Christ,' I said. June was standing by my chair, patting me ineffectually on the shoulder like I was a nervous dog. 'Oh Christ.'

'Sophie,' said Leonard. 'I mean it . . . we can help you.'

I shook my head in disbelief. 'What, give me millions and millions of pounds?' Then I regretted my sharp tongue in response to their genuine and instinctive kindnesses. 'Sorry. Sorry. Sorry. Oh God, what a mess. What a horrible, horrible mess.'

June patted me again. 'You've had a terrible shock.'

'Why didn't anyone warn me?'

Leonard shrugged. 'Oh, your dad had had setbacks before. He'd never let anything worry you . . . you were his princess, you know.'

I felt the tears prick again.

'Plus, he always said, "She's so beautiful, she'll probably marry the King of England."'

Silence fell. I did feel, suddenly, like clinging to the shiny leather armchairs; the understated luxury of Leonard's house; throwing myself on their charity, begging for them to bring me up, like little orphan Annie.

But I was twenty-five. My life was my own. I was completely on my own, and staying here, in warmth and comfort, was only a harsh reminder of everything I no longer had.

'I should go,' I mumbled.

'Stay for dinner,' said Leonard. 'Please. The girls are coming over. They'd love to see you.'

The idea of Leonard's family, all love and warmth and affection and babies sitting down to a lavish Sunday dinner and spending their time being kind to the poor little rich girl was more than I could bear.

'I can't,' I said. I was going to make up some polite excuse but I couldn't even manage that. 'I . . . I can't.'

Leonard's face was very sad as he looked at me. 'I understand,' he said. 'But Sophie, if there's anything – *anything* – I can do. A place to live, a job, some money . . . please, please, please come to us.'

I nodded. 'Thanks,' I said, meaning it. I didn't have anything left in the world, after all. 'It's good to know that.'

And it was, I suppose. When everything else had turned to ashes. June gave me a hug and gently stroked my face in a way that was the complete opposite to every rough caress of the night before – it was maternal I supposed. Not that I'd know – and I took my leave. As I made it to the end of the

170

street a huge Audi estate turned in, with Leonard's eldest daughter and her handsome husband and two sticky dark-haired children in the back. I waved cheerily, as if I was just passing, but they didn't see me, as I made my lonely way back to the end of the street, and out into a teeming, cold, cold world.

In the end, I walked home. All the way home. Well, there was hardly any point wasting a bus fare when I had nothing else to do, except contemplate the ruin of all my hopes, the emptiness – the complete and utter emptiness – of my life. Or what was left of it. What was left of it? More picking up sweaty G-strings, chasing invoices from newspapers and picking Wolverine's hair out of the plughole in the shower. Or perhaps, to cover my living costs, I could get an extra job and work all night in some bar until I got too old and was just a miserable old hag with a tale to tell.

Everything had gone. Friends – not really worth the candle, in the end. Family – nope, gone too. Money – all gone.

The view from Waterloo Bridge, all the great sights of London politely lined up in a row for you to admire them one by one, usually raises my spirits. Today I thought seriously about what would happen if I simply jumped over the side. Would anyone notice? Maybe I could leave a note saying that Wolverine could have my room. Maybe I could leave behind my dresses and Cal could make them into curtains. I wouldn't even ban Carena and Philly from my funeral. Would it hurt much, I wondered. Probably. And I am a coward. Maybe a bath and a razor blade. I thought of the motley collection of blunt razor blades in the Old Kent Road. Best not. The septicaemia would probably get me before the blood loss.

Oh God, Oh God. I didn't know what I was going to do.

When I finally, quietly, let myself in, the boys were round the kitchen table, all together. This was unusual. I looked around. They'd picked up all the empty bottles from the night before and put them next to the back door. This didn't exactly constitute cleaning up but was something of an advance on before, when Eck once left a Weetabix bowl right by the front door. As an experiment I left it there. Every single person entering the house fell over it immediately. Not one person picked it up. This went on for three days.

And finally, they were eating a meal which, judging by the bizarre array of implements filthily scattered around the room, they'd cooked themselves.

'Hey,' I said, not wanting to get drawn in. My misery was best kept to myself. It would mean nothing to them; it might even be insulting, the idea that to live like they did was the worst possible fate one could imagine.

'You do not,' said James finally, tucking into what might once have been a Brussels sprout but was a very unusual colour, 'look exactly like a woman who's recently been taken to the edge of sexual ecstasy and back.'

'Shut it, fusilier,' said Cal shortly.

'Quiet, the both of you,' said Eck. 'Sophie, are you OK? How are things?'

Cal shot him a look. I wondered how much had passed between them about last night.

'Uh, come and have lunch. We made it! We all did different bits! James did the sprouts!'

'We like them this colour in the army,' said James.

'Cal did the potatoes.'

'Those are potatoes?' I found myself asking, weakly. There was a grey swill in a pan dunked on the table.

'I never know how long to leave them on for,' said Cal.

'So what did you go for?'

'About two hours?'

I shook my head, confused. 'And who did the meat?'

'I cooked it, Wolverine carved it,' said Eck, proudly. It looked like those plastic hams you get in doll's houses.

'With his teeth?'

'Fine,' said Cal. 'Turn down our very kind invitation to Sunday lunch.'

I thought of the smells of gravy and roasting garlicky chickens that had been coming from Leonard's kitchen and suddenly felt hungry. Could potential suicide victims be hungry? Maybe I could eat lunch but just add some poison to it.

'Let me push it around my plate for a bit,' I said, trying to sound at least a little grateful.

'Uh, we're slightly out of plates,' said Eck who, I now noticed, was eating out of a saucepan lid. Not a saucepan lid that fitted any of the saucepans we had though. 'But Wolverine's licked his clean.'

Wolverines plate was a plastic bowl. I think maybe it was a dog's bowl.

'No, thanks,' I said. 'Maybe I'll just pick bits from the saucepans.'

173

For want of anything to do that didn't involve GBH – to myself – I sat down on the pile of newspapers supposedly for recycling, which had now got so high we could use it as a chair. Eck passed me the roasting tin (a bunch of old Chinese takeaway foil boxes, crushed and formed into something vaguely square) and I attempted to hack my way into what might have been beef. Or pork. Or camel. Or crocodile. Or baboon. I wanted to cry.

'So what's new?' asked James politely. 'Apart from –' Cal shot him a look – 'Uh, good day?'

Maybe ... maybe I should just tell them. Save them thinking I was moping around for Cal. Or just a total misery guts. It would be good to tell someone. I felt... I just felt my whole life was a fake. Fake money, a fake job, fake friends – the fakest, and I was no princess there myself – fake sex. It was all fake and shallow and pointless and dishonest. Maybe, just for once, I should come clean. And they might despise me even more, for looking down on their lives. But at least it would be real. Who I was.

'Something has happened,' I began. I realised I'd been angrily stabbing the mystery meat all this time. I'd made absolutely no impression on it whatsoever. Just then, however, the doorbell rang.

'Who's that?'

Everyone shrugged.

'Maybe it's a furious lover,' said James. 'Come to take her revenge on Cal with a pair of pinking shears. And she'll have to duke it out with you, Sophie.'

'The use of the term pinking shears gives us a lot of

insight into your pathetic but well-organised fantasies, Gardener,' said Cal. 'Someone stop Wolverine barking, I'll get it.'

He was back in two seconds, with a puzzled look on his face.

'It's for you,' he said, pointing at me. 'He's got a camera.'

I stiffened. 'What do you mean, a camera?'

Cal shrugged. 'I don't know. It's just a bloke asking for you, standing there with a camera.'

It must be Julius. What did he want with me on a Sunday though? I put down my fork with a clang and headed through the hallway towards the door.

It wasn't Julius. It was an unhealthy-looking man with three days' worth of growth on his beard and a grubby leather jacket. He was carrying a big paparazzo-style camera, with a powerful zoom lens on the front.

'Sophie Chesterton?' he said.

I tilted my head a fraction. He squinted his eyes at me. 'Oh, yeah.' Then he picked up the camera and started firing off shots.

'What the fuck are you doing?' I said, going to shut the door. But as I did so I saw a very slim, elegant blonde woman step out of a car. She looked oddly familiar, and marched up to me in a very over-confident fashion.

'Flick Abermarle,' she said, shooting out her hand, so I'd shaken it before I'd had time to think. What the hell was this? '*Daily Post*.'

Uh-oh.

175

'Can I come in?' she said.

I recovered just in time. 'No,' I said. 'What do you want?'

'Charming,' she said, jotting something down in her notepad. 'Well, Sophie, we'd like to run a story on you.'

She said this as if she was giving me a birthday present.

'On *me*?' I said. I turned up in gossip columns occasionally – one drippy songwriter had written a dirge about me that went top ten, and I was often to be found in the back of the weekly mags, milling about at some charity affair, and of course there'd been the big party, but I wasn't a *proper* It girl, like Tara or Tamara or that lot.

'Yes,' she said. She looked like a very well made-up fox. 'Why don't we go inside and discuss it?'

I didn't want to say it was because inside smelled like a wet dog's kennel.

'Out here is fine,' I said.

Her face took on the fakest expression of mock concern I'd ever seen in my life, and I know Carena Sutherland.

'Now, Sophie . . . you know you've been through a few tough times recently.'

'I'm fine,' I said automatically.

'And we wanted to run a very sympathetic piece . . . about how you've been affected by your new life.'

'No thanks,' I said. 'If I wanted the publicity I'd have an agent, like everyone else.'

'It's not for publicity,' Flick said, trying to open up her tiny tiny eyes to look like she was being sincere. 'It's about human interest and understanding.'

And I've had a cheese sandwich made out of the moon.

'No thanks,' I said. The photographer was still snapping away; I was very conscious of my unwashed hair, greasy pull-over, tear-stained grey, shagged-all-night face.

'Something terrible has happened to me. And I don't want to talk to you. Goodbye.'

'But we've come all this way on a Sunday,' wailed Flick, her fake sweet expression dropping like she'd thrown it on the floor.

'The Old Kent Road is very central actually,' I replied, closed the door and went back inside.

'Who was it?' said Cal.

'Oh, nothing. Work. They're a double D down for tomorrow.'

'And they wanted you to stand in, what?' said James excitedly.

'No,' I said.

'Not fair,' said James. 'Cal's seen them.'

After hours of tossing and turning on my narrow single bed, sleep finally crept up on me, but my nightmares were back with a vengeance that night. My dad was shouting out to me, and I was spinning around in a nightclub till I started to fall deeper and deeper down through the floor.

I was in hell. I was in jail. There was nowhere left to fall. There was nothing of my old life left to grieve, because it was all gone.

I was woken by a heavy banging on the door.

'Sophie! Sophie?'

'Unf?' I grumped. It was the boys, all roaring like ele-phants.

'What is it?'

'Look, look!'

I blearily focused. Eck was holding up a copy of the *Daily Post*. Emblazoned above the headline (something about immigrants affecting house prices) was a gruesomely hideous picture of me, all lank hair and treble chin, like Britney Spears at a custody hearing.

POOR LITTLE RICH GIRL! ran the strapline. FROM IT GIRL TO BEDSIT GIRL.

I rubbed my eyes. That was quick. 'What the hell?'

'Why didn't you tell us you were famous?' said James. 'Gosh!'

'I'm not famous,' I said, my heart pounding.

'You are now,' drawled Cal. 'Here you are, darling, I've made you some tea.'

'Do you want some tea?' Eck said at the same time. 'Oh.'

Without waiting for an invitation they all came into my room and sat down on my bed as, hands shaking, I turned to the middle pages. There I was – on the left a picture of me at some charity ball last year, wearing a red Gharani Strok number. I was so slim! I'd completely forgotten; I must have got used to the new me. That girl didn't look like me at all. I was flashing lovely white teeth and looked like I was having a fabulous time, wherever I was.

On the right was me yesterday. You wouldn't have known it was the same person. My hair was a complete disgrace, my skin covered in a rash – a snogging rash, though it could have been anything. I was clearly at least a stone heavier, and wearing the daggiest clothes imaginable.

Once the toast of Mayfair's super-set, ran the introduction, *Sophie Chesterton now scavenges a living from the fringes of porn, and squats in a derelict flat.*

'That's a bit harsh,' said James. 'I mean, we pay rent.'

'That makes it worse,' I murmured, my heart pounding.

Her father was implicated in the great banking runs of 2008 and, after his untimely death several months ago, it is reported that he has left the family with huge debts. So what now for the poor little rich girl who once had the world at her feet? Her former best friend, Carena Sutherland, is now set to marry one of London's most eligible bachelors, the Right Hon Rufus Foxwell-Brown in society's wedding of the year. But Sophie has been cast out of her fast-living set . . .'

'No wonder you didn't want to bring any girls to the party,' said Cal.

'No, that was still because you were disgusting about it,' I said faintly.

'I feel sorry for her really,' said erstwhile friend Philly Thompson (twenty-six). 'Ha,' I said. 'That'll get her to stop telling everyone she's twenty-two'. *'She always wanted to fit in. But now we know it was all a sham.'* Hang on, I thought. That was YOU.

Sophie was a familiar face on Bond Street, flashing Daddy's black American Express card and attending lavish product launches and parties. Now her highlighted hair is dull and matted and her . . .

179

That was it. That was enough. They could slag me off to the high heavens, but when they got started on my hair . . . I got up, went through to the bathroom and threw up. It took a while.

When I finally came back, the others were staring at me like I'd just beamed down from another planet.

'You're a *celebrity*,' said James, using the same tone of voice in which he might have said, 'You're a *hermaphrodite*.'

'Now she is,' said Cal.

I bowed my head. 'Some bad stuff happened to me.'

Eck came over. 'What?'

'Things . . .'

'So are you rich?' said James.

'No, that's the point,' said Eck. 'She used to be and now she isn't. Right?' He leant over and said, 'You'll get it back. Don't worry. Those bastards.' Which made me feel a teeny, teeny bit better.

'What's it like being rich?' said James.

'James,' said Cal. 'Shut up.'

'Just asking.'

We all sat around in silence. I could tell they were a bit stunned.

'I mean, you're obviously posh,' said Eck.

'Yes, but there's posh and fake posh,' said Cal. 'I thought you might be that.'

'Thanks very much,' I said. 'Anyway, I wasn't posh, I was rich. There's a difference.'

'The fact that you know there's a difference makes you a bit posh,' he shot back. 'God. Did you think you were just going to be slumming it with us, then you'd find some rich guy and head off again?'

I looked down. 'I thought I'd get the money back.'

Cal shrugged. 'Typical bourgeois scum behaviour. It makes me feel really dirty and used. And normally I like feeling like that. A little real-world vacation from the –' he read from out the paper – 'glamorous Kensington town house and luxury holiday villa in Majorca.'

'The villa isn't that nice,' I said reflectively.

'No,' said James. 'I've heard that about luxury holiday villas.'

We lapsed back into silence. I knew it. This was why I'd never said. It was as if a barrier had opened up between us. Now I wasn't Sophie their flatmate. It was as if I'd perpetrated some sort of fraud, pretending to be something I wasn't – i.e. a normal person – but now, with everything that had happened to me I was a normal person who was somehow looking down my nose at them. Which I wasn't. Well, maybe at Wolverine, a bit.

'I'd better get to work,' I mumbled. Nobody said anything. They were all still looking at me like I came from Mars. Then, when I was at the door, Eck said, 'So, when you cleaned our toilet . . . was that the first time you'd ever cleaned a toilet, ever?'

I stared him straight in the face. 'Yes,' I said. 'Yes, it was.'

'Well, that's something,' said Cal encouragingly. 'We all just thought you were a lunatic.'

*

I knew within ten seconds that Julius had seen the paper. Then I heard the twins squeal and realised that they'd seen it too.

'That's *you*??' said Grace. She was wearing lime green feathers.

'What *are* you wearing?'

'It's *Burlesque*. Like Dita Von Teese, innit?'

I absolutely would never had said how much she didn't look like Dita Von Teese.

'So you're rich and that?' went on Grace. 'I'd never have guessed.'

'That's because you don't pay attention,' said Kelly. 'Delilah told us about all her clothes, remember? So you're an idiot.'

'Oh, stop being immature,' said Grace.

'Just because I'm younger than you.'

'Uh, yes, well, it doesn't matter,' I said. I was back in my tracksuit bottoms. After dressing up on Saturday night it felt like all I deserved. Saturday felt like a long time ago, even though it was still making me yawn.

Julius looked at me for a long time. 'You didn't tell them about me, did you?'

'You've read the piece. Does it mention you?'

'No. Well, only that you used to hang around top photographic studios.'

'Oh Jules,' I said, sadly, wondering if he was going to sack me again. 'Let's pretend I still do.'

Julius looked at me for a long time. Then he handed me a camera. 'On you go then.'

'What do you mean?'

'Well, if you're grafting for a living, you might as well make a start. Why don't you take the twin's first set? I'll take a set too, and we'll see how they do.'

He started snapping. Kelly started rubbing the feathers between her legs like she was vigorously towelling herself dry. And I, highly excited, started lining up shots.

'Is that what Dita Von Teese does?' Kelly asked.

'Kind of,' I said. 'But bend down a little . . . and smile. A bit cheeky. That's it. You've got it.'

And I let the camera click.

When I went to the caff at lunchtime, I could see the well-thumbed paper lying open on one of the tables, they slipped an extra slice of bacon in my roll and the friendly server said, 'I am very sorry for you to lose everything.'

'Thanks,' I said, genuinely grateful for a bit of well-meant sympathy.

'In my country I was an engineer, and taught at the university. I had a big house, many nice things. Then they decide they no longer like universities. Here I cook greasy sausage for fifteen hours a day. Lots of people have hard things in their lives.'

I looked, for the first time really, at the man who served me every day.

'Thank you,' I said, holding out my hand, which he took and shook vigorously. 'Thank you very much. I do feel better.'

Chapter Twelve

I went through the rest of the day in a dream. The shoot went well, and Julius reckoned some of my shots would be fine for *Zoo*, no problem.

But this tiny shred of optimism was quickly replaced when I found myself cleaning up. Back to sweeping the floor and picking up little pieces of cloth covered in spangles. Today was different. Today was cleaning up for good. For ever. It wasn't a theme-park ride. It wasn't slumming it for a bit. This was the end.

Mopping took longer than usual. Partly because of the feathers, partly because I could see the future stretching out drearily in front of me. The girls had tarted themselves up super-posh, i.e. they looked like baby drag queens, because they were going to 'pull a suit', i.e. they were headed to All Bar One.

'You must have, like, gone there all the time,' said Kelly, slightly awe-struck. I didn't correct her.

'Or maybe Tiger Tiger,' said Grace.

They invited me, which was really sweet of them, and Grace had even said she'd buy me a drink if I talked really posh. But I just wasn't in the mood. Julius left me to lock up, so I took my time as the shadows climbed the walls of the studio, with its abandoned, slightly greasy mirrored bulbs, the little tubs of opened sparkly lipgloss, the talc on the floor. I put some mournful French music on the stereo and meandered about, straightening up the array of clothes we kept there – tiger-print sarongs; mini kilts, boas and love-heart sunglasses. It looked so tawdry in the half-light. I finished with the mop, pulled on my coat and headed for the door.

'Uh, hi,' said Eck.

I jumped out of my skin. 'Fuck!'

'Uh, sorry, I was just looking for the doorbell.'

'There isn't a doorbell. I think everyone who comes here has a really loud voice.'

'Oh,' said Eck.

'And all the girls have gone home, so you're dead out of luck.'

'I didn't come to see the girls,' said Eck, going very pink. 'I came to see you. I thought you might want some company.'

I looked at him. He was absolutely right.

'Uh, thanks,' I said. 'You did give me a fright though.'

'I try not to be too frightening,' said Eck. 'As a rule.'

'Well, I think that's a very good way to be,' I said. I was half in my coat and half out of it. Eck made a really complex and difficult attempt to help me on with the rest of it, which was doomed to failure, and between us we wriggled our way out of the door with lots of 'sorrys' and 'whoops, just theres' and 'oh, never minds' until we were giggling so much we gave it up as a bad job.

Outside it was nearly dark; I hadn't realised how quickly the nights were setting in. But it was a mild night, the kind that, say I'd been at someone's house in the country, would have seen lots of brown leaves blowing across the path, and a vibrant pink sunset illuminating the corn fields. Here it just made the dog poo harder to see.

'It's a nice night,' said Eck. 'And the buses all smell. Shall we walk?'

'OK,' I said.

We strolled along in silence for a little while. It looked like Eck was trying to tell me something. Finally, after crossing the road to avoid a pack of feral hoodies who – surely not – looked like they were trying to set a dog on fire, Eck took a breath.

'I'm sorry you're an orphan,' he said.

As he did I realised I'd never quite thought of it that way, even though it was technically the case. My mother had died so very long ago that I'd got used to it. For me, having one parent you loved very much was just kind of the way of things.

'My mother died a long time ago,' I said. 'I don't remember her. You don't really miss what you never had.'

That was a barefaced lie I'd developed over the years to stop people feeling sorry for me and, occasionally at parties, playing me drippy songs on the guitar. I had a complete fantasy of what my mother must have been like in my head and thought about her all the time.

'My . . .' He swallowed hard, as if this were difficult to say.

'Um. I lost my dad too,' he said. 'When I was eleven.' He kicked at the pavement with his dirty old trainers.

'Oh yeah?' I said. 'I'm sorry. What happened?'

Nothing, I've learned over the years, is worse than people asking about it then shying away from the topic like they've just been handed a poisonous snake. 'Cancer,' he said, looking down. 'It was horrid. So, I just wanted you to know that I'm here if you need me.'

I looked at his big brown eyes. His tufty hair had fallen forward. For a split second I wondered what it would be like to tuck it back behind his ears. He peered up at me, giving me an apologetic half-smile in the half-light.

'Must be quite a shock, coming down to all this,' he said. 'I thought there was something different about you the first time you came to the door . . .'

'Did you?' I said, with a tiny amount of tease in my voice. 'Did you think, There's a girl worth a couple of million quid?' I couldn't keep the quaver out of my voice.

'Shit,' said Eck. 'Shit.'

'Looking after myself was meant to be good for me,' I said. 'Character building. You know, for a while.' I looked down at my dirty hands.

'Well, I'm impressed you've managed not to call us all plebs and demand that we bring you champagne cocktails every evening.'

'Ooh, that never even occurred to me. Would you?' I said.

There was a long pause. 'I'd do anything you asked,' said Eck simply. I glanced at his tall, dark profile silhouetted in the streetlights.

I glanced up at him. What I'd thought was a mild flirtation suddenly seemed to take on a deeper, more serious hue in the autumnal twilight.

'Hey, Cinders,' came a voice. 'If we bought some cider and got Wolverine to fart in it, could we call it champagne?'

And Cal loped over to join us from the shadow of the dodgy bookies.

'What are you doing here?' said Eck. He didn't look in the least bit pleased to see him. Cal gave him a furrowed look.

'Well, nasty stuff about Sophie in the papers, dark, cold, wet night . . . I thought I'd just check she hadn't thrown herself on the railway line.'

'Well she's fine,' said Eck crossly.

'And actually here,' I volunteered. 'Only, with you guys talking about me being suicidal and stuff . . .'

'I never thought you were suicidal,' said Eck. 'Though after a night with Cal, most girls are slightly sadder than they were before . . .'

'Yeah, yeah, yeah,' said Cal. They stood there, not saying anything. The tension between them was palpable. I piped up.

'Shall we go eat?' As I said it, I wondered if maybe I was too sad to eat. I did want this famed misery weight loss to start kicking in. 'Or, maybe not. I'm just not hungry.'

'Yeah, let's get you home.' Eck made as if to put his hand out to me, and I nearly took it.

'Come with me then,' said Cal, ignoring Eck. 'I'm starving. You can watch me eat.'

Eck glanced from Cal to me. Then, 'Let's all go eat,' said

Eck, looking a bit pissed off. Cal raised his eyebrows as if he wasn't bothered one way or the other.

'Right, I know where. Follow me,' Cal said, disappearing down a dark alley next to the bookies. Eck and I looked at each other. Then I thought, what could possibly be worse for me than what had already happened. So I followed after him, Eck bringing up the rear, looking around dubiously.

'Here we go,' said Cal. We were in a street where at least half the street lamps were missing, and the shops had been boarded up. I didn't like the look of this at all. It looked like a scene from a video game set in a post-apocalyptic world where zombies jump out at us. I had a sudden flashback – once upon a time, I'd been to the launch of a game like that – God knows why, something to do with Philly. Yes, the drinks were lavish and expensive but we were surrounded by geeks the whole night, practically humping our legs like little dogs. We were quite mind-blowingly rude to them, but I don't think they noticed. Happy days.

At the end of the derelict row was one little building with a light on.

'Hello, Memento,' said Cal, pushing open the door into a roomful of deafening music.

The room was lit by a fluorescent strip buzzing overhead. There were about six tables, the white plastic garden type, with cheap plastic mats over them and mismatched chairs. Four were occupied by large groups of people of all colours eating, shouting and drinking beer. It didn't look like anywhere I'd ever been before.

'Hello,' said the large lady behind the counter. 'You've

brought friends.' She looked me up and down with a judge-mental air which I found a bit insulting considering she was about four-foot square. 'But still no girl, eh, Cal?'

Cal rolled his eyes. 'Stop worrying about me, Memento, you're not my mum.'

'Usual?'

'Yup, two . . .' He turned to me. 'Are you sure you won't eat?'

Actually, the place smelled fantastic. It was making me hungry. Not quite the Michelin-starred places I normally toyed over salad in. But no. I was too sad.

'No, thanks,' I said. Memento raised her eyebrows then looked more closely at me.

'Hey . . . aren't you that girl in the paper?'

'She's been getting that all day,' said Cal smoothly. Eck pulled out a chair for me. I sat down on it, trying not to notice that one of its plastic legs looked like it was bending over.

'Yes,' I said, wearily. 'Yes, I am.'

Memento raised her eyebrows at Cal. 'Well, she looks like she needs to eat.'

Frankly I felt like I needed a full sauna, steam and spa day, possibly followed by a colonic irrigation to undo the damage done by all those sausage sandwiches, but I wasn't in the mood for arguing and threw my hands up in submission. Ten seconds later three steaming plates of curry were set in front of us. They smelled absolutely wonderful.

'You don't have to eat it if you don't want to,' said Eck, gently.

'Yes she does,' said Cal. 'Look at the girl. She's practically in shock. Get it down you and you'll feel a lot better.'

'Has anyone phoned the house?' I asked weakly. Without thinking, I forked a load of the curry into my mouth. It was delicious.

Cal's brow furrowed. 'Not phoned as such,' he said.

'Actually, they're camped outside,' said Eck. 'Waving lots of money for exclusives.'

'Really?' I briefly perked up. 'How much money?'

'Ignore them,' said Cal. 'They're vultures.'

'They're not,' I said. 'I got papped once. They shout at you all the time and all the flashbulbs go off and it's brilliant.'

'Well, those days have gone, sweetheart,' said Cal. 'Eat your goat.'

'Eat my *what*?'

'Don't you think . . .' said Eck, trailing off. He wasn't eating, but playing with his food, pushing it round his plate. Weirdly, my appetite was voracious. As if my body was telling me not to give up. I ate the whole thing and when I looked up, Eck was talking. Cal was looking at me as if he couldn't believe how much I'd just stuffed my face.

'Don't you think it's possible you'll get the money back?' said Eck. 'After all, it can't all have gone, can it? Surely they'll just sell the house and sort it out then you'll be OK? Plus your dad must have had tons stashed away in offshore accounts and things that they'll never find.'

I thought back to what Leonard had said.

'I don't think so,' I said. 'He was kind of betting his own

money. Which means we owe the banks something like a billion squillion dollars or something. Nothing you'd get back from the house.' I couldn't quite believe it.

'So you have to go and talk to your stepmother,' said Eck. 'She'll know.'

'So why hasn't she called me?' I said. 'Why won't she pick up the phone?'

I noticed that while Eck was being quietly organised and reasonable and trying to help me out, Cal was getting betting tips from the guys at the next table who were talking about three-legged greyhounds and smoking indoors.

'I don't even know where she is,' I said. 'Does it say in the paper?'

'It says . . .' and he took it out of his jacket. Oh God, had he been hauling it around all day to show to people? *It is not known whether Mrs Chesterton is close to her stepdaughter, whose tabloid antics must often have embarrassed her.*

'Dancing on tabletops is not "*tabloid antics*",' I said, finishing my food. 'It's youthful exuberance. Everyone knows that.'

'Uh-huh,' said Eck.

'We haven't always got on,' I admitted, 'that's for sure. But I'm sure she wouldn't hide my dad's money from me.'

'Money does strange things to people,' mused Eck.

'Not having any money is much, much stranger, believe me,' I said.

'Neh, you should just say "Sod it",' said Cal, feeding Eck's curry to a mangy-looking dog who'd wandered in. 'Forget all about it. It'll just piss you off. Why don't you just get on with life?'

'Because my life sucks,' I said.

'Oh yes, I forgot how hellish it was for you, living with us,' he said, raising an eyebrow.

'You could do it, Sophie,' said Eck. 'We could help. Show those bastards what for.'

'Thanks for the vote of confidence,' I said. The bill came. It was a sum of money that wouldn't have covered one cocktail in the old days, but it still made me a little anxious. 'Us against all the lawyers and bankers in the world who have cash and actual rightness on their side.'

'Sure,' said Eck. 'I'll get the bill.' Then he winked at me. 'You can pay me back later.'

I couldn't help it; my confidence perked up a little.

Back at the flat, Eck put on the kettle, but I was knackered; I'd barely slept in forty-eight hours.

'No, thanks,' I said. I glanced round at the kitchen. The floor was covered in cereal. I raised an eyebrow.

'Did Wolverine get into the Cheerios again?' Eck asked Cal in an accusing voice.

'Looks like it,' said Cal.

'I'll do it in the morning,' I said. I guessed I was still on cleaning duty, because if anyone tried to up my rent this month I was completely stuffed. 'Goodnight, everyone.' I turned round and headed for bed.

As I reached the door of my bedroom, I heard footsteps behind me. It was Cal.

'Hey,' he said.

'What?' I said.

'I dunno . . . just thought you might want some company.'

Actually, a night of good but completely emotionless sex was exactly what I didn't need right now. I could do with a cuddle, and being cherished. I could do with a long heart-to-heart with a close friend. I could do with sitting and having dinner with my dad. I could do with a lot of things, but tonight, pointless screwing wasn't one of them.

'I'm fine, thanks,' I said. My mind flashed briefly to Eck. He would never give such a rough come-on. He'd be respectful. A gentleman.

'Oh,' said Cal. 'It's just after the other night . . .'

'I thought we weren't going to mention the other night?'

'Oh, yeah, right. OK.' He paused. 'You seemed to like it at the time.'

That made me cross for some reason. 'Look,' I said. 'OK, my life is not in a great place right now. But you should know that I'm actually a very cool and sorted person. When things aren't completely in the shitter. So I don't need pity shags, or you're-very-convenient shags or whatever you think this might be, OK?'

'I never thought that.'

'You're ordering me up like pizza!'

'I'm just standing in the hallway.'

'Yes, your hallway! How convenient. Why don't you spend the evening doing something useful like . . . I don't know. Washing your duvet cover? It's this thing that's on your duvet and, amazingly, it comes off! Then—'

'OK, OK,' he said, retreating. 'Sheesh.'

I watched his long body slouch off. For a moment I felt regret. Then, as if to remind me what a tomcat he was, I heard the front door slam, and watched him lope off out, somewhere into the dark grimy city, up the Old Kent Road.

Chapter Thirteen

'What about my diamonds?'

'Covered by the insurance policy. Never left the house. They've gone too.'

'Should I have stolen them?'

'Probably,' said Leonard ruefully. 'Oh. I never said that.'

I was scrubbing the skirting boards and talking to Leonard at the same time. I wasn't making a particularly good job of either task.

I'd been calling him everyday. I just didn't believe there was nothing we could do. Well, there was, but it meant mounting an appeal and funding lawyers and, basically, we couldn't win. My dad had bet all his money. And he'd lost. It hadn't stopped Eck encouraging me, but throughout that long, dark winter, I just felt crappier every time the subject came up, as I boiled up noodles for the fourth time that week.

I knew, at some point, I was going to have to go and find

Gail. I was trying to put it off, like a smear test. But if there was anything left, anything at all, she'd know. Obviously I was putting it off because I didn't want to see her. But also I was putting it off because she was the last ditch solution; the last chance saloon.

So far, so not exactly jolly. Which explains why, when Philly called and left a message saying a new restaurant had opened in St James that did the most unbelievable sashimi and people were flying in from Japan to taste it, and you couldn't get in there without donating a kidney and your firstborn and even then it took two years, *and* she was doing the PR, I was absolutely tempted beyond endurance. Though slightly embarrassed, obviously, that I could forgive the most horrible betrayal if there was very lightly battered tempura involved.

'Come on,' she said. 'I'll stick it on expenses. You can fill us in on all the goss.'

Which I *suppose* meant, tell us lots of miserable stories and we'll buy you a nice lunch. Well, everyone has a price.

Plus, Cal had gone off on some ludicrous international shag fest which meant that every morning there was a nine-foot blonde, or a short Amazonian pygmy, or a sloe-eyed beauty in the kitchen exclaiming over how pleasantly clean the teacups were. But Cal and my paths rarely crossed, he'd become nocturnal again.

Eck and I, though, had taken to eating our breakfast together. It was just kind of nice to come downstairs and find that someone had made you a cup of coffee, not because they were being paid to do so, but because they liked to. I would have made Eck coffee too, but he grimaced once too often and said it was all right, he knew I was trying and that was enough but twenty-five was probably too late to learn how to make a decent cup of coffee so I should just wait till I got my money back and could afford to buy him Starbucks every day. I rather liked this idea of his; that one day in the future all would be well, and we would still be friends and get to go to Starbucks. I liked it a lot. Plus, Starbucks seemed an achievable goal when all my other goals – get back all my money, win a new fabulous boyfriend to annoy Philly and Carena with and get over the fact that all my previous friends and old life were actually a bit horrible – seemed a little tricky.

Eck agreed that I should see the girls, and not just for the sashimi. That maybe my life was different now, but bitterness wasn't going to help it. And I thought he was right about that.

'OK,' I said to Philly, and we planned for next Saturday. She booked the table, I just thought about the pickled carrots.

I spotted Philly and Carena at the corner table, the best one in the room, and sidled my way over to them.

'Ah, the prodigal daughter,' said Philly, getting up and giving me a kiss.

I chose to ignore her.

'Now,' said Philly once we'd seated ourselves. 'You must have what you like, no expense spared.'

A part of me wanted to order very little, to show I really didn't give a toss, that I didn't think this might be the last time I ever got to eat here. But then I thought, Well, sod that, and ordered so much – starting at the dim sum and moving up to, I think, fried horse – that the girls' eyebrows moved further up their faces (well, Carena's did; Philly had had a recent Botox top up).

'Thanks,' I said finally, once I'd got stuck in. 'So how is everyone?'

'Do you mean Rufus?' said Carena quickly. 'He's fine.'

Actually, I realised, I had been asking quite generally. Ever since the party, he hadn't taken over my thoughts anything like as much.

'Good,' I said.

'Everything's great,' jumped in Philly. 'Preparations for the wedding of the season continue . . .'

Carena shot Philly a look.

'Oh, nothing,' Philly tailed off.

I was stuck with a prawn tail half hanging out of my mouth.

'The thing is,' said Carena, putting on her sensitive voice. 'I've been putting the guest list together, and I thought . . .'

'What?'

'Well,' she looked at me.

I took the prawn tail out of my mouth.

'Sophie, I know we're friends, but . . . I mean, under the circumstances. When we met, Rufus and I . . . it was as if, suddenly, true love had shown the way, and we had to follow our hearts, regardless of the consequences. When true love happens to you, you'll see that's right. Do you understand?'

I eyed her suspiciously. Not the Bolt of True Love That Excuses Everything again.

'Anyway, I just feel that I don't want the spotlight to fall on you . . . after all this terrible negative publicity, and, you know, the wedding is at the Dorchester, and it will be quite dressed up and I wouldn't want you to feel lacking in any way. And, well, it's not very nice to remind Rufus that *technically* he was seeing you when he and I were hit with a thunderbolt, and . . .'

I put my chopsticks down. Bum. I mean, I was never in a million years going to *go*. But I had thought at least I'd be asked and be able to smugly decline. This implied that they thought I'd turn up wearing a wedding dress and pitch myself into the cake in a crying fit!

'Here, have some more seaweed,' said Carena, passing it over. 'It's very naughty, but *so* yummy.'

'*Thanks*,' I said.

'We'll send you the photos,' said Carena, as if trying to cheer me up.

'Who's taking the photos?' I couldn't help asking.

'Oh, we're going for a top fashion photographer, not a snaps/wedding photographer type. They're so naff.'

'Hmm,' I said. 'What about Julius Mandinski?'

'You think we'd get him?' said Carena, eyes widening. 'I mean, he's so cutting edge . . .'

'I'd have thought it would be just the thing,' I said. 'Maybe not,' I added. 'He'd probably cover you in dead fish or photograph you upside down on a rope or something.'

'Hmm,' said Carena, which worried me a bit. It was a 'Hmm I think I'd like to do that'. And I knew what usually happened when Carena wanted something.

'Anyway,' said Philly, getting a bossy look on. 'Sophie, we've – I've – got a proposition for you.'

'Oh yeah?'

'You know, there's a lot of interest in you.'

I looked around the table to see if there was anything else to eat.

'Yeah, I do. They hang about my house trying to take pictures of me crying in my sweatpants.'

'Did they get any?' asked Carena.

'That's not the point.'

'*Well*,' said Philly, dragging the focus back to her. 'Why don't you capitalise on it?'

'What do you mean?'

'You're the Poor Little Rich Girl! Society Darling fallen on hard times! Why aren't you cleaning up?'

'What on earth are you talking about?'

Philly started talking to me as if I was really thick. 'Well, you've been in the paper. Now there's a whole career out there for you. Tearful interview with *OK!* Follow-up confessional in *Mail on Sunday*, triumphant appearance on *I'm a Celebrity*, a book deal, then *Dancing on Ice* . . .'

'What are you talking about?'

'Stop being an idiot,' said Philly, exasperated. 'Something happened to you. You're a commodity. There's money to be made. From you. Uh, I mean, *for* you.'

I stared into the middle distance, chopsticks halfway to my mouth. 'You mean . . . what, tell my tragic story, whore myself out to the media.'

'If you lost some weight,' said Philly pointedly, 'you could do some modelling shoots too. They can do a lot with airbrushing these days. A *lot*.'

I ignored this. 'So, I have to give lots of sobbing interviews about losing my dad and all my money and then everyone feels sorry for me and gives me money and stuff?'

'That's kind of how it works.'

'Then I could get to be a Z-list celeb like those desperate horrors that clutter up charity balls that we always laugh at because they're so desperate to get photographed they spend all night sidling up to an ex-game show host?'

'Everyone wants to be a celebrity,' said Philly huffily. 'What makes you so special?'

'So by trading in my own misery I could make a better living?'

'Ironic, don't you think?' said Carena.

'All jobs are like that,' said Philly dismissively.

'And you get, what?'

'Twenty per cent,' said Philly.

That was it. That was the last straw. I stood up.

'You two,' I said. 'You are just disgusting. All of you. Point-less, desperate, leeches. You –' I pointed at Carena – 'steal a man off someone else and are too pathetic even to make up with her properly. And *you* –' I pointed to Philly – 'are just a pimp. And you just spent hundreds of pounds on a meal you didn't eat, didn't enjoy, and if you had eaten it would have spent half an hour in the toilets trying to vomit it up again. You are completely pathetic.'

I felt better.

'Oh, and thanks for lunch. If you could let go of your terri-ble self-hatred for a minute, you'd see it was absolutely delicious.'

They sat there, not saying anything.

The waiter came over. Madly I thought he was about to congratulate me on telling those witches a thing or two.

'Would you,' he said discreetly, 'like me to bag some of this up for you to take home?'

Feeling slightly sick, I boarded the bus home. Somehow I'd become completely oblivious to the noise of the children, and I quite liked the chatter of the pensioners. It was comforting, the way they worried about the price of potatoes and talked about their grandchildren. It was a relief to get to the flat.

'They want you to do *what*?' Cal said, when I told him about lunch.

'I'm not sure exactly. Do interviews. Get my photo taken looking sad. It doesn't matter anyway.'

'What for?'

Cal had been, unusually for him, alone in the kitchen when I got back, and had enquired why I didn't want dinner (pie and mash by the looks of things). I'd ended up telling him everything then, when Eck wandered in, telling it again.

'Everyone wants to be famous, don't they?'

'Do they?' said Cal.

'Well, look at you,' said Eck. 'You think you're a rock star.'

'I'm an artist,' said Cal. 'That's different.'

'So if Damien Hirst invited you down the Groucho Club to get paparazzied you wouldn't go?'

'Well, that's different.'

'How?'

'It's different if you were famous for painting magnificent work or building superb sculptures or being the next person to

203

do the Turbine Hall. But for . . . what, for a bit of bad luck that happened to you . . . surely that's just embarrassing.'

'It wasn't "a bit of bad luck",' I grumbled. 'My life is in total ruins. And with everything that's happened to me I'm kind of beyond embarrassment. But I really, really need cash.'

'Well, why don't you put on a basque and parade up Shepherd's Market?'

For fuck's sake, Cal always had to cheapen everything.

'That's different.'

'What, selling yourself?'

'OK, maybe I don't want any more advice from men who like to call me a whore.'

Cal rolled his eyes and went back to his dinner.

'I think it's quite a good idea,' said Eck. 'Get your picture in the paper, get back into that world where you belong. Plus, you'll have everything on record if you manage to sue for your money back.'

'Sue what?' I said. 'The world recession?' Although there was still a tiny, tiny flicker at the back of my mind that suspected Gail had possibly stolen all the money. No. It wasn't possible. Of course not. Just wishful thinking.

'I mean, what would they make you do?' said Eck, trying to pour oil on troubled waters as usual.

'Knowing Philly, probably the most embarrassing things possible,' I said. 'It doesn't matter anyway, I told them all to piss off.'

'Well, how bad could it be?' said Eck. 'I think you should give it a shot.'

'Not in a million years,' I said.

'OK,' said Eck. 'Oh, by the way, I hate to do this to you. But the electricity bill's come in.'

I picked it up. I couldn't believe how much it was for.

'Christ,' I said. I turned to Cal. 'Are you running a full-on aquarium up there for all your exotic animals?'

'Yes, but it's solar powered,' he said lazily.

'I can't afford this.' I looked at Eck in a pleading way.

'We're all on loans, Sophie,' said Eck. 'None of us can. We all have to chip in, that's how it has to work.'

'I know,' I said, feeling my stomach turn over sadly. I trudged to the kitchen cabinet. 'I'll get the mop out.'

Eck looked awkward. 'And the windows could do with a wash.'

And it was perching outside, precipitously high in a howling gale, desperately scrubbing at a smeary window with a piece of newspaper with my face on it that I found myself thinking, Could Philly's proposition really be worse than this?

Yes, as it turned out. Much.

Chapter Fourteen

There are moments in life when you wonder whether you aren't the punchline of some enormous galactic joke. That, in fact, the whole universe is having an enormous laugh at your expense. That your very existence is part of a bet two aliens are having to see how much unbelievable humiliation one human body can put up with before it actually spontaneously combusts in an orgy of embarrassment. That must be it, I was thinking to myself. That must be why I kept getting myself into these situations. Surely it couldn't all be my fault . . .

'Yeah, move a bit, to the right, that's right. Lift that left tit up . . . gorgeous.'

Julius was squinting at me from behind the lens. Yes. At me. It had been a month since my sashimi lunch with Carena and Philly. A very, very long month.

'You scrub up all right you do. Course I prefer more than a handful, but that's me, innit.'

I grunted in response. I didn't want Julius talking to me really. Didn't want any reminder of where I actually was right now – half naked in a draughty lock-up garage in south London. Selling myself. The thing I really, really hadn't meant to do. I felt the colour rise to my cheeks again.

'That's lovely, bit of a flush, pretty, nice, nice . . .'

I did my best not to cry.

'You can still see a bit of chunky fat around the side,' yelled Philly from the far side of the studio, where she was also hollering down the phone at someone from a newspaper. 'Well, that's a ridiculous sum, Jeremy, no point to us, we've got the broadsheets breathing down our necks . . . can't you hoik that left tit up a bit more? She looks like some old rock star's wife.'

'Yeah, I'll just get my invisible tit-hoikers, you daft cow,' said Julius, quietly.

I'd been so desperate. So desperate. I couldn't eat another bean. I'd had horrible, seriously threatening letters from the council tax people, and I'd been turned down for housing benefit, on the grounds of actually trying to work for a living. I'd eaten humble pie. I hadn't even had any phone credit, I'd had to phone Philly from a phone box. She was *delighted*.

Of course, it hadn't been anything like what she had said it would be. There had been no sympathetic newspaper spreads; no kind interviews, or the media picking up an investigative torch on my behalf. It hadn't been like that at all.

Although after the *Daily Post* feature I had received a letter in a slightly creased envelope. Inside was a card with a picture of a kitten wearing a hat and, in badly written English, a note. *Dear Sophie*, it said. *Sorry I has no been in touch with you.*

Things were hard. Your stepmother was very sad. I hope you are no too sad also. You're Friend, Esperanza. There was also a cheque for twenty pounds. I'd sat down at the kitchen table, holding it in my hands. I bought her granddaughter a dress and sent it back. It soothed the pain a little.

But after that, nothing, except a couple of weekly magazines that said, actually, if I didn't have a disabled baby whom I'd given up for adoption, whom I'd met when grown up and then accidentally fallen in love with, they weren't that interested. Finally, Philly took a call from a magazine who said if I could lose some weight their readers might be interested in seeing me with just a bikini top on, which wasn't topless, after all.

She was delighted. 'It's the big time!' she yelled down the telephone. I winced. Grace and Kelly thought it was the big time too. It wasn't really what I'd dreamed of when I thought of the big time. In my wildest fantasies I'd imagined *Vogue* doing a photoshoot with me where they dressed me up in lovely clothes again. Taking my clothes off for a men's mag? Absolutely no way. Definitely, absolutely not. I would rather drink non-brand-name bleach than put on a bikini and . . .

Then she told me how much they were paying. It was the difference . . . I mean, it was everything. Rent arrears, bills, some credit for my phone. It was money I didn't really see any other way of getting. It was . . . well. I didn't have much choice. It was wretched.

Two days earlier I had been walking home with Eck. He'd got in the habit of turning up on his way home from college and walking me home from the studio. I sighed.

'How are you feeling?' asked Eck.

'I know,' I said, 'that Grace and Kelly do it every day. I don't know why it bothers me so much. I've had such a cruddy day.'

'Did you never have cruddy days before? I don't know – fire at the gold and diamonds factory?'

'Yeah, yeah, yeah,' I said. 'Actually, no. It was all right. So, change the subject. How are you?'

Eck didn't look that happy either, come to think about it.

'The show is going really badly. I don't know. The last couple of months, I've really lost my appetite for this art thing. I don't know why. Find myself dreaming of the old nine-to-five. Mad. Anyway, it doesn't matter. It'll be fine. Let's talk about nice things, like bunnies and kittens and stuff.'

I sighed again, thinking about the shoot. At least they'd agreed to let Julius do it.

'You know, it won't be that bad,' said Eck. 'I mean, people like that Isabella Hervey do them. Not that I would ever know or have ever seen them or anything like that, never, not ever no. Once, by mistake, at the dentist.'

'You saw Isabella Hervey in a bikini at a dentist's?'

'Or it might have been very strong painkillers they were giving me.'

I kicked a stone on the pavement.

'Have you spoken to your stepmother again?' he asked, more gently.

'No!' I said. 'I'm . . .' I felt so safe with Eck, like I could tell the truth. 'I'm frightened. She was my last hope.'

Eck punched me awkwardly on the shoulder in that boyish way of his. 'She's not. Never lose hope, Sophie.'

It was Esperanza who'd managed to track her down for me. I don't know what I would have done without her. It turned out my stepmother was living in a rented mansion flat in Battersea. I wasn't sure what to make of this. Maybe she was lying low until the lawyers went away. I squeezed myself into my old Max Mara suit and took the bus to Battersea Rise.

I was incredibly nervous. This was a woman I'd dedicated most of my life to ignoring, sneering at, answering back to. The one I was never going to let in my life. And now, she held the only key to anything that was left.

Her voice on the intercom sounded nervous and querulous. There was a long pause when I announced myself. I thought for a moment she wasn't going to buzz me up at all. But she did.

The hall smelled of lavender, and small dogs. Fake flowers covered the surfaces and the mailboxes were grey with dust. The lift was tiny and dark and I followed the signs to the fifth floor. The door was on the latch. I knocked, tentatively, then entered.

Gail's flat was tiny. Two strides would take you to the kitchenette. Two other doors led off the minute corridor; obviously bedroom and bathroom. Into the space she'd tried to shoehorn some ornaments from the old house – a large stuffed kestrel my father had liked (God knows why), an ornate vase; but the effect was a bit overcrowded and spooky.

There wasn't much light in the flat, and the carpet had a horribly swirly print which made my eyes prickle.

She was sitting in the corner. Having always looked so soft and young and slim and nothing like being in her mid-forties now, it was as if her face had just collapsed into middle-age. She was painfully, pitiably thin, with long grooves running down her face, right down the middle of her cheeks. I felt sorry for her at once. Sorry for her, and sorry for myself; that there would always be a gulf between us, and that I had not only dug it but maintained it.

'Hello, Sophie,' she said, getting up, her face kind. I felt like we were two old opponents in a war neither of us could remember the reason for.

'Hello,' I said, stepping towards her, but we didn't touch. 'Would you like me to make some tea?'

Her eyebrows lifted. I rolled my eyes. 'I know how to make tea,' I said.

'Of course you do,' she said. 'I never doubted it for an instant.'

I half-smiled and headed towards the kettle. Before I got there, however, I turned round. There was something I really, really had to say. That I should have said a long time ago, before it corroded everything.

'Gail,' I said. 'I'm really, really—' But before I could get the word out, Gail's face collapsed. It looked like it was melting into grief, the tears running down the grooves already marked in her cheeks.

'Oh, Sophie!' she said. 'I'm so, so sorry.'

I knelt down by her chair.

211

'What do you mean?' I said, as she sobbed. 'Why are *you* sorry? I want to say sorry to you!'

'No,' she said. 'How could I turn you out of your home like that? I thought it's what your dad wanted ... please, please believe me, I had no idea, no idea at all about the situation.'

I glanced around the mean little apartment again.

'I believe you,' I said, exhaling a long breath. My last hopes – that she had sneakily done a runner, and held some back for me – had pretty much dissolved in the scent of the dusty hallway.

'If I had known,' she said, 'I would have stuffed your pockets with every diamond in the house. Everything. All of it.' She hid her face in her hands.

'They took all of it?'

'Everything. I'd put it all in the safe just as I was meant to ... I wanted to protect your inheritance, Sophie. I knew you didn't trust me or like me, so I wanted to have everything accounted for properly.'

'And they took it all.'

'I'm such an idiot.'

I couldn't think of what to say to that.

'Do you take sugar?' I asked, finally, aware that I should probably have known.

'No,' she said. 'Just milk.'

She took the tea and heaved a sigh.

'I mean, I've been poor before, but it's so much harder for you ... I can pick myself up again, I've done it before.'

'I can do it too!' I said, stung.

'Can you? Can you, Sophie?'

'Why didn't you answer the phone to me?' I said.

'Because I thought you were going to be so furious with me for not saving your things . . . I couldn't take your venom, Sophie, not when I was in such a state about your dad. I know you hate me. But you have to know, if I'd known . . .'

I nodded. 'I didn't hate you.'

She grimaced a smile. 'Oh, Sophie,' she said, taking a sip of her tea. 'You've no idea how much I hoped and hoped and hoped that we'd be friends. I dreamed of you being the daughter I've never been able to have. When I fell in love with your father I used to imagine you coming to me and telling me what you were up to in school, and we could watch girly movies together and I could maybe, maybe, just in a tiny way, be there for you somehow in a way a mother should . . .'

Her voice trailed off again tearfully.

'I know you didn't want to share your dad. And he was great. I don't blame you.'

Well, she should do. Shamefully I flashed back to the way Carena and I mocked the clothes she chose, and the way she ate, and how much we would talk about how much we hated her and wouldn't let her come near us. We even had a WE HATE GAIL club and used to leave the badges lying around. I just didn't give a shit. He was *my* dad, and she wasn't my mother.

'You know, in your dad's eyes you could do no wrong, so I couldn't talk to him about it. I couldn't tell anyone, it would make me sound so wicked.'

'Is that why you used to drag me to the shops all the time?'

'I thought you'd enjoy a little mother-daughter bonding expedition, we could try things on and have tea at Fortnums and it would be fun.'

'I thought you were punishing me.'

'Is that why you'd never try anything on or eat anything?'

'Prisoner rules.'

'And drag your feet all the way up the King's Road?'

'I was being punished! Of course I wasn't going to make it easy for you.'

She laughed. 'Oh, Sophie! I promise, you never did that.'

'I'm so sorry.' I didn't know what else to say.

'Good,' she said. 'I'm glad. And I'm sorry, too; that I couldn't be what you needed. I was so jealous of you too. My good intentions never lasted as long as I hoped they would. He loved you so much, Sophie. More than anything. Much more than me.'

I felt a lump in my throat.

'But he loved you too.'

'Yes, he did,' she said.

'I can't . . . I can't get rid of the guilt. That I should have answered the phone that night.'

She regarded me for a long while. She looked like she was going to say something – that it didn't matter, or that it was OK, or something, but finally she just said, 'I know.'

And we sat there for a little while, and drank our tea, and told stories. Stories of him. How Gail had met him, and their courtship. I told her what we used to do before she came. She told me how he used to talk about me. Little bits and pieces of daily family life; things we should have been sharing for years and years and years. But maybe it wasn't too late to start.

Before I left she said, 'I do have one thing for you.'

I raised my eyebrows.

'They didn't think it was worth anything. But I knew better. Hang on.'

And she went into a little cupboard and brought out the clunky black Leica that had belonged to Daddy.

And that evening I'd gone back to Eck, who had been watching *Top Gear* in the sitting room, sat down next to him, and cried and cried and cried; and he'd put his arm around me, and the feel of his warm strong body next to mine made me feel a million times better.

So, after the visit to see Gail, I knew there really was no secret stash of diamonds, which is why I was now half-naked in a freezing cold garage in New Cross.

At least Julius had started to look a bit uncomfortable asking me to do all this stuff.

'Sorry, love,' he was saying. 'It's just what the punters are after, isn't it?'

'No matter,' I said. 'I let Delilah do my bikini line. I'm never going to be in that much pain again. Psychic trauma is piffling.'

Grace and Kelly had turned up to provide moral support. They arrived in a limo for a set of shots for *Playboy*. They really *were* moving up in the world.

'How did you get a limo to bring you to New Cross?' I said, from my perch on a high stool.

'It's to make us feel like princess bunnies, innit,' explained Grace. 'The Playboy experience looks after you every step of the way.'

'Just relax,' said Kelly, tossing her hair. 'Stop worrying about it.' She was probably right. She'd recently had pink extensions put in, followed the next day by Grace getting identical ones. I don't know what had happened, but the next day they'd arrived Kelly had no nails and Grace had no extensions and they both looked sad. Now Grace had baby blue ones but she kept tugging them and grimacing in the mirror.

'Now the thing is, sweetheart,' said Julius. I stiffened. He never called me sweetheart. I glanced at Philly at the back of the studio. She was still pacing up and down in a pair of killer boots, glancing at me occasionally and giving me a thumbs up.

'This is a men's mag, right?'

'Uh-huh.'

'Which one?'

I mentioned the name of it, and Julius sucked his teeth.

'What?' I said.

'Well, did she not mention it?' he indicated Philly.

'Mention what?'

'Well, they're going to want nipple shots.'

'Not from me,' I said. 'Philly's got it all sorted out. Bikinis only. No more than Natalie Portman would do.'

Grace and Kelly both snorted.

'Philly,' I said, shouting across the studio. She lifted a finger to tell me, hush, she was on the phone.

'PHILLY!'

Julius glanced at his watch. 'Sorry, Sophie,' he said. 'It's just . . . no tits, no tips. No nips, no tips. No bazongas, no wonga. No twins, no pins. No bust, no crust. No—'

'OK, OK, I get it. I *get* it. PHILLY!' I shouted, panicking.

With a sigh, Philly muttered something into the phone and walked over slowly. 'Is there a problem?'

'Yes, there's a problem. You said this was a bikini shoot. You told me categorically definitely no tits.'

Philly sighed. 'Yes, but, darling . . . I mean, look, you know the ropes. You hang out here. I figured you'd work it out.'

'But, I—'

'What are you saying, Sophie?' said Philly, swinging her expensively cut, short coat expansively. 'Are you saying that you're too good to get your knockers out? That it's all right for Kelly and Grace here but actually you're too good for it? Too posh?'

'Yeah,' said Grace. 'Is that what you think?'

'What's she talking about?' said Kelly. 'I like getting my tits out.'

'No, no, not at all,' I said, desperately backtracking. 'I don't mean that at all. I respect what you do.'

'Doesn't sound like it,' said Philly, looking critically at her mobile phone and preparing to fire it up again. 'Sounds like she's dissing you lot.'

'Come on, love,' said Julius, uneasily. 'You want to just do it? Just get it over with, yeah?'

'Well, it's that or you don't get paid,' said Philly. I thought in terror of all the bills piling up, day by day, every time I took a shower or turned on a light or ate a meal; things I just couldn't pay for.

'She really thinks she's too good for this,' Philly was saying in a disbelieving tone to Grace, who was nodding in agreement. Oh no. Oh God. Hand trembling, I gradually lifted it to behind my neck, in order to undo the straps of my bikini top. I found myself fumbling for the clasp. It wasn't like I hadn't gone naked on the beaches of Porto Cuervo, St Kitts or St Tropez a thousand times. But this was different. Different, and much, much colder. I stifled a sob. I could do this. The world wanted to grind me to dust. Did it matter any more? It wasn't like I'd embarrass my dad . . .

Suddenly, the door to the studio flew open with a bang, letting in even more freezing air from outside.

'Sophie?'

Everyone froze. In strode Cal, looking tall, and blinking in the lights. 'Eck said you'd be here. Are you here?'

I squeaked an assent as he blinked in front of the arc lamps. Philly's mobile phone dangled from her fingers.

'Oh. Thank goodness. That could have been embarrassing,' he said.

'Hello, Cal,' said Philly in a cool tone. 'This is, like, a closed set, yah?'

Grace and Kelly raised their eyebrows at each other; Cal completely ignored her and walked up to face me.

'Look, Eck told me . . . he was worried about you. He said you guys discussed it and thought it was all right . . . but it's not, is it?'

Meekly, I shook my head.

'You don't want to do this, do you?'

I shook my head again.

'I mean, loads of girls don't mind and want to do it.'

'Yeah!' said Kelly.

'Not people who are just desperate, like you.'

I looked at him, suddenly feeling desperately, horribly humiliated. Why did I have to be so desperate, so helpless and pathetic? Suddenly I felt furious.

'That's easy for you to say,' I spat. 'Want to pay my rent?'

'OK, OK,' he said. 'Sorry, Miss Hostility. I just ...' He looked around, as if recollecting where he was, and rubbed the back of his neck. 'Er, I guess I got a bit carried away.'

'I guess you did,' I said, just wanting him to *leave*, for Christ's sake, not to see me like this.

'But, I guess ... I mean, I'm just sticking my nose in. You don't need me, obviously.'

He looked around, embarrassed and pink. 'Er, sorry everyone. Carry on.'

And he started backing out of the studio. But before he reached the door, I'd made a decision.

'Stop!' I shouted.

Everyone froze.

'Stop,' I said again. 'Julius, Philly, everyone. Stop. This has to stop.'

'Eh?' said Philly.

'Cal, you're right.'

'Huh?' said Cal.

'You're right. I don't want to do it. There's nothing wrong

with it if you want to,' I said in Grace's direction, who humphed audibly. 'But I don't want to.'

Julius put down his camera.

'Sorry, Jules.'

'It's all right, love, you don't really have what it takes anyway.'

'Oh. Really? Uh, I mean, never mind. Sorry, Phil.'

'You're throwing away a terrific career.'

'Really? Honestly. Tell me the truth.'

Philly sighed. 'Oh, Sophie, there's no room for divas like you in this business.'

'I think you're probably right about that,' I said. I smiled gratefully at Cal. He smiled back and gave me an awkward wink. It was the first time I'd ever seen him less than a hundred per cent sure of himself. It was cute.

'OK, then,' I said, glancing around for my clothes. 'What? Why are you all still looking at me?'

'Uh, your bikini top,' said Cal. Philly sneered. I clutched at my neck. Sure enough, the cords had unslid from my grasp. My bikini top was round my waist and I hadn't even noticed.

'That's how I knew you'd never make it,' observed Julius.

'What – you've all just been staring at my tits for the last ten minutes whilst I've been talking about how I'm not going to get my tits out?'

'Not me,' said Cal. 'I've seen 'em.'

'Oh for *fuck's* sake.'

'Oh, come on, it was funny,' said Cal, walking me home later.

'Funny wouldn't have been my first description ... did Julius take any sneaky shots?'

'Oh, yeah, definitely. He pretended he was setting up the lights.'

'Really?'

'No! Julius is all right.'

'I know.'

After I'd got dressed again, Julius had taken me aside and said he'd really liked some of the shots I'd been taking, and he hadn't realised how desperate my financial situation was. So, if I liked, he'd take me on more full-time, doing more photography with him, and less of the cleaning up. There'd be a bit of a boost in salary, and he could give me an advance if I needed to cover things right away. I was overcome with gratitude. Cal had bought me chips on the way home.

'Well,' I reflected. 'At least I won't have to worry about whether or not my boss is wondering what I look like under my clothes.'

'Exactly. Everything has an up side.'

When we arrived back I noticed something quite bizarre. Eck was standing on the top step. Even stranger, he had a brush in his hand.

'What are you doing?'

Eck looked nonplussed. 'Uh,' he said. 'I knew you were working today. So I thought I'd have a bit of a clean up for you coming back.'

He'd been cleaning. I was completely taken aback.

'Was it . . . was it OK?'

'She didn't do it, actually,' said Cal, with a hard edge to his voice.

Eck put down the mop. His face looked concerned.

'Why, what happened?'

'Well, she didn't want to. You gave her bad advice.'

Eck's eyes widened. He looked really perturbed.

'He didn't give me any advice,' I said. 'I made the decision. It turned out to be wrong. OK. End of.'

'Oh, Sophie, I'm so sorry,' Eck was saying. 'Honestly. I thought it was what you wanted, I thought it was, I don't know. A break for you.' He looked absolutely stunned. 'Oh no,' he said. 'This is awful.'

Cal snorted and stalked upstairs, treading his huge feet through Eck's fresh mopping. Eck didn't say anything.

'I think he's a bit embarrassed,' I confided in Eck. 'He kind of burst in and made a scene. Very strange.'

'Oh, bugger. Maybe I should have done that,' said Eck, staring at his feet. 'Damn. I just . . . I just didn't realise.'

'That's all right,' I said heading for the kitchen. I hadn't eaten properly in about a week from nerves and bikini prep, and I was absolutely starving. 'Now, what *shall* I have for supper. Toast or crackers? Toast has more of a comforting feel, I find, whereas crackers make it feel like more of a festive occasion.'

Eck followed me through, still holding the mop. 'No,' he said. 'Come out to dinner with me.'

'That's really kind of you,' I said, 'But honestly, I don't think I can handle any more goat stew right now.'

'No,' he said, looking decisive. 'Let's go into town. Somewhere posh. College is nearly finished. So. My treat.'

'Are you *sure*?' I asked, looking at him. He was a bit pink in the cheeks.

'Unless you need the money to pay the rent?' he said.

I shook my head. 'Actually, Julius is taking me on for more things. Isn't it great? I should be celebrating.'

'Then we shall celebrate!' he said. 'I mean it.'

'Will it be just you and me, or you, me and the mop?'

A pleased look passed over his face and he turned to the mop. 'Are you being rude about my butler?' he said.

We grinned at one another.

'Can I change?' I said. 'It's not really bikini weather.'

'A man can dream,' said Eck, and we headed off to our separate rooms, excitement in the air.

Eck had his floral shirt on again and still looked pink.

'Where shall we go?' he said.

'Well, I don't know,' I said. I'd squeezed into a purple top that came down over my jeans but hung off my shoulders. It was a bit chilly, but it looked quite nice. 'We could have Chinese, or go for a curry . . .'

'No,' said Eck. 'Let's go up West. I mean it. Get out of here for a bit. When you were rich, where did you like to go?'

I thought about it. Then I remembered what they charged for a cup of coffee.

'It doesn't matter,' I said. 'Really. Anywhere round here is fine.'

Eck stood opposite me in the hallway. 'Look,' he said. 'I've been living in poverty since I became a student again. And so have you, since all this happened. But we won't for ever. Things will change. I'll have had my time trying out this art stuff, and you'll get your money back, or something will turn up, and we'll forget that we ever lived on one pot of chilli con carne for a week.'

'In the future,' I solemnly swore, 'I will never eat a kidney bean again.'

'Is that a promise?' said Eck.

'Oh yes,' I said.

'We might even look back on this and think it was quite funny.'

'Funny? Trying to get people to write down their phone calls in a little book with a pencil attached to it?'

'Well, maybe not funny, exactly. But what I'm saying is, we won't be brassic for ever.'

'We won't?'

'You can't believe that, Sophie. I won't let you.'

I sniffed.

'So, to prove it to you, I'm taking you out. Proper out, actually, so jeans won't do. You get a frock on and we're taking a cab. A *black* cab. And you tell me where we're going.'

I can still see Eck's face as we drew up in front of the lovely restaurant I used to go to with Daddy. Thank God, the maître d' remembered me, and welcomed me as if nothing had ever happened, otherwise we might not have got a table. Eck's eyes were pretty wide.

'Oh God, isn't that . . .' and he named a famous actor. 'Wow,' he said, turning his head to look at the massive chandelier hanging overhead. 'Oh,' he said to me as we got to our lovely table in the middle of the large room. 'Am I acting like a hick that's only just seen electric lighting for the first time?'

'No,' I said. 'You're fine.'

And he smiled at me and opened the large leather menu.

'Well, that's good. And now, I want the suckling pig. Stuffed with diamonds. And a Tia Maria and Coke. And a Toblerone. And some chips. And . . .'

'Excuse me, sir?' said the waiter.

'Uh, two glasses of the house champagne please,' he mumbled, politely. And I looked straight at him and grinned.

'This is the best bread I've ever had in my life,' said Eck, scoffing. 'Shit. We're ruined. I don't know how I'm going to go back now. Maybe they'll let me sleep in the kitchen, like in *Ratatouille*.'

'I know,' I said, inhaling the fragrant, warm, fresh bread. When in my life did I think that I didn't want to eat the bread? If I've learned anything, it's that life is too short not to eat the bread.

Eck sat back as his soup arrived and sniffed the steam greedily.

'Oh God, I'm going to have to chuck the art in and go back to doing something I completely hate just so I can come here every day, aren't I?'

'Can't you just become a horribly successful artist and come here all day *and* all night?' I asked.

Eck squirmed a bit. 'I dunno. Not many folk do.'

'But some do though. Why won't you let me see any of your stuff?'

Eck looked around as if he was about to confide a terrible secret. Then he leaned forward across the table.

'Can I tell you something?'

225

'Uh-huh.'

'They're not very good.'

'What do you mean, they're not very good?'

'I mean. I'm not a very good artist.'

I stared at him. It had never actually occurred to me that the boys weren't good at what they did. I mean, they were art students. I kind of assumed they were reasonably good at what they were doing.

'But you got into art school,' I said.

'Yeah,' said Eck. 'Copying my Warlord comics, mostly.'

'You are joking.'

'I wish.'

He bent back to his food.

'But why did you go?'

Eck squinted. 'Well, I just hated the accountancy, and I just wanted to do something more fun, more interesting, you know? Plus in those days mortgages weren't interesting, nor was having a nice car or anything like that.' He paused reflectively. 'I find them more interesting these days.'

'I know what you mean,' I said as my oysters arrived, on a huge place of crushed ice, with the onion vinegar perched on top. I couldn't help smiling with delight. Eck smiled to see me smile.

'That's how I know you're posh.'

'Oysters aren't that posh,' I protested. 'Have you really never had one?'

He shook his head. I think he was just pleased to have changed the subject. 'I'm a bit scared of them.'

'Oh, come on. You can do it. Try one.'

'I'm not sure . . .'

'Go on!'

'You know, the last time I tried something out of my comfort zone, I ended up at art college living in an unheated hovel.'

I ignored him and put some lemon and vinegar on the oyster.

'Oh, yes, yes, you do,' I said, giggling. Finally he closed his eyes and tilted his head, and I poured the oyster down his throat.

Well, I don't know if it got stuck, or if he was already constricting his throat or what, but anyway, mass panic ensued. Coughing, choking; thank God for the friendly waiters who flooded over, whacking Eck hard on the back, till the oyster flew out, shot halfway across the room and bounced off Ralph Fiennes. He was very nice about it, considering.

When all the hacking and retching had finally subsided, we sat down again, trying to look inconspicuous. Eck was red-faced and his eyes were popping slightly. Nobody said anything for a little while.

'Well, that could have gone worse,' I proffered finally.

'Yeah,' said Eck. 'It could have been Sir Anthony Hopkins.'

I grinned up at him. 'So,' I said. 'Another?'

'Or I could just poke this fork in my leg,' said Eck.

'Tell me about your degree show?'

'Actually, I will take that oyster.'

'What's your stuff like?'

Eck sighed. 'Well, I try to express the frustrations of contemporary life,' he said. 'The chaos of industrialisation. The politics of pain.'

'That sounds kind of interesting,' I said.

'But they all come out looking like big twisty metal spiders,' said Eck.

'Oh yeah?' I said.

'Even if they came out like twisty metal flowers,' said Eck gloomily, 'that would be a teensy bit more commercial.'

'What's Cal's stuff like?' I asked.

'Well, it depends what you like,' said Eck. 'He mostly smashes things up and kind of half jams them back together.'

'That's a *job*?' I asked. 'Sounds more like what I'm doing with my life.'

'He does beautiful figure work too,' said Eck. 'When he can be bothered, which isn't often. I mean, some people don't care about being skint. They really don't care. Look at Cal. Banging on about bourgeois scum and living on cider.'

'Yeah, but Cal doesn't give a fuck about anything, or anyone.'

'Well, that's a good way to be though. At least, I think for an artist it is.'

'Not for a human being,' I said.

'Well, I do care about it,' said Eck. 'I care a lot.'

I looked at his strong, gentle hand lying on the table top and wondered what it would be like to hold it.

'So I was thinking . . . after graduation. I might go back and get a proper job. A real job.'

'Are you serious?'

'Back to accountancy, or recruitment, or something like that. Something real. Something that I can earn a living at, get a mortgage, do something useful with my life.'

'Art is useful,' I said.

'Not the way I do it,' he said.

When the bill came he took out his credit card and paid with a flourish.

'See. That would be nice to do more often,' he said, as the waiter took it away. Then he stole an anxious glance at the waiter's retreating back as he took the card to the machine.

'Are you worried?'

'Bricking it.'

'Well, thank you. That was lovely,' I said. And it was. After careers we'd talked about our upbringings, and school, and he told me funny stories and we just had a lovely, easy-going time. He made things so easy, Eck, just by being gentle.

Outside the restaurant, we turned without thinking into St James's Park. It was dark and quiet under the moon; the bright lights of the West End fading quickly back into the night.

'Tell me about your dad,' I said, finally. I wanted to probe how it felt. And whether it got easier.

Eck paused for a long time. It was obviously still difficult.

'Uh,' he finally started, stiltingly. 'He always wanted me to go to college. He was a gas fitter. Not a bad job or anything, but not much money in it. He was disappointed when I wanted to go to art school.'

'But you were eleven when he died, weren't you? Did you know even then?'

'Uh, yes. Kind of.'

'Wow. You know, Eck, you shouldn't give up too easily. It may be a vocation after all.'

He shrugged.

'Do you still miss him?'

'Yes,' said Eck. Then he added softly, 'I think your dad would be very proud of you.'

'For the floor scrubbing?'

'For how well you've coped. A lot of people just wouldn't have made it through.'

'Where would they have ended up though?' I said. 'I mean, it was get through or, I don't know, debtor's prison.' I had a sudden vision of myself sharing with my stepmother in that tiny room. 'Or hell. And look, I got to meet you. And that makes it all better.'

He looked at me, a smile playing on his lips.

'Do you mean that?'

'Yes,' I said. I meant it. Eck was the only decent thing that had come into my life. All those nights of coming in knackered and dispirited, he'd been there, making me tea. All those times Cal tried to put me down he'd been there, standing up for me, being on my side. The only person who'd really been there for me through all this had been Eck, a near-stranger – and he was standing right here in front of me. I took a step closer.

'Thank you,' I said.

'What for?' he said.

'For this,' I said. Then I turned my face up to his and let him kiss me as if it were the most natural thing in the world.

'Ooh, hope it's me next,' said James chirpily, as we finally fell in the front door, arm in arm, wrapped up in each other. Blokes.

'At ease, Corporal,' I said, as Eck ignored him.

'Tea?' I said.

'God, no,' said Eck, looking at the light on in the kitchen. I agreed. Too late. Cal was pushing through the door. His head was caught in silhouette as he was looking behind him, laughing hard at something a petite, drunk Icelandic girl was saying. They were both in hysterics as she seemed to be trying to imitate a puffin. Then they caught sight of us and pulled up short.

'Uh, evening,' said Cal. He didn't look pleased to see us at all. Then he blew air out of his mouth. 'I thought you two must have headed out together. Lovely,' he said.

'Hello,' said Eck, with a set to his mouth.

'You two having fun?' said Cal.

'Leave it,' said Eck. I could feel Eck's arm in mine go stiff.

'Still a party girl, then?' said Cal to me.

'I said, leave it,' said Eck, more firmly. 'I'm *sick* of it,' he went on. 'You and your patronising asides and little remarks. Your blithe assumption that you can just sleep with anything.'

Cal's raised eyebrow made it clear that he did feel this was a fair assumption.

'You treat girls like meat and you don't give a shit about their feelings. Watch out for him,' he said to the Icelandic girl.

'Treat girls like meat? You're the one who lets them think topless modelling is OK.'

Then Eck pushed him. 'Shut up.'

231

Cal pushed him back. 'You shut up.'

'Pathetic low-life shagger.'

'Pathetic low-life failure.'

'You just think with your dick.'

'And you are one.'

At that, Eck pulled back his hand and clenched it into a fist. Cal actually laughed at him. Eck was red and trembling and was just about to throw a punch when, shocked, I jumped in the middle.

'What the hell is going on?' I yelled. The little Icelandic girl looked alarmed.

Cal and Eck instantly drew back and immediately looked ashamed of themselves.

'Sorry man, OK?' said Cal. 'I've just been stressed out about my degree show. So should you be, incidentally.'

'I'm sorry too,' said Eck. 'Too many things . . . you know.'

Cal nodded. 'Friends?'

'Friends.'

'Hey, is no one going to apologise to me?' I said petulantly. Everyone in the house turned to look at me in surprise.

'Well, I was very frightened,' I said.

Cal shook his head.

'Girls,' he said. 'Nothing but trouble.'

'Isn't anybody going to fight?' said James. 'I have a lance.'

'Nope,' said Cal. 'Show's over.'

And he headed upstairs to the room at the top of the house, the little Icelandic pixie scampering behind him.

'Well . . . that went well,' I said.

Eck held out his hand to me. I stared at it, confused for a moment as to why my flatmate was offering me his hand.

'Oh,' I said.

He took it back.

'Sorry, not if . . .'

I took it.

'Yes, please,' I said.

Eck and I lay together in the bed, kissing and stroking each other. He smelled of Plasticine and something slightly metallic. It was nice. Weirdly, though, I couldn't quite get into the mood. It was exciting and new, being so close to Eck. But I couldn't help thinking about the last time I was in this situation – just a floor above – and I somehow couldn't quite get my mind to switch off. Plus, of course, knowing Cal was upstairs doing exactly the same thing with someone else. What was she like? Was she better than me? I didn't want Cal, but I couldn't close my mind off, especially in a new situation when I was nervous anyway.

Eventually, after having to shift about a bit in Eck's narrow bed, we reached a comfortable position where we were just kissing, and tickling a little, and giggling and chatting. Eventually Eck said, 'Do you just want to sleep here? You know, not rush anything?' and I realised straight away that this what I wanted after all.

'That would be lovely,' I said. 'As long as you don't mind?'

Eck tried to intimate that obviously he did mind terribly but it would be very bad manners under the circumstances, which I thought was extremely gentlemanly of him. The truth, I suspected, was that he was nervous too. Which was comforting. So, kissing and nestled in each other's arms, we drifted off to sleep. I felt warm and calm and looked after for the first time in a long time. There would be no nightmares tonight.

Chapter Fifteen

I woke up before Eck in the morning, and for a long time looked at his sweet face and brown hair strewn out on the pillow. I felt, for the first time, better waking up in the morning than I had the night before.

I sat up. The morning light was coming through the dirty windows. I felt a momentary shaft of positivity. Right. Eck and I ... oh, I quite liked that. The sound of it, like we were boyfriend and girlfriend. OK. I was going to work as hard for Julius as anyone ever possibly could, take over the twins' shoots and anything else I could get my hands on. I'd start building up my own portfolio and have a proper job. A real job. And a bloody cleaning rota. I'd never thought it could ever be a dream of mine to have a cleaning rota, but we all have to adjust our expectations as we grow up.

I left Eck to sleep. I suspected I'd probably given him a dead arm and he'd need his rest to restore his circulation.

Downstairs, there was no one else in the kitchen apart from baby Bjork.

'Hello,' I said, a little shamefacedly. We must have seemed horribly rough, barging into the house last night and then Cal and Eck squaring up to each other.

'Hi,' she said softly.

'So . . . er . . . good night?' I asked, then felt stupid immediately.

She shrugged. 'Oh, you know. Cal. He is like the wind.'

'What, quick and farty?' I asked, but then realised that arty girls in love don't always have the best sense of humour, so I pretended I'd been coughing and put the kettle on.

'He must fly here and there . . . he can't be tied down.'

I thought she was putting a very romantic spin on the fact that Cal was basically a slut.

'He cannot be tamed . . .'

'Cause he's a feckless arse I wanted to say, but didn't.

She smiled ruefully, then her face took on a dreamy look. 'Still, to be with him . . .'

'Eck is lovely too,' I said quickly.

'Who?' she said.

'Eck. The other boy who lives here.'

'The soldier?'

'No, my boyfriend . . . never mind. Tea?'

'No, thank you,' she said. 'I'm just in to get two glasses of water . . . then, back to bed . . .'

'Fine,' I said. 'Yeah, me too.'

She looked up at me. 'Have you . . . I mean, do lots of girls come through here?'

'Don't worry about it,' I said. She was terribly pretty, in a wounded penguin kind of a way. Maybe this one would hang around longer than the rest. Longer than me, a little voice inside of me whispered, but I tried to ignore it, as I waited for the kettle to boil.

'Good morning!' I walked into the studio holding a cup of my usual café's takeaway coffee. It wasn't Starbucks, but I still felt oddly optimistic holding it in my hands as I walked – like a real working person, with a real job, that enabled her to buy coffee.

Julius looked up from his camera.

'How are you?' I said.

Julius grunted something into the lens of his Nikon. 'You've perked up. Don't tell me – bloke?'

'Maybe,' I started rearranging the costumes with a smile playing around my lips.

'That guy yesterday? The vampire pirate? Dashing in to save you from the evils of tittage?'

'Cal isn't a vampire pirate,' I said. 'He just looks a bit like one. Anyway, no, not him. Someone much nicer.'

I hugged the thought to myself. Someone nice. Someone lovely. Someone dependable.

Julius raised an eyebrow. 'Well, anyway. I've had a friend of yours on the phone.'

'What do you mean, a friend of mine?'

'I knew it,' said Julius. 'Look, you can't let this get out, Sophie. If the whole fashion world knows I work glamour on the side . . . well, it's bad for my image, innit?'

'What on earth are you talking about?'

'Carena Sutherland.'

'What? What about her?'

He gave me a dark look. 'She wants me to take her wedding snaps.'

'No way.'

'I told her, Julius Mandinski doesn't take wedding snaps. But she wasn't taking no for an answer.'

'Well, that does sound like her . . .'

'Julius Mandinski is a high-end fashion creator. I don't need fucking weddings.'

'Just Page Three.'

'Page Three is a fuck of a lot more honest than most weddings.'

'There's probably something in that,' I said. 'So, did you say no?'

'Well.'

'What?'

'She threatened me.'

'Threatened you? What with?'

'Exposure. She threatened to go to all the glossy mags and tell them about my little jobs on the side.'

Only Carena would stoop to blackmail on her wedding day.

'Tell her to fuck off! You don't care! And by the way, I didn't grass you up. She got it all from that cow Philly.'

Julius looked a bit sheepish, kicking his expensive trainers. I forget sometimes, that just because I've had every bit of dignity and privacy stripped from my life, that other people might feel they had appearances to keep up.

'Yeah, but, well, it's useful, like.'

'Won't it do your career a lot worse to be seen taking wedding photos?'

'She says it's a big society bash, is that right?'

'Yes,' I said. 'She'd have liked David Bailey.'

Julius hated anyone mentioning David Bailey. He kicked the chair leg.

'Plus, she's offered a lot of money,' he said.

'She has a lot of money,' I said. 'Ask her for more.'

'You're invited to this wedding I take it?'

'Me? No. No. Carena and I aren't friends any more.'

'That's right, it were in the paper, weren't it? She's marrying your ex—'

'Yes, well *that* doesn't matter, I've got a new boyfriend now.'

There was a pause.

'How likely is she to carry out her threat?' asked Julius finally.

'Very. She is quite evil,' I said, honestly.

He rolled his eyes. 'Look, for what she wants . . . I'll need a full-time assistant to take portraits of all the guests in groups, as well as "casual" shots. Posed and unposed.'

My heart started to beat extra quickly and my brain was racing. Julius was going to take me out on a job! A proper one, with me working! But, but, but, but. It would be Carena's wedding. I couldn't. I just couldn't. Of course not. It would be unthinkable, awful, upsetting.

On the other hand. Did I care? I carefully prodded my heart to see how it reacted at the thought of Rufus getting married and Carena walking down the aisle towards him. There was a sting, definitely.

And would Carena even let me come? I'd already been strongly disinvited, and I certainly wasn't going to beg. On the other hand, what was she going to do, have me removed by security? Oh, yes, that wasn't beyond Carena in the slightest.

'I'll pay you . . .' And Julius named a figure that would – well, it would solve a lot of my problems. A *lot*.

I blew out my cheeks. 'OK, you're going to do it?'

'Yeah,' said Julius.

'And I can work with you on it?'

'Yeah.'

'Right,' I said. 'Let's do it. I'm going to text her and let her know.'

'Yeah, OK. My fucking art, wasted on a wedding.'

'A very expensive wedding,' I pointed out, taking out my phone.

' Right, hurry up about it, Pinky and Perky are on the way.'

As if on cue the twins burst in. '*Sophie!* Who was that totally hot bloke yesterday? He was at your party too!'

'No one,' I said. 'My flatmate. No one, really. Someone with too much time on his hands.'

'God, I'd love a bloke to charge in and tell me to stop doing stuff like that,' said Grace.

'What about that bloke in Southend last year?' said Kelly.

'Yeah, bozo, but that was like my *stepdad*. When I was fifteen. So it doesn't count.'

'Come on, you two,' I said. 'We've got rabbit costumes to get you into, and time's a wasting.'

'I want the pink one,' said Grace.

'The pink tail is for the smallest arse,' said Kelly. 'So good luck with that.'

Eck left a text message on my phone. It just said: *tx for lst night. dnr? Cant do posh restaurant again. Spag bol?*

I smiled to myself as I cleared up. I was going home to someone. Someone who would be pleased to see me. Someone who wanted to make me spag Bol. I really ought to learn to cook, I thought. I imagined us – I knew I was getting ahead of myself, but it was so long since I'd had something to hope for, I couldn't help it – I imagined us, maybe, in a little house, like those cottages in Chelsea, maybe not quite in such a nice area. Though maybe Eck could go do accountancy for one of those big firms that charge lots of money then get caught in billing scandals.

'Hey!' I said when I got home. Carena hadn't texted back, but I had the right number, so I'd have to assume she'd seen it. Thinking about the wedding made me nervous and a bit excited at the same time. Somehow, being there with a camera round my neck, with Julius Mandinski – well, it showed I wasn't begging in the gutter, didn't it? Even if it didn't show how close to the gutter I actually was.

Eck smiled back at me, from where he was balancing two candles stuffed in wine bottles on the rickety kitchen table. 'Hey,' he said. 'I'll just light these.'

'I can't believe you can cook,' I said, looking at the two mis-shapen pots bubbling on the stove. He gave me a funny look.

'It's spag Bol, Sophie. That's not cooking.'

'It bloody is,' I said. 'Smells great.'

'Thanks,' he says. 'I was going to bribe the others to go to McDonald's to get them out of the house for the night.'

'How old are they, four? Did you say they could have a happy meal?'

'No,' he said. 'I didn't have enough cash to bribe them. So I just resorted to begging. James has gone to the Campsie Fells anyway.'

'Good,' I said. I could relax. We weren't going to get interrupted by Cal bringing home a girl, or Wolverine snuffling around the skirting boards. I didn't feel very relaxed, though. I suddenly felt nervous. Eck's hair flopped over his brow as he concentrated on lighting the candles.

'So, sweet girl,' he said. 'How was your day?'

It had been a long time since I'd wanted to tell anyone how my day was. I felt my heart open and my cares fall away.

'It was good!' I said. 'I've got a proper job! A wedding! Actually, Carena's wedding!'

And I told him all about it.

'Won't that be a bit strange?'

I opened the cheap bottle of red wine that was sitting on the sideboard.

'Have we got two glasses?'

'Matching?'

'No, that doesn't matter.'

'Still, er, no. One pint glass nicked from a bar, one Arsenal mug.'

'I'm a Chelsea supporter.'

'You would be. Pint of red for you, then.'

I poured out the wine.

'Yes, it will be strange. A few months ago the idea of it would have made me want to hide in a cupboard for a week. But, actually . . . I think it'll be OK.'

'I think it will too.'

I smiled, enjoying the couple-at-home-fantasy.

'So tell me about *your* day, darling,' I said, expansively.

'My day was . . . interesting,' said Eck. He gave me a sideways glance, going back over to stir the bubbling sauce. 'I thought a lot about you.'

'Oh yes? You may have crossed my mind too.'

Eck smiled, then came over and kissed me. I kissed him back as enthusiastically as I could manage whilst trying to balance a pint glass and an Arsenal mug full of wine.

'Ooh,' I said, when he'd finished.

'And . . . I don't know. I don't want to freak you out.'

'Why? Have you got a gimp mask under your bed?'

'A what?'

'Never mind.'

He looked at me. 'This sounds stupid . . . well, anyway, it's nothing to do with you. OK, how does that sound?'

'Fine . . .' I said, not sure what to expect.

'You know, if I applied for jobs now I could start after the final show,' he said.

'You've thought about all this, just today?'

Eck looked pained. 'I knew this would freak you out.'

'No, no, it's interesting.'

'It's just, well, when we were talking last night . . . I felt I kind of admitted it to myself. I'm no artist, Sophie.'

243

'Except of spaghetti Bolognese,' I said, as he dished me up a plate.

'Be serious, please.'

'Sorry.'

'It's been going round my head for a long time, but talking to you . . . I mean, the degree show is in a couple of weeks, then I could find a job over the summer, then . . .' He glanced up at me. 'Well, I might look for a flat somewhere, and you never know, you might . . .'

'Hang on, hang on,' I said. 'You figured all this out today?'

'It was a quiet day,' he admitted.

'Every day is a quiet day in the world of gigantic metal spiders.'

Eck's hand went to the back of his neck. 'I know . . . I know . . . sorry . . . I just . . . I couldn't help myself . . . after last night.'

I thought about it. I mean, obviously he was projecting far ahead, but his enthusiasm was galvanising.

'No, I'm teasing,' I said. 'I think it's brilliant. If you're sure. If you're sure it's what you want?'

'I think it is,' he said. 'Don't panic, I was just lying awake, thinking about my future, that's all.'

'I know,' I said.

He looked at me, over his nearly finished pasta.

'Actually, forget all that.'

'What do you mean?'

'There's only one thing I want,' he said. 'You.'

And I took a final swig of the rough red wine, then we went to bed. And it was sweet, and comfortable, and oddly familiar, and I drifted off to sleep feeling as warm and cosy and safe as I think a girl can living on nothing on the Old Kent Road.

It rained every day that week. I didn't mind at all. I hurried home every night, and Eck would have something delicious simmering on the stove and we would sit and have dinner and after the second night we had to have the rest of the boys in, because otherwise they would just hover round the kitchen door looking pitiful and starving. The situation with Cal seemed to have settled down – it's amazing how boys can do that. Square up for a fight then forget all about it. Whereas when girls fall out it's *omertà* for about two years. Sometimes I wish I was a boy. Cal was annoyed that Eck hadn't mentioned he could cook.

'I've been living off frozen peas for three years.'

'Well, I knew if you guys knew I could cook I would have to cook every day, like Sophie has to do the cleaning.'

I smiled weakly. Actually, since I'd moved into Eck's bed I'd practically stopped doing the cleaning. Nobody seemed to have noticed yet.

Cal tucked into his shepherd's pie.

'How's the polar pixie?' I asked mischievously.

'Inga? She's good, I think.' He grabbed another piece of bread. Poor Inga. 'So, Eck, ready for the show?'

Eck shrugged and looked down at the teapot he was holding.

'Oh, kind of. I don't know.'

'What do you mean, "I don't know"?'

Cal looked over and explained to me. 'You realise this is our degree show? Our one chance to get into the West End, to get proper buyers to come and have a look at it? You're not bamboozling him with hot moves and stopping him working are you?'

'I am not!' I said. 'I think he should be there too!'

'I'm just not too sure . . .' mumbled Eck. He'd talk to me about his future, but not to the others. 'I'm not sure I'm really cut out for trying to pursue an artistic life.'

There was silence round the table.

'Eck. You've been at art school for *three years*,' said Cal. 'This is not the time.'

'I know,' said Eck. 'I know.'

'I mean, this is what all this is for, isn't it? Our Bohemian lifestyle . . . living like this . . . so we could follow our artistic dreams.'

Eck nodded reluctantly.

'So why are you here?' I asked James, who was scarfing down shepherd's pie like he'd been freezing his arse off on manoeuvres for forty-eight hours while surviving only on packet soup.

'Saving up for a deposit on a flat,' said James. 'Saved me a fortune dossing here.'

'Oh,' I said.

'I want a flat,' said Eck.

'You want to be a creative genius lauded throughout the world,' said Cal.

'I'd like a new cooker,' said Eck, looking unhappy.

Cal looked over at me. 'You've done this,' he said, pointing his knife at me.

'*Me?*' I said, stung by the unfairness. 'How come it was me?'

'You've given him lots of dreams of being able to buy you nice things and stuff.'

'That's right,' I said. 'That's why I keep dragging him down Bond Street and standing, sighing in front of Asprey. Shut up, Cal.'

'It's not that,' said Eck. 'Although it would be nice to have a girlfriend I could take out once in a while.'

'See,' said Cal.

After supper, when Eck had headed upstairs and I was following him, Cal waylaid me.

'I mean it,' he said.

'What?' I said. 'Take your hands off me, please.'

'Don't fuck Eck up. Please.'

'I've got no intentions of fucking anyone up, thank you. Eck is a great guy.'

'He is,' said Cal. 'That's why I don't want you to fuck him up.'

I glared at him and shook his arm off. 'I don't fuck anyone up, you idiot. That's you.'

I wasn't quite sure why I said that. So tired, I suppose, of his troupe of lovesick honeys mooning about at all hours, and still, I suppose, upset that he'd discarded me in the same cavalier fashion.

Cal stood back, as if I'd slapped him.

'I didn't . . .' then he got himself together and shook his head.

'Well, just . . . Make sure you mean it this time,' he said, heading off to the kitchen.

'And what's *that* supposed to mean?' I said.

He didn't answer.

'Nothing,' I said. 'Just another sarcastic remark from our great, bitter artist who thinks anyone not from exactly the same background as he is, is completely worthless and pointless, who believes in the nobility of man but treats women like complete shit. Thanks for the advice, Cal. Thanks.'

Later, I lay in Eck's bed, still thinking about what Cal had said. It was so unfair! What, I didn't deserve a nice guy? Because of my class?

'I've been thinking,' said Eck.

I hadn't even realised he was awake.

'Oh yeah?'

'You know, the guys who repossessed all the stuff from your house?'

'Uh-huh . . .'

'Well, they shouldn't have taken your diamonds.'

'What do you mean?'

'That was obviously not your dad's, was it? It was obviously gifted to you. They've stolen your property. I'm sure of it.'

'Oh, Eck,' I said, with a sigh. 'I'm sure they did everything exactly right.'

'Shouldn't you at least talk to a lawyer again?'

'You really are sounding like an accountant now,' I said, smiling.

Eck was sounding quite awake now. He'd obviously been thinking about this.

'I mean, it would be worth asking, surely. There would be

enough if you sold them for, I don't know. A deposit on a flat.'
He tickled me. 'Big enough for two?'

I tickled him back, but didn't answer. I wasn't sure I could
face tackling it all again.

'Maybe if I sold any pieces at my degree show we could
hire a lawyer.'

'Maybe if you finished them,' I said. I did feel a bit guilty
about that, Eck was always rushing home to make supper for
me rather than staying late at the studio, like Cal was doing.

'Actually, I have a lawyer,' I said, thinking about Leonard.
He had offered to help in any way he could. 'I suppose I could
ask him again. Just for advice. But I'm sure if there was any way
at all he could have helped . . .'

He took my face in his hands.

'Brilliant! Sorry for pushing so much about the future. It's
just, sometimes, when I see you . . . well, I just think you're so
amazing. I get carried away. I'm sorry.'

'That's OK,' I said. 'But you know . . . if I got my diamonds
back. I'd keep them. They were gifts. From Daddy. They'd be
all I have left of him. At the moment I don't have anything at
all. Apart from my camera.'

'Of course,' said Eck, stroking my shoulder. 'Of course you
would.'

We settled down to sleep.

'We should definitely go and see your lawyer though, don't
you think? He might even know what's happened to your diamonds.'

'Of course,' I said, thinking of the 15-carat pendant with
the blue-tinged teardrop he'd fastened round my neck on my

twenty-first birthday. I remember at the time being slightly peeved because I'd wanted the rose cut. God.

'Everything is going to work out all right,' said Eck solemnly, taking my head in both his hands and planting a kiss on my forehead. 'I promise.'

'I know,' I said.

Chapter Sixteen

It felt like it had been raining for about six thousand years but finally it cleared up. Spring was now definitely in the air. I could probably take off the hideous fleece I'd borrowed from Eck about a month ago and which he'd now said I could keep. I threw on a couple of vest tops, sniffing them suspiciously. Sometimes the washing got mixed up, and the boys liked to dry out their clothes by leaving them soaking in the wet tub as long as possible. Thing was, I wasn't exactly a laundry expert either. I was improving, but things were, on the whole, pinkish and occasionally a little musty.

The wedding was taking place at the Dorchester the following day. Only Carena could book the Dorchester with less than a hundred year's notice. I wondered what to wear. I didn't want to look like a guest, or like I wanted to be a guest. On the other hand I didn't want to look like I was making a massive point by wearing jeans and boots. They were having a separate, more traditional photographer for the church. Only Carena would book two sets of photographers.

'What should I wear?' I'd asked Eck. 'Come on, you're artistic.'

'You look gorgeous in anything,' he said, not helpfully. I'd called Delilah.

'Hello, Fairy Godmother,' I said, answering the door.

'Bleeding 'ell,' she said, taking one glance at my hair. 'Look at your roots.'

'These aren't roots,' I said carelessly, as if nothing could be of less interest to me than my hair. 'It's directional.'

'It's a freaking liberty,' she said, dumping her huge beauty suitcase on the bed. 'Right, let me see.'

'You have bleach in there?'

'Yeah . . . you never know.'

I was too frightened to watch and couldn't have seen in our tiny mirror anyway as she set about me with a small paintbrush. I just concentrated on psychically beaming pictures of Gwyneth Paltrow into her head.

Unsuccessfully, obviously. Oh God, oh God, oh God. I missed a hairdresser. The *first* thing I was going to do with my wages was go to the hairdresser. The FIRST thing. When I had a chance to examine it in full daylight, my head was the colour of Big Bird from *Sesame Street*. A huge, Day-Glo yellow sheet.

'Boy,' Eck said.

'You look like a golden retriever,' said Cal.

'What Cal said,' said James.

'Shut up everyone,' I said. 'I did this on purpose.'

'On purpose for what?' said Cal. 'To attract passing shipping?'

'So *where* are you off to again?' said James, shaking his *Daily Telegraph*.

'The Dorchester,' I said. 'It's a five-star hotel in the West End—'

'We know what it is,' said Cal, interrupting me. 'Shall we crash it?'

'No!' I said.

'Ooh, yes,' said James. 'Just think of all the totty! Girls always get mental at weddings and start panicking about their ovaries and things. What are ovaries anyway?'

'They're like womb monsters,' I said. 'You have to stand well clear or they start popping at you. Don't come, please.'

'It'll be easy to find,' said Cal. 'Just follow the glowing Belisha beacon.'

Shut up boys!

I woke with a start. Today was the day. It was hard to get the Belisha beacon comment out of my mind while I got dressed, Eck still snoring loudly in the bed. I had thought about sleeping in my own bed, mostly as a way of keeping Wolverine out of the room or, worse, to stop Eck renting it out to someone else. I was terrified he was going to suggest something like that. Also, weirdly, I'd kind of wanted to spend the night in my own bed. It wasn't because I didn't think Eck was amazing or anything, I just wanted a little space. The problem – which I'd never had before – of starting a new relationship with someone who lived in the same house was that you jumped over the dating stage and straight into living together before you'd got to know each other's freckles. It was a little peculiar.

All black? No. I'd look like I was in mourning for Rufus. Red? A harlot from the past. Finally, sighing, I settled on a grey chiffon top over skinny jeans, which toned down my hair a tiny bit, and made me look professional without being too scruffy.

It was the most gorgeously sunny morning. Julius was travelling separately, in the van full of kit that I'd have to unload, but for the moment it was nice heading up to town on the bus, watching the sunlight bouncing off the river, the South Bank flooded with tourists wearing Union Jack top hats and looking slightly lost on their way to the wheel. I got off at Trafalgar Square, enjoying the walk. The back roads of Piccadilly were thronging with staff on their way to work; chefs outside of restaurant kitchens having cigarettes; waiters yammering to each other in a dozen different languages; smartly if cheaply dressed girls on their way to the arcade shops; or the more glamorous ones, dressed to the nines. The only giveaway that they weren't off for a day of leisure, but instead to man the tills at Armani or Tiffany was the hour. I treated myself to a cup of coffee to sip whilst I strode along the W1 streets I knew so well. I was one of them now. I swung my lenses case. A working girl.

The ballroom at the Dorchester holds five hundred people, and we were going to be photographing most of them. Carena had requested a 'grotto' where people could come in pairs or groups and get their picture done. It sounded a bit unusual – just a way of being able to go through the photos in ten years' time and say, 'Who the hell was that? Didn't they get divorced?

How fat are they now?' but it was plenty of work for me, so I was excited.

I almost skipped up the steps and smiled cheerfully at the doorman.

'The ballroom wedding please.'

He eyed me up and down. 'Oh, yes,' said the doorman, pointing a finger. 'The staff entrance is that way.'

Well, that burst my bubble. I slouched slowly off round the back. As I did so, a van zoomed into view, hurtling down Park Lane and beeping loudly. It was Julius. He skidded into a left turn to pull up just outside the main entrance.

''Ello, darling,' he said, jovially. 'Good to see you're here on time.'

'They've sent me round to the back door!'

He screwed up his eyes. 'Well, of course they did. We've all got to work for a living, darling. Even you.'

I sniffed. 'I know. It's just, the last time I was here . . .'

'Never mind about that,' said Julius kindly. 'All you have to think is, they're all a bunch of nobs anyway, aren't they? That's all you have to do. Just think, What a bunch of utter wankers.'

'They are *mostly* wankers.'

'Neh,' said Julius. 'They're all wankers. And don't you forget it. Right, hop in the van and we'll pop round the back.'

Oh my, the room looked beautiful. Perfect. Every lily in the world had been used for the occasion, and there were great streams of flowers and ribbons hanging from every table. The mezzanine was cleared for champagne and cocktails, hundreds of bottles of Dom P. ready to be popped when the party arrived from the church. I hadn't seen Carena in a church since she used to paint her nails in assembly service, but I'm sure any vicar would have been delighted to welcome them. I wandered over to look at the seating plan whilst Julius made some vital decisions about the lighting. Sure enough, name after name I recognised, double barrels all the way down the listing. The only person missing, it seemed, from everyone I'd met my entire life, was me. Oh, and my stepmother wasn't there either, although my father certainly would have been invited if he'd been alive. Another tiny snub. I thought for a moment, Well, at least I'll get to see it, but that was stupid and wistful.

Julius saw me gazing at the table plan.

'*All wankers!*' he hollered to me loudly. '*Don't forget!*'

'I won't,' I said, shaking my head.

The 'grotto' was in a side room off the main ballroom. There was a chaise longue surrounded by flowers. I was to hang about there gathering groups whilst Julius did 'reportage', i.e. the arty black and white photographs everyone had to have these days that were supposed to make them look like they'd got married in the 1950s. I suppose the idea was that if you looked like you'd got married in the fifties, you'd have similar divorce rates. The grotto was pretty too. Everywhere in the main room staff were scurrying to and fro, carrying champagne and flowers and vases and lights, all ready to make everything perfect. At one end was a huge five-tiered cake, icing-sugar roses spilling over it in a heady profusion. The whole room smelled of orchids and lilies and the heady scent, coupled with the fact that there was no natural light in here (on such a sunny day – what were they thinking?), made it feel a little overwhelming. Or perhaps I was just feeling light-headed. I winked at one of the Filipino waiters and he grinned back and wandered over.

'Haylo.' He smiled politely.

'Hello,' I said. 'I'm starving. Is there anything to eat?' I wondered if he'd be able to get someone to knock me up a sandwich or if I could just call room service.

He looked shocked. 'Oh no. Staff can't touch the food.'

'Oh. OK,' I said.

'I can get you a menu.'

A twenty-six-pound club sandwich. I didn't think so.

'No, I'm all right,' I said. 'Can I get a glass of water?'

He nodded his head discreetly towards a door and I slipped through it.

At once, I entered chaos. In the ballroom all was quiet and serenely floral. In here, it was madness. Dozens of chefs were lined up alongside great steel rows of huge ovens and stainless-steel chopping stations, all going ten to the dozen. Acre after acre of exquisitely dressed hors d'oeuvres were being arranged on plates, as horseradish was squirted onto smoked salmon and caviar appetisers. Olives were being expertly stabbed into rolls of prosciutto. Rows of pheasant with their legs tied together were being roasted on spits or taken in and out of ovens, and veg was being chopped at blurred speeds by young skinny men and women – it was impossible to tell what sex they were beneath their huge white hats and terrified expressions. The noise was incredible and it was at least ten degrees hotter in here than outside. I mouthed 'water' to the nearest boy/girl and they, without pausing in their chopping motion, hurled me a bottle of water, much re-filled. I didn't care and drank from it anyway. Suddenly a loud hooter went off. Everyone immediately stopped what they were doing and stood to attention. The door behind me clanged, and dozens of waiting staff burst through it and filed up in lines.

A huge man with a frightening expression (not helped by the huge cleaver he was holding in his hand) shouted out, 'All in your places? You bastards better be ready. Good luck, and have a good service. The party is starting to arrive. And, one two, three – *go*!'

With that, the whole place leapt into action. Two waiters at a time darted forward to receive a pristine tray of canapés, then another two, and another. I managed to slip out of the door just ahead of the relentless onslaught, and just in time to see the double doors at the head of the room open up, and the first guests arrive. Adrenalin shot through my body. This was it.

Amazing. Of course, the hair, and the plain clothes, and my very obvious status as staff all contributed, but still, not a soul recognised me. Everyone swam past me wearing the most incredible outfits. It had been so long since I'd seen people properly dressed up for going out, I'd slightly lost the point of why anyone bothered; especially now I had no money and Eck waiting for me at home. Clothes were fun, I supposed, if you didn't care how much they cost, and wore a sample size.

There were lots and lots of women with fragile ankles and wrists, wearing tiny buttoned jackets over their delicate bodies and sporting elaborate fascinators and discreetly expensive earrings. They greeted each other with a kind of exhausted delight, remarking upon the last time they'd been there. All the women were blonde, different shades of blonde but all had poker straight, perfectly styled hair.

The men, red-faced and choleric, hung around chatting about money and grumbling about not being able to smoke cigars. 'She's a pretty filly all right,' I heard one of them say.

'Yes, lucky bastard,' said another.

'Oh, had one wife, had them all,' said the first, and they all guffawed in unpleasant tones. I searched the crowd for Julius. He was at the very front, walking backwards in the best tradition of the paparazzi. The wedding party was arriving. I went back to take my place at the grotto room, but couldn't resist stopping to stare. Then the orchestra – none of your string quartet low-key nonsense here – struck up a wedding march and they walked in.

Carena looked exquisite. A proper queen. Her dress was a shimmering fall of palest cream satin, a little exquisite beading on the bust and straps; a huge diamond necklace and tiara the real glowing stars of the outfit. Her arms looked like two sticks down her sides holding the elegant black lilies of her bouquet; but very much from the Angelina Jolie school of beautiful stick arms and legs so it didn't matter.

Behind her Philly and Carena's cousin Samantha were radiant in Schiaparelli pink prom dresses, showing off vertiginous heels. Philly had a smaller version of Carena's tiara. I wondered whose idea that was. They were carrying lilies of the palest pink, and they glowed like princesses from a fairy tale. The throng parted and Carena gave a smile designed to make her look beautiful and modest. I sighed. It was working. Behind her, reaching for her hand, was Rufus, as wolfish and roguish-looking as ever in his grey morning suit. He was being mobbed by a gang of his school friends. They were all laughing uproariously and passing a hip flask, and they all seemed pretty drunk already. The whole tableau looked beautiful and carefree and joyous, and even this jaded crowd clapped as they passed into the room; the couple's happiness was palpable. Yep, OK. I had to admit it. I was jealous. I was so jealous I wanted to explode. I was so jealous I wanted to take my back-up camera and hurl it at them. Throw tomato juice all over the tulle layers of that beautiful dress. Scream 'IT'S NOT FAIR!' over and over again to the ceiling. Yes, things were getting a *little* better for me. I had a nice boyfriend and something approaching a future was beginning to take shape. I wasn't trailing in the gutter.

Yet somehow that was worse. When everything is as bad as it can possibly be at least you stand out for being a complete disaster. You're still special, just special for being such an unbelievable fuck up. People speak about you in vaguely hushed tones all the time. Whereas when everything is patently going to be average and you're just going to have to get through it – that, in a funny way, is much harder. I couldn't throw my hands up in the air and go to bed for a week. I had to soldier on. I raised my camera like a gun and sidled back to my room, just as I heard Rufus announce, 'My wife and I . . .'

A great cheer went up, and the waiters and waitresses converged, like a swarm of petite wasps, dispensing champagne and canapés. The sound of laughter loudened as the orchestra launched into something light and lovely. It was gorgeous. I wanted to cry.

'*Sophie?*'

Of course. It was Philly, bearing down on me like a glamorous pink truck.

'You got Julius! What's up with your hair? You look like a golden—'

'Labrador, I know.'

'I was going to say retriever.'

'Oh.' I stood there.

'So are you *working* here?'

'Of course.' I'd never been to a party where I hadn't seen Philly hand out business cards, but I didn't mention it.

'Wow, that's amazing.' She shook her head. 'It's a shame the fame thing didn't work out.'

'I'm over it.'

'Well, Good For You!' she said as if talking to a slow child. 'That's brilliant! Does Carena not mind you coming here? I thought, you know, it was insensitive . . .'

'I'm Julius's assistant,' I said. 'It's up to her to object.'

'Oh, I'm sure she wouldn't have you *thrown out*,' said Philly in a way that suggested she wasn't sure at all.

'Well, that's what friends are for,' I said.

'Of course,' she said. 'Well, you know, I do have a lot of duties to do . . .'

'Off you go,' I said as cheerily as I could muster.

The dinner seemed interminable, course after course of tiny things with sauce smeared on the plates. Nobody would want their pics taken till later, till they were a bit pissed. I amused myself by watching the amazingly fluid choreography of those manning the tables; the way they whizzed in and out of the huge kitchens bearing dozens of plates and mountains of dirty crockery, re-emerging seconds later with a whole new tray. The level of chatter in the room was high and spirited, rising to a crescendo by the time Rufus rose to his feet, tapping a glass sharply.

'Hello, everyone,' he said in that ridiculously posh baritone I'd once known so well. There he was. Rufus the doofus.

'I just wanted to say how delighted I am that you're all here today – and how thrilled I am to have my beautiful bride seated beside me.'

A huge roar went up. He thanked his parents, his friends, his farm manager, his relatives and his dog. I waited patiently, but he didn't thank me for so gracefully stepping aside the second he met someone he liked a bit better. My mature tolerance could only take so much backslapping, and I retired to my grotto and sat there on my own. Oh well. All the cameras were ready and set up. There was absolutely nothing to do. I wandered about and finally turned off the main lights, sat down in a corner (the chaise longue was wildly uncomfortable) under a table and, like a bored dog, sleepy after sharing Eck's bed for a fortnight, simply dozed off.

I wasn't sure how long I was there before I came to and realised there was someone else in the room. They couldn't have seen me, I was tucked away in the corner. And they were sobbing. I rubbed my eyes and got up slowly and quietly, worrying about startling whoever it was by appearing out of the half-light.

'Hello?' I said quietly. 'Are you all right?'

'Who's that?' Came a startled voice I knew very well.

'Carena?'

'Sophie?'

My eyes adjusted to the light. There she was on the chaise longue, the beautiful dress spread out behind her like a queen's train.

'What are you doing here?' she hiccupped, rubbing at her eyes.

'I'm helping the photographer. I texted you.'

'Yeah, I change my number once a fortnight!'

'OK, good for you,' I said. 'Well, I didn't sneak in, if that's what you were thinking.'

'Oh, for fuck's sake, it doesn't matter,' said Carena savagely. I looked at her more closely.

'Are you . . . are you all right . . .?'

That's when I realised. Honestly, I'd never seen her cry, not even when she broke her shoulder the year we skied at Vail. You could say what you liked about her, but she was incredibly brave. I think the long years of parental neglect had taught her that crying didn't help anything terribly much.

She looked at me for a moment, as if about to dismiss me once more. Then her face wobbled and crashed.

'Oh, Sophs,' she said, which she hadn't called me for years. 'It's just so much crap.'

'What? How?' I said, going over and sitting down next to

her. I patted her shoulder ineffectually, and she leaned in and started to seriously cry; my chiffon top was getting wet.

'It's OK,' I said. 'It's OK.'

I glanced nervously at the door.

'It's OK,' she said, stuttering. 'I've locked it. So none of *them* can get in. They'll think I'm doing my face. They think that's all I do.'

She stuttered and coughed a little more, and I gave her the clean dusters from the camera box to wipe her face with.

'Thanks,' she said. She pulled a bottle of champagne from under her skirt.

'I liberated it,' she said. 'I thought I'd drink it quickly by myself and then things wouldn't seem so bad.'

'But . . . it's *gorgeous*,' I said. 'You look so beautiful, and you all seem so happy, and you've got this big posh wedding, and everyone's so pleased, and you're going to live in his beautiful house . . .'

Carena uncorked the bottle and took a huge long swig. Then she passed it to me.

'He's an idiot, of course,' she said.

'Well . . .' I didn't know what to say about that, so I took the bottle and took a long swig myself, which gave me enough time.

'He's so handsome,' I said. 'And so successful – he's the one everyone wanted. Everyone envies you. I wanted him so much.'

'Who cares about that?' she said. 'And he's getting stuck in to the other women already and we're not even married – I'm sure he's slept with Philly.'

'Oh, God, there's about two people in SW3 who haven't slept with Philly,' I said. 'I wouldn't let that worry you.'

She half-smiled. 'They do say fidelity is a terribly middle-class concept.'

I thought about Eck, who would never cheat on me. And then, strangely, I thought about Cal, who would never do anything else.

'Don't worry,' I said.

In the early days of scrubbing the floorboards, I had often fantasised about a time when Carena would have nothing and I'd have everything and the tables were turned and I'd be cool and dismissive. That was all bollocks, of course. She was horrible, and difficult, and all the rest of it, but she was still my friend. My oldest friend, and I cared about her.

'It'll be OK,' I said, not sure whether it would. It had never really occured to me – if he could leave me that fast, it didn't say much for his staying power.

'Oh, forget it, it doesn't matter. He's done it before. He is completely indiscriminate. Honestly, we get through cleaners like you wouldn't believe. He'll quite happily snog any old boot. He's like one of those dogs you have to get neutered.'

'But you love him,' I said.

'I'm wearing the dress, aren't I?'

She looked down at what I estimated to be sixty-thousand-pounds worth of glorious haute couture – Galliano, unmistakeably – now looking a little watermarked.

'I mean, I told myself that it doesn't matter. And it doesn't. It doesn't mean anything. This is everything I ever wanted. Gorgeous husband, huge wedding, plenty of money, beautiful house, all of that.'

'And you look amazing,' I added, helpfully.

'I do,' she nodded, entirely without vanity. 'I look amazing. I've eaten nothing but oranges for three weeks.'

'That sounds fun.'

'What happened to your hair?'

'I'm dating a golden retriever.'

A smile touched the ends of her mouth.

'What are you going to do?' I said. 'Do you want me to get your mum? Do you want to go home?'

She threw back her head, laughed, then quaffed another load of champagne.

'You are joking.'

'Uh . . .'

Carena stood up and found a mirror. From a secret pocket somewhere she drew out her make-up bag and started assiduously re-applying her face.

'It'll be fine, darling. We'll have a lovely life and be as happy as people can be. I may even take a lover myself one day. It's all for the best.'

In almost no time at all she'd got rid of the effects of crying. Trust Carena to be a pretty crier.

'No, it will all work out fine. You won't mention this . . .'

'Of course I won't,' I said. Carena came forward and gave me a hug.

'Thanks,' she said. 'I just needed . . . a little time . . .'

'Of course you did,' I said, hugging her back. 'You'll be fine.'

'I always am,' she said. Then she took another huge swig, finishing the bottle. Burping in a most un-bridelike fashion, she threw the bottle aside and unlocked the door.

'*Darlings!*' I heard her say as she threw it open. 'You must get your picture taken in our gorgeous grotto! Isn't this *such* fun?'

Eventually, word got round, and people did come in and get their pictures taken and a lot of them did recognise me, but amazingly, lots of them were kind (apart from comments about my hair, which I took in good spirit, even whilst internally deciding to have it all shaved off that night à la Britney Spears), and to the rest, I think I gave off good funky photographer chick attitude. As soon as people see you really don't care, they leave you alone. So it was a very successful day, in fact. I took some young farmers in a big group, all of them howling at me like a bunch of prepubescent owls; a couple of dashing young troubadours, and Rufus himself, who demanded he have his pic taken surrounded by 'all the totty at the party' which didn't include his wife. He smiled happily at me, friendly again, and a bit too pissed and too stupid to care who I was or what I represented. I smiled back at him as best I could.

By 10 p.m. I was exhausted with smiling, corralling, snapping. Julius was delighted though. He could send all the pics round and sell them individually. Even the little waiter had smuggled me in a plate of utterly delicious food, which I guessed Carena had ordered for me. In fact, it was probably hers so she didn't have to eat it.

The crowd had thinned to a trickle, and I was preparing to start packing away, when a bunch of people burst through the door.

'Take our picture! Take our picture!'

I glanced up expecting another crowd of young London bucks. Which it was, I supposed. It was James, Eck, Cal and Wolverine, all completely pished and collapsing with laughter.

'*What* did I tell you?' I said. 'I said, *No*. No, no, no, no, no!'

'You're not our real dad,' said Cal, giggling and clutching a half-full bottle of champagne. I had a feeling Carena's parents may have slightly overcatered.

'You're going to get thrown out,' I said, trying to stop Wolverine sniffing round the camera box.

'We are not,' said James proudly. 'Carena recognised us and invited us in.'

I took a little breath. I couldn't help it, I was touched by the gesture. Not that I was that pleased that this bunch of scruffs were turning up as *my* . . . I took a closer look.

'*What* are you guys wearing?'

'We broke into drama club!' said James. 'They have a wardrobe and everything!'

'I told them not to,' said Eck, his eyes going in slightly different directions.

'No, no,' I said, starting to giggle. 'You look great.'

Technically they all adhered to the black tie dress code: a red velvet smoking jacket on James, a frilled shirt on Cal (bit Adam Ant, but in a good way), and a pre-tied bow tie on Eck, who came lurching up to give me a big snog.

'We even got a pair with a hole in the back for Wolverine's tail,' said Cal dryly.

'But now *I* feel rubbish!' I said, looking forlornly down at my jeans.

'We thought of that too!' said James, as Eck produced a dress from his messy rucksack. It was red velvet, a belted number, completely over the top but weirdly, rather nice.

'Oh my,' I said. Then, 'No. This is my first professional engagement. I'm not going to ruin everything by misbehaving all over the place.'

'Champagne?' said Cal.

Curses! Felled by my terrible weakness. My hand stretched out of its own volition.

'Go on, love,' said Julius, who'd been putting camera parts away behind me. 'You deserve a bit of a laugh tonight.'

Suddenly, I heard a sound I recognised, though I couldn't believe it. It sounded like the opening chords of 'Pray' by Take That. My favourite band. But it didn't sound like a record. It sounded . . . I flung open the door.

Sure enough, standing at one end of the dance floor, waving to everyone, were the four remaining members of Take That. Now *that's* what I called a wedding band!

As I was watching, Carena turned round and caught my eye. She smiled at me and beckoned to me. That was enough. I certainly wasn't going to get up close to Take That in my work duds.

'Give me that dress and get out,' I hissed at the boys.

'Even me?' said Eck.

'And me?' said Cal.

'And me?' said Julius. 'I've seen 'em too.'

'This is getting *so unfair*,' howled James.

'Out! All of you!'

And I hopped into the red dress, which, amazingly, fitted

pretty well. I added a bit of cheap lippy, tied my hideous hair back in an elastic band we used to keep film stock in, and ran out onto the dance floor.

I didn't care that people stared at me, and talked behind their hands as the five of us waltzed up past the cleared-away tables. Take That were here! And they were great! And all we wanted to do was dance. I went up and stood next to Carena and squeezed her hand.

'I know!' she whispered back. 'Best day of my life.'

Just as she did that, Gary got her up on stage to serenade her and all the girls in the room screamed, even the scrawny, perfectly groomed, posh birds who thought themselves so superior. We all screamed. And I realised: I was happy. I didn't want what Carena had. I didn't want to fit in with everyone else. I wanted what I had. No, put that a better way: I wanted what I'd earned.

I couldn't dance with just one person, so I danced with everyone. Then gradually the whole floor filled up so it didn't matter. Philly sidled over and tried to start dancing with Cal, but he managed to sidestep her gracefully, until she ended up dancing with Wolverine. Well, she was dancing, he was capering, but it seemed to be going all right. James showed off some pretty swanky moves for someone whose idea of a good time was crawling under a muddy net. Rufus spun in and out, leading a very foxy-looking waitress. Carena wouldn't care; she was still on stage staring into Mark's eyes. It was brilliant, and we danced through the whole set and the two encores and yelled for more, until finally, still carrying bottles of champagne, we swept out of the building.

Wolverine and Philly seemed to have disappeared, as had the bride and groom, of course, and the four of us left in a cloud of happiness and laughter as we strolled down Park Lane, ferreting about in the pockets of borrowed clothes to see if they had any small change we could use for a cab. 'OK, OK, I'll get it,' said James finally. 'Sheesh. Students. And you.'

'I believe I made money today,' I said, adding quickly, 'but I haven't seen any of it yet.'

A cab drew up almost immediately. Eck and I sat on one side, James and Cal on the small seats opposite. We were all giggly.

'I never put you down for being such pop fans,' I said. 'What happened to that industrial grime stuff you like?'

'I like it a lot,' said Cal, stretching his long legs out. He turned to the cabbie. 'Can you drop me in New Cross after, mate?'

'Not coming home?' I said. I'd been hoping we could all sit up and drink champagne all night and have a fun time.

'You're not the only one working today,' he said, suddenly looking impatient. 'It's the degree show in a week. All systems go.'

Eck shifted uncomfortably. 'It doesn't matter to me,' he said. 'I'm moving on anyway. Going to get a real job. Live in the real world and everything. I've got a future to think of now.'

He took his hand in mine and I squeezed it hard.

'I never pegged you for a swot,' I said to Cal.

'You never pegged me for a lot of things,' he said darkly, and proceeded to stare out of the window all the way home.

It wasn't quite so much fun after that, as we straggled into the house. Eck and I went straight to bed, but I couldn't sleep and lay staring at the ceiling for a long time. It had been a big day. And, I decided, a good one. So why did I feel so weird?

Chapter Seventeen

I was chivvying and nursemaiding the twins. Sorry, I was running my own photo shoot with the twins.

'I still can't believe you didn't invite us to that posh wedding,' Grace was grumbling.

'I wasn't *there*,' I said, for the nineteenth time. 'I was working.'

'God, we could have pulled there,' said Kelly, pulling disconsolately on a pair of rabbit ears. I hated the stupid rabbit ears. It was so demeaning, somehow. Like they might as well be donkey ears or a stoat's tail, or anything that just completely negated any need for any brains whatsoever.

'*Take That!*' said Grace. 'My mum loves them!'

'Yeah, yeah, I know you're wildly young,' I said. 'But they were fabulous actually.'

'Julius, why don't you take us to your weddings?' said Kelly. Julius snorted loudly.

'Because I'm *not* a wedding photographer.'

Actually, it was interesting looking at the contact sheets when they'd come back. My work really wasn't half-bad. And, when we'd sent the sheets to a society mag, they'd chosen one of mine, not Julius's! Julius was very sweet about it under the circumstances, and it meant a little extra cash for me. I was beginning to wonder if there was any way for me to move into that business.

'We could add glamour,' Kelly was pouting.

'Yeah, glamour and chlamydia,' grunted Julius.

Kelly tutted. 'That's offensive, you know. I could report you.'

'Be my guest,' said Julius. 'Right, spread your cheeks, I'm taking the pics from behind, Sophie can do the pretty face shots.'

Kelly obligingly bent over. 'I could, you know.'

Suddenly Eck appeared at the door, looking excited. He was early to pick me up.

'Hello, gorgeous . . . everybodies,' he said. He still got a bit flustered around the girls, it was sweet.

'I'm not ready,' I said. 'I've got to finish this.'

'Julius, can I take Sophie?'

'Hey, no,' I said, a bit peeved. 'This is my shoot, OK? It's my work. I'll finish it, then we can leave.'

Julius and Eck exchanged glances, but I didn't care, and Eck took a chair at the back of the studio and pretended to be checking his texts whilst actually watching the girls the whole time.

'Where are we going?' I said finally, stepping out into the

spring sunshine. The days were definitely getting longer, and it was raining less.

'It's a surprise,' said Eck, perky mood back.

'Yay!' I said. 'Where?'

'Never you mind.'

We swerved off the Old Kent Road onto Trafalgar Avenue, a much nicer street with huge houses. There were several old, large Georgian properties on it, in varying stages of repair. Eck led me up it.

'Ta dah!' he said, stopping in front of one.

The house was painted white, with huge sash windows and a front garden full of rubbish. It was potentially nice but looked terribly unloved.

'What?' I said.

Eck looked a bit hurt.

'Well,' he said, 'this house. It's for rent. Or, rather, the bottom two floors are. Like a maisonette.'

Sure enough, a tattered old 'To Let' sign hung out of the front of an overgrown hedge.

Eck turned to me and took both of my hands in his.

'You know,' said Eck. 'The flat's about to break up. College is finished. Everyone is going to go their separate ways. James is getting posted. Cal and Wolverine and I are graduating. That's it, it's the end.'

Somehow, weirdly, this came as a bit of a surprise. It should have been obvious; student life doesn't last for ever, however long Cal and Eck had tried to drag it out. But still, the old flat was ... well, it was the closest thing I had to home.

'Oh God,' I said. 'I never thought of it like that.'

'Yeah,' said Eck. 'Well, I thought, maybe . . . you and I . . . we could come and rent here. It's easy for me to get to the City when I get my job, and it's still close to Julius's for you and we could do it up and make it nice – I'm sure I can still use my art skills for something.'

I felt slightly taken aback. 'Eck . . . I mean, we've just started dating . . .'

Eck looked awkward. 'I know, I know, I keep pushing a bit too fast, but I just thought . . .'

He paused, and I realised this was my cue to jump in and shout, 'Darling! It's amazing! Wow!' But I hadn't quite processed leaving the flat yet. And, I wondered, had I really processed Eck and I? Together? As much as he thought we were?

He echoed my thoughts.

'Oh, Sophie,' he said. 'I'm sorry for being such an idiot. I just . . . I thought we were together.'

And he was right, of course. Why wouldn't he think that, when we ate and lived and slept together every day? And he made me feel safe and loved and looked after? This was what it was, wasn't it? I thought back to Carena, tearful in her wedding dress. About Rufus dogging about, and Cal bringing back every girl in town. There weren't many good guys about. And Eck was definitely one of them.

'I'm sorry,' I said. 'It's a lovely idea. I'd love to move here with you. I just . . . you know, it's been so hard getting over my dad, and the idea of moving and leaving another home is just quite scary.'

'I understand,' he said quietly. 'That's why I thought we'd stay close by. For now. You know, I lost my dad too.'

Instantly I felt bad for not being more enthusiastic. As if he didn't know what it was like. As if he wasn't just looking for a home, just like me.

'We'll make it beautiful,' I said. And I squeezed his hand hard and reached my face up to meet his familiar lips.

The next morning, Eck bounded out of bed before I had barely stirred.

'What are you up to?' I said, half-opening my eyes. No tea for me today I noticed. Eck was hopping about trying to get his trousers on in the half-light.

'Curses,' he said. 'I was trying to leave before you woke up.'

'Why?' I said. And then, 'Are you wearing a suit?'

He smiled nervously. 'Oh, I wasn't going to tell you in case it went wrong. I've got an interview!'

'No way,' I said. 'Wow. You are full of secrets at the moment.'

He stopped dashing about and grinned at me.

'You've spurred me on, Sophie Chesterton. It's all for you.'

'Well don't do too much on my account . . .' I started to say, but he'd vanished to the bathroom.

He looked very smart and handsome in a suit.

'You know, maybe being a City boy will suit you,' I said.

'I hope so,' he said. 'It's nice not to smell of turps.'

'I'd got used to it.'

I got up and made tea whilst he finished shaving.

'Good luck,' I said.

'Thank you,' he said, smiling at me in the mirror, which made him nick himself. He winced painfully. I watched him wander up the street towards the bus stop trying to look non-chalant, and smiled.

'Ahh. Watching hubby go off to a hard day at the coal face,' said a sneering voice behind me. It was Cal. He looked pale and skinny, he'd obviously been up all night. 'Is there any of that tea left?'

'No,' I said snottily, pulling Eck's big jumper closer round me. 'He's got a job interview actually. Have you?'

'Artists don't have *job interviews*,' said Cal dismissively.

'At the Job Centre they do,' I said.

Cal checked to see if there was any water left in the kettle. There wasn't.

'He's doing all this for you, you know,' he said.

'He's not,' I said, hotly. This was unfair. 'It's nothing to do with me. I told him to keep on with his art.'

'It's everything to do with you. He just wants to offer you a decent standard of living.'

'Did I ask for that?'

'You crave it,' said Cal. 'You can't help it. You were brought up with everything. It'll never leave you.'

'Well, that's hardly my fault, is it?' I said. 'I've been existing on a seventy-nine-pence lipstick for months and you're telling me I shouldn't want anything better.'

'It's not your fault at all,' said Cal. 'Everyone wants something better than they've got. I just mean, before you tie Eck down to a life of indentured servitude, make sure *he's* what you want. Don't make him give it all up for you, even if he thinks he wants to.'

I was furious suddenly.

'*Thinks* he wants to? I can't bloody stop him. If he wants to go and get a job he can go and get a job and it's not for me, it's for him. There's nothing I can do about it, so leave me alone, OK.'

'OK. Sorry. I didn't realise you were so serious about him.'

'We're moving in together,' I said, before I'd really decided in my heart that we would.

Cal raised his eyebrows. 'Well, well,' he said. 'I knew he was keen but I didn't realise it was so strong on both sides.'

I dropped my eyes.

'Because no one would ever move in with someone just because they were desperate to belong somewhere.'

'No,' I said, with finality. 'They wouldn't.'

But Eck wasn't rushing for me. I knew he wasn't. Or at least, not entirely. The fact was, it was nearly summer. On the day I should have been coming in to my inheritance, I'd stayed at home all day, just in case it had turned out all to be a horribly convoluted test, or if they would discover some codicil which meant that all my money had been ring-fenced after all. No call had come, of course.

Cal was right that, of course, I missed material security – who wouldn't? I wouldn't be human if I didn't get apprehensive when I didn't know if I had enough money to buy cheese *and* soap powder. But he was wrong if he thought I was after Eck as an easy mark. So wrong it made my blood boil. In fact,

I was getting more and more work all the time. The models liked working with me, and one of my acquaintances from my old life had called me after she saw Carena's wedding shots and asked me to do her engagement party. I was going to have some cards printed up and start lobbying in earnest. It was exciting.

All the boys had vanished. Finally it was their end of year show. Eck, I sensed, was in such a state about it that he could hardly talk. Cal looked ridiculously drawn and intense.

The show was on a Thursday in May. It was quite a big event; the London papers were coming down to have a look, to see if there was anything particularly hilarious they could sell to the *Daily Mail* that year, ideally made out of elephant dung. In fact, when I saw the invitations I realised that I'd been invited before, but, of course, I'd never have attended something so far south – why did you have to when Frieze was so much handier in Regent's Park?

I'd asked Eck if his mum was coming, but he'd said no, there was no point when he was giving it all up – she could come to his office Christmas party, he'd joked. He hadn't heard back about the job yet, but had his fingers crossed.

All the boys dressed smartly – in fact, when we realised nobody had bothered to take the borrowed theatre costumes back, I stuck the red frock on again and Cal went for the tux.

I looked for a long while at the cheque I got from the magazine for Carena's wedding photos. This could go down as the deposit on the new flat. Or maybe towards buying some furniture when we were in there. It would be odd living in a house with bought furniture, as opposed to, say, stuff nicked out of skips. I could pay off my share of the council tax bill. I looked at the cheque for a long time. Then went straight to my old hairdresser.

He was gratifyingly pleased to see me again and, very sweetly, gave me a ludicrously huge discount, whilst telling me how he'd followed my extremely brief tabloid career to the letter.

'You should have come to me, sweets,' he said. 'You could have been one of the salon girls or something. At least we could have kept your hair in order. Whilst *this* makes it look like you're about to bark. Your hair! Your beautiful hair!'

'I know,' I said, shamefaced. Yet another person whose kindness would have helped me in my darkest hour, whom I hadn't even considered. 'It was so awful with my father gone and everything . . . I didn't know what I was doing.'

'But to hook up with that awful Philly,' he said. 'I shiver when she heads in here. Grey pubes, can you imagine?'

'No way!' I said. It made my day, although not nearly as much as it did when Stefano whirled me round and let me see my reflection in the mirror. I looked . . . I looked like me again. I thought I was going to cry.

'There you are, girl,' said Stefano.

I looked more closely at the reflection. It wasn't quite the same girl as before. But she was all right.

Stefano gave me a kiss on the cheek and I stepped out onto the streets with a spring in my step and a bounce in my locks.

*

281

'What did you do?' said Eck.

'Got my hair done for your degree show. Don't you like it?'

I swirled the pale, corn-coloured shiny sheet around as I did a twirl.

'Did it cost a lot of money?'

'All of it,' I said. 'But it's OK, wedding season is upon us. I reckon I'm going to be quite busy.'

Eck looked worried. 'I was hoping we could save some of that money towards the deposit,' said Eck.

Instantly I felt terrible. 'Oh, I'm so sorry, Eck,' I said. 'I just wanted to look nice for your event. It's the first time I've had any money in . . . well, a long time. I'm so sorry.'

'It doesn't matter,' said Eck, slightly sullenly. 'Your hair is much more important than our home together.'

'It's not!' I said, desperate to placate him. It was the first row we'd ever had. 'I'm so sorry. I won't spend money again without mentioning it to you.'

'Well, I'm not the police,' he said. 'It's your money. I just thought our future might be as important to you as it is to me.'

'It is!' I said. 'It really is.'

But he'd left the room. I put it down to all the pressure he was under with the show.

'Hey, blondie,' said Cal, swinging by with a mysterious object shrouded by a sheet under his arm. 'Looking good.'

Eck couldn't be cross with me for long, thank God. He came and kissed me and told me I looked beautiful and we headed out for the show. James emerged from his room last of all as we were clattering down the stairs. He was wearing full dress uniform.

'No way!' I said. 'Look at you!'

James shrugged. 'Actually, I have to wear it. I'm on active service now. Leaving in the morning.'

'You're kidding. Where are you going?'

'The Balkans, I think. Heating up again. At least it's not Iraq.'

'You're leaving *tomorrow*?'

He nodded. I gave him a huge hug. Our house was breaking up so much quicker than I'd thought.

'Don't get killed,' I ordered him strictly.

'Absolutely not,' he said. 'I refuse to get killed before I've seen your tits.'

'Glad to hear it,' I said. 'You've just guaranteed it's never going to happen.'

'Confound it!'

The second shock came in the cab. Wolverine was wearing a full graduation gown, complete with hat.

'We're dropping Wolverine off,' explained Cal. 'He's not coming to the view. It's his graduation day.'

'Graduating in what?' I said, looking after him as he scampered down the steps. 'Forage Studies?'

'His PhD in Industrial Chemistry,' said Cal. 'He's a super-brain, actually. Got an amazing research job at Cambridge coming up. They think he's found something harder than a diamond or something.'

'No way,' I said, laughing.

'Good at chemistry,' said Cal. 'Human skills, not so much.'

'Bloody hell.' I stared after him.

Eck was wearing his interview suit and looking nervous. 'I shouldn't really bother coming,' he said. 'I don't care about this now.'

I knew he'd done almost no work on it in the last month or so, because he'd mostly been in bed with me.

'It'll be fine,' he said, staring fiercely out of the window. 'I don't care anyway.'

Cal was also uncharacteristically nervous. He kept shooting glances at me.

'What?' I said. 'Does this dress look weird in daylight?'

'No, no,' he said, fumbling with his hands. Then both the boys lapsed into silence.

The college was a large red-brick building, packed with contemporary bits and pieces (if you saw a fire extinguisher you had to be careful in case it was actually a priceless piece of conceptual work), full of terrifyingly weird-looking girls and smelling of pottery. And it was buzzing. There were press, arty people wearing bizarre hats, patrons of the art scene who flitted in and out secretively, trying to gauge the work without being noticed by their rivals. They would, I assumed, all have been in earlier anyway, making their choices and planning who was going to be the next big thing, just as people would be doing at degree shows and fashion shows and music shows and end of year plays all across the country right now, as everyone dashed about looking for the star.

All the students were nervous, I could tell. And the work . . . there were photographs of people in and out of focus;

of women on beaches looking sad as the sky turned green; videos of people doing things slowly and discordantly; a smashed piano looking miserable in the middle of the room; paintings of pigs eviscerating humans and slide shows of peculiar tents. It was weird, but rather fabulous. There was a painting made entirely of apostrophes and semi-colons. I liked it very much. It already had a red sticker beside it indicating it was sold. But I couldn't see Eck's . . . oh yes, there they were.

'Indicating life' the first one was called. It was a wrought-iron spider next to lots of wrought-iron eggs.

'"This work is about the circle of life even in ugliness, pain and despair",' I read off the card next to it.

'Yeah, they help us write that stuff,' said Eck gruffly. His work was rather tucked away in a corner. One of his bigger spiders, one with red legs, was a bit more prominent, careering down one wall. 'A great attack in the vengeance of a burning world' it was called. It hadn't sold either.

'The spider thing,' I said, shaking my head.

'I know,' he said. 'I wish they didn't put so much stress on representing your inner consciousness. I wish they'd just told me to paint pictures of horses and flower-covered bridges.'

'It looks brilliant,' I said, kissing him. I remembered him when I had moved in to the flat. So cheerful and always busy; smelling a little of his welding kit. What had happened to him? Now he was constantly checking his mobile, to hear about a job, or checking me, to make sure I was OK. Was it my fault? Had I dragged him down, or was life doing it?

I left Eck standing forlornly by his spiders and moved through into the second gallery. I wandered through a little garden of sculptures. I stopped to look at them more closely. Then more closely again. The works were of feet and hands, sculpted in the purest of pure white marble. There were two hands holding a mop. A foot, with chipped nail varnish next to a part of a toilet bowl. They looked like pieces broken from some large work, but somehow they were complete and beautifully made of themselves, despite their lowly subject matter. It wasn't just that, though. The more I looked at them, the more I realised that the hands and feet looked familiar – they were mine.

I didn't even have to look at the label, although I did. 'Cal Hartley', it said. And neatly, beside each one, 'Cinderella i, Cinderella ii, Cinderella iii and so on. Each of the pieces included, somewhere, a lock of long, blonde hair. And every single sculpture had a red dot on it. I could hardly breathe.

'What do you think?'

Cal's voice came out of the spotlit shadows. It didn't, for once, sound sarcastic or amused. He genuinely wanted to know.

'Mad,' I said. Then I reconsidered and turned round. 'They're beautiful,' I said. 'You've sold them all.'

'I've kept one or two,' he said.

'Is it me?'

He rubbed his quiff in a nervous way. 'Well, no, there was this other posh bird who came in with nothing and did the cleaning.'

A chap wearing black horn-rimmed glasses came up.

'Very nice, very nice,' he said. 'The classical and the quotidian. Perfect little pieces.' He shook Cal's hand and gave him his card. 'Come see me soon, please.'

He glanced at me and then at the pieces, one of which had the tailend of long pale hair resting on its heels. 'Is this your muse?'

I tried to look modest.

'You look familiar . . . Ah, well. Look after him,' he said. 'He has a bright future ahead.'

I could barely glance at Cal, who was staring at the card in his hand as if he couldn't quite believe it.

'Who was that?' I asked when he'd gone.

'Sloan . . . only *the* most influential guy on the London art scene . . . oh my God! Sophie, God, do you know what this means?'

I shook my head, but his utter joy was bubbling over, and he picked me up and spun me round in a big bear hug.

'It means . . . I don't know what it means, but it's exciting and an adventure.'

'I'm so pleased,' I said, meaning it, all our bickering dissolved suddenly. 'I'm *so* pleased for you, Cal.'

'Thanks,' he said, completely choked. 'Thank you.'

Just then Eck came running up. 'Where have you been?' he said, a little impatiently. 'I've been looking for you everywhere. Ernst and Young just rang.'

'Who?' I said, distracted.

'The accountancy firm. *You* know.'

'Oh. Oh, yes.'

'They've got a training position for me! It's opened up early! I can start next month and sit my exams with them and everything.'

'That's . . . that's great,' I said. 'Are you pleased?'

'Yes,' he said. 'I am.'

'OK,' I said. Then I went up and tried to give him a kiss but slightly misjudged it and caught the side of his nose. 'That's great! Brilliant! Good news all round.'

Eck took in Cal's little line of pieces, glowing in the low light.

'Well done,' he said honestly, taking in the stickers. 'You deserve it. You worked hard for it.'

'And the same for you,' said Cal, staring steadily at me all the time. I felt like a washing machine inside.

'Hey, is this Sophie?' came James's loud voice. 'Why couldn't you have done one that showed her tits?'

Eventually, after there had been lots of congratulations and farewells and excited squeals from the other students (and some envious looks – Cal had obviously been the hit of the show), we wanted to leave for a drink in the union so, arms linked, we made for the door. Just as we did so, James nearly tripped over an elderly couple who were staring at Eck's spider.

'Sorry,' said James.

'That's all right, young man,' said the old chap, turning round. He was dressed in an out-of-date double-breasted brown suit and a slightly odd blue tie. 'I'm looking for Alec Swinson . . .'

Then he caught sight of us.

'Alec! There you are! We've been looking for you everywhere.'

'Oh, yes,' mumbled Eck. 'Hello, Mum. Hello, er . . . Dad.'

Dad?

'Did you just say . . .' I started, thinking, it must be his step-dad but Eck had moved over to kiss what were obviously his parents – you could see it a mile off. His father's hair may be grey now but it fell over his forehead in exactly the same place; they even had the same stance.

'I didn't know you were coming,' Eck was saying.

'Would we miss it?' said his mum, who looked nice, and a merry sort. 'It was in the paper.'

'Can't get rid of us that easily,' said his dad. 'Not after three years of this, eh? And are these your friends?'

I smiled, struck numb inside.

'Eh, kind of,' said Eck. His face was puce, a mixture of confusion and upset. 'But I think they have to go.'

'But Eck . . .' I said, looking at him, trying to get some understanding.

Seeing the situation was helpless, Eck grabbed me and pulled me over to the door.

'Sophie . . .'

'But . . . but . . .' I couldn't get a hold on my emotions at all. 'But that's your dad!'

Eck buried his face in his hands. 'I know.'

'But . . . how could you have been so *wicked*? It was *wicked*, Eck. *Wicked* to do that.'

'I know, I know . . . I was just trying to . . . trying to get you to like me.'

'But I already liked you!'

'I thought you liked Cal. I was . . . I was being a fucking idiot. I said it out of desperation, and then, well, it just kind of

289

snowballed, and I couldn't tell you the truth, because I'd told such a stupid lie.'

'But did you think I'd never find out?'

'I just kind of put it out of my mind . . . I hoped that when we were living together maybe you'd love me enough . . .'

I looked at his sweet face. 'I would have loved you enough.'

Eck swallowed heavily. 'Does that mean . . .'

I didn't answer.

'Of course it does,' he said. ' Of course. Christ. God, how can I have been so stupid?'

'I don't know,' I said, frozen, hardly able to speak.

'Alec?' the voice came from the next room.

'I think you should go to them,' I said, as firmly as I could, trying to hold back the tears.

'Sophie?'

I shook my head.

'Please. Go.'

'What happened?' said Cal as I stumbled into the bar. James went to fetch us some drinks. 'You look like you've seen a ghost. Why won't Eck introduce you to his parents?'

'Because,' I said, and I nearly couldn't say the words. 'Because he isn't meant to *have* two parents.'

James handed me a glass of wine, then retired. I took a large slug.

'Oh God. Cal. He told me . . . he told me his dad was *dead*.'

'What do you mean?'

'He told me . . . he told me his dad was dead, and that he knew how I felt. But Cal . . .' I felt like I was five years old. I couldn't get the words out at all. 'My dad really *is* dead!'

And I burst into huge miserable sobs, so loud the fashionable people around us moved away. Cal wrapped me up in his long arms.

'Oh, oh, darling. Are you sure you can't have been mistaken and he meant someone else?'

I shook my head as he found us a couple of chairs out of sight.

'You know,' he said, 'I know how nuts Eck is about you. He's been crazy about you from the second you arrived. Oh God. I mean, he would have said anything to get on with you.'

'But that's . . . that's like the *worst* thing he could possibly say.'

'I know. I know, sweetheart. He was so excited to meet you . . . thought you were way out of his league. He must have got carried away. I think a life with you – glamour and money and all that. He was dead into it. And you, of course.'

I shook my head, the tears dripping all the way to my lap.

'That must be why he kept pestering me to go and look for the money or talk to the lawyers, or all that bullshit about the jewellery. Maybe he thinks there's money in it.'

'I don't . . . I'm sure it's not like that.'

I thought about my gentle, sweet Eck. I'm sure that's not what he meant. But he had told a lie, and it had just spiralled more and more and out of control.

'Oh no. I miss him so much.'

'Eck?'

'God, no. My dad. I miss him, Cal. He'd never have let me get taken in like this.'

'I know,' said Cal.

I sat bolt upright. 'You don't, Cal. That's the thing. Nobody does. Except my stepmother, and I don't know if she'll ever forgive me.'

'What? What could be so awful?'

'He called me, Cal. When he was having his heart attack. He called me, and I didn't want to talk to him. And I could have saved him, and I didn't, because I was at a party. I killed him, Cal! It was all my fault.'

Cal took my face in his hands. 'It wasn't your fault, Sophie. I promise. It wasn't your fault. A heart attack – they're terrible, terrible things. There's nothing you could have done.'

'I could have saved him.'

'You couldn't have. You couldn't have.'

Then he took me in his arms and held me very, very tightly. For a long time.

'We should go,' said Cal eventually. I'd lost all track of time.

'Oh yes, we must,' I said. 'You'll miss your big party and everything.'

'Oh, that's finished now,' he said. 'It doesn't matter. I'll be much better off being mysterious and not turning up and everyone can talk about me.'

I swallowed hard. 'I'm so, so sorry,' I said, rubbing at my face. I felt much better. Weirdly. Cathartically cleansed, somehow, inside. Just telling someone. Naming the nightmare I'd been living through might make it go away a little. I could never forgive myself completely. But perhaps I could learn to live with it.

'No, I mean it,' he said. 'Oh, there's your mate Philly over there, chivvying Jay Joplin. Shall I go and tell her to fuck off?'

'Neh,' I said. 'It'll keep.'

He kept his arm around me as we walked out of the union, supporting me.

'I don't want to go back home,' I said.

'I don't think Eck will be there,' Cal said.

Oh Eck. I'd liked the idea he'd represented: of comfort, and stability, and security. Everything I'd lost. But it had all been a lie.

'Oh God. I don't want to talk to him. Everything I thought about him. None of it . . .'

There was a long pause.

'I probably shouldn't say this,' said Cal. 'But I knew you two weren't right. Not really. It's just good you figured it out before you went and did something stupid, like moving in together.'

'Oh God,' I said, weary and sad. 'What am I going to do now? I'm going to have to start all over again.'

'So what?' said Cal airily.

'What do you mean, "So what"?' I said.

'Well, life is unpredictable. One day you're up, one day you're down. I'm sure you'll be fine,' he said.

'Well, thanks for that.'

'You've done it once. You can do it again.'

I sniffed. I suppose he was right. I could pick myself up. I'd learned a few things; I was no longer the spoiled ignoramus who couldn't make herself a cup of tea.

We turned into the long road home.

''Course,' he said, finally, 'you could always take me along for the ride.'

'You?' I said. 'You and your constant cheek to me and your millions of girlfriends?'

'Well, first of all,' he said, 'constant cheek is maybe my way of telling you I like you.'

'A stupid way,' I said, but I felt something strange happening to me. The corners of my mouth were turning upwards.

'And secondly, not millions of girlfriends, no. Just me. I mean it, Sophie. You and me. Of course, after you ditched me, I had to drown my sorrows somehow.'

'I didn't ditch you!'

'Course you did. One night, and that was me, history.'

'I thought . . . I mean, I woke up and you were gone.'

'I'd gone to get myself a cup of tea. *And* make you one, in fact.'

'But I thought it was your way of saying I was dumped.'

Cal shook his head. 'Oh God, Sophie, tell me that's not true.'

We stopped and he turned me round to face him. A sudden bolt of electricity raced through me, just as I'd felt when I'd first moved in. God, I fancied this man. I was, I had to admit it, utterly crazy about this man. But it was madness. I couldn't have him. He belonged to all the women of the world, apparently, and I had to set my sights elsewhere. It struck me. I'd known it wasn't right with Eck. I had known, Cal had known, but I couldn't admit to myself that I was failing again.

This, though . . . this was completely different.

'You couldn't be with just one woman,' I said playfully.

'Surely you of all people might believe that people can change?' said Cal, quietly. 'Oh, I tried to forget about you, but I couldn't.'

'Well, I was right there all the time.'

But Cal wasn't listening; he obviously had to get this off his chest.

'I'll never make you any false promises, Sophie. I won't promise you the happy ever after, or a little country house, or a steady job or any of that kind of thing. I can only promise you my heart and soul and all that kind of stuff. The girls . . . well, I was single, they were there, and I couldn't have the person I really wanted, so I figured it didn't matter. I know this is hard to believe, but I'm actually not a bad boyfriend. Probably.'

I smiled. 'I'm no picnic, you know.'

'Oh, I know,' he said. 'But from the second I saw you with your head stuck down that toilet . . .'

'Oi, none of that.'

He was back to his grinning, mocking ways. But I could feel that beneath his light-hearted tone, his heart was thumping. I took the lovely, lovely liberty of moving towards him again, and pressing my body against his. His heartbeat mirrored my own.

'Can I?' I said, looking up at him.

'Can you what?'

'Can I have all of you?'

'All that I have is yours. Of course, that is basically a hundred per cent of fuck all.'

'Ah, we'll manage,' I said. 'Night bus?'

'Let's walk,' he said. 'We'll save money.'

'Yeah, all right,' I said. And he pressed me into him, and we half-stumbled, half-kissed, and clumsily, in no hurry, and filled, at last, with a kind of strange, fierce joy I'd never, ever known before, we made our slow way up the whole length of the Old Kent Road.

And that night I dreamed about my dad. And he was smiling.

Part Three
Now

Chapter Eighteen

'What are you laughing about?' says Cal, as he heaves back up the beach. 'It's not easy, carrying fish and chips – and *you*!'

May, our two-year-old, giggles in delight as her daddy bounces her up and down.

'I've had to walk *miles*!' he says.

'MILES!' yells May happily.

'We had to walk for miles. But here you are, my princess. Our first fish and chips of the year. Only . . . oh, never mind what it cost. We can put it down as a work expense seeing as Mummy had to take so many stupid photos of me.'

May turns her father's face to hers and gives him a big smacker on the lips.

'Mummy take photos of me now,' she confides to him.

'Well, that's fine.'

I open the steaming packet and stare out to sea. It smells so good.

'What were you thinking about?' says Cal. 'I've been watching you all the way across the dunes. You were miles away.'

'Oh, just about how we met,' I say.

He looks at me in confusion. 'Well, you moved in to my flat and jumped my bones.'

'*Not* in front of May, please.'

'Hot, hot, hot!' May was saying, trying to throw a chip to the seagulls.

'I thought we were always going to be honest in front of her.'

I grin up at him and he ruffles my hair.

'Well, there was a bit more to it than that.'

'Nothing that matters. Give me a chip.'

Of course, it wasn't always easy at first; living on nothing and budgeting. But God, it was fun. We worked out of a series of studios Cal's new patron helped us find in the East End, and we survived on loads and loads of fierce sex and cheap sandwiches. And the loads and loads of sex took their toll and we got pregnant, and thought, Well, you might as well bring a child into a loving home without central heating as anything else, so we had May, who was born in May obviously, but is also as beautiful to us as a spring garden.

James came back safely from the Balkans and finally bought his house, quite near us in fact, and he let Wolverine move in, and he has a big garden, so that works well. Wolverine has been sleeping with Philly for years now but we must pretend she's only at James's by coincidence. And James always seemed to pop by ours just when I was breastfeeding.

The photography went from strength to strength really – well, we'll never be rich, but after May came along Julius offered to go into partnership with me, so while I run the wedding side of the business, he can devote even more time on his weird fashion supplements. Grace, Kelly and Delilah are May's godmothers and she adores them to pieces and wants to dress like them all the time. This worries me a bit. And she absolutely loves Gail, who is back working for a travel company again. She clambers on to her lap and demands stories and sweets and chitchat and orders her about, and in every way is the little girl, I think, that Gail would have liked very much, and I'm oddly touched to have been able to do that for her, however late.

Cal's pieces have started to sell a little more – particularly the work inspired by May's feet and hands, because it turns out that babies' hands and feet all look rather similar and people are willing to pay quite a lot of money to be reminded of the crooks of their precious one's elbows, or the dimples on their knees. It's still pretty chilly in the winter without the heating on and I still have to be reminded not to use every drop of hot water if I ever have a bath, but all our friends are skint too, so having people round for the spag Bol I've now learned to cook and cheap wine is just what we do, and I look over at Cal in his grubby old shirt throwing his head back and laughing, or winding someone up on purpose, or tossing May in the air, and I think, Christ, I'm so lucky.

Oh, when my poor Eck came to pick up his stuff on our last day in the flat, he was embarrassed and as sorry as a schoolboy caught stealing. I gave him a hug and told him it was all right – I didn't want to make him feel worse than he clearly did, worse, even than me, once I'd got over the pain of the deception. He winced a bit when he saw Cal and I had got together, but over time he and Cal got reacquainted – they'd been good friends once, before I'd come along and buggered it all up – and we were at his wedding not too long ago, to a nice girl; a very well-off accountant with her own house in Battersea and a BMW convertible and the nose of a fox, according to Cal, but I think he was just a bit pissed off from having to listen to six million conversations about house prices at the wedding when we were still renting and thus doomed to eternal penury, according to Eck's new stuffed-shirt banker friends, and so Cal got drunk and told them they were all bourgeois dick brains which went down fantastically. He can still be the rudest man I'd ever met. God it's sexy.

But then a couple of months ago, Cal got offered the Tate Modern space. He was one of the youngest artists ever to be offered it, it was an amazing breakthrough; Sloan had pushed him like crazy. The day of the unveiling was mad; everyone turned up – there were press and art world grandees every-where. Carena came, without Rufus – 'He's up country most of the time these days, darling, whereas I miss London too much.' Or the twin boys she'd had, whom I'd never met and I think spent most of their time with a nanny. I over-mothered May terribly, I couldn't even bear to send her to bed without telling her a million times how Mummy and Daddy would be right there for her in the morning, as indeed we would as we invari-ably woke up with her small body sandwiched in between ours for warmth, but I think Carena left most of that to the help. Twins are tricky, I suppose.

At the launch, Cal had peppered the space with sculptures of people looking at pieces of sculpture, so beautifully done it was hard to tell who was real and who wasn't, and many of the guests ended up in conversation with someone who turned out to be made of stone. The whole place had been turned into a forest. Critics were muttering words like 'kitsch', but the dozens of children there were running in and out of the trees like it was a wonderland. There were also two of Eck's metal spiders integrated so subtly into the design they didn't look unpleasant at all. Anyway, at the launch, Leonard came up to me. We'd stayed in touch over the years, so of course I'd invited him, along with Stefano and Avi from the greasy spoon. I'd never forgotten their kindness. And Esperanza, of course, who hugged me like a long lost relative. Leonard, a wise grand-father several times over, had sweets in his pockets for May so she jumped on him like a small happy monkey.

'Sophie,' he said, tickling May. 'You have a birthday next week, don't you?'

'Turning thirty,' I said. 'Getting old.'

'Well, please come and see me after that,' he said. 'Lovely installation, by the way.'

And so today is my birthday at the beach, and tomorrow we're going to see Leonard. I don't know why.

May sleeps all the way home back to Hackney and Cal and I don't even make much conversation, we're too dazed and tired by the fresh sea air and the running about and the beers we had after the fish and chips and the splashing in the chill water and May's unsuccessful attempts to trap a WIDGEON to take home. I took tons of photos and Cal tickled us both in the

303

sand dunes and called us his best girls in all the world. It was such a happy day.

Now May and I are waiting in St John's Street for Leonard. June is pleased to see us and immediately rustles up cakes and tea. The last time I'd been here seemed a long time ago.

'Sophie,' says Leonard, sweeping into the room with his little glasses on and kissing us both fondly. 'I have something for you.'

'You don't need to get me anything,' I say. 'I don't like being reminded I'm thirty! Thanks, though.'

'Actually, it's not from me,' he says, handing me a box. Instantly, I feel my heart pounding and set May on the floor.

'What is it?'

Leonard shrugs at me. 'Open it.'

I do.

Inside, nestled on a box of ice blue satin, sits a huge, multi-faceted, multicarated diamond.

I can't breathe.

'What the hell is this?' I demand, finally.

Leonard still says nothing, but simply hands me the envelope that came with it.

My darling Sophie, it reads.

I don't know why I'm writing this – I think I'm a little drunk. I'm sure it's not necessary, but sometimes I do worry. Anyway. This is for you, and I wanted to keep it safe until you turned thirty. In case anything happens to me or, my darling girl, and I'm sure this won't happen, but just in case you fritter away

your inheritance, or marry a bad sort or make some bad
investments . . . I know you won't do anything like that, my good
girl, but I am a silly old worrier. Anyway. If you are doing well,
this should be a nice surprise, if not, it may even prove useful.
Please carve off a chip and make yourself something pretty to
remember me by.

I'm sure I'll be whooping it up with the best of them at your
thirtieth (IF I'm invited – I haven't forgotten your twenty-
first!!!) but if I'm not, Sophie, you should know I love you more
than life itself. You are everything to me. I wish you and Gail
could be better friends, and I wish you every happiness in life.
Sometimes I look at you, with your parties, and your dresses,
and your glamorous friends and your crazy life, and I wonder if
you really are as happy as you ought to be.

I do hope so, my darling, darling girl.

Always yours

Dad. xxxxxxxxxxxxxxxxxxx

I look up at Leonard, face streaming.

'Why didn't you tell me about this?'

'I didn't know what it was,' says Leonard, gently. 'Anyway –
client/ attorney privilege, remember?' He looks at the diamond,
with a broad smile. 'Oh, I'm so pleased for you, Sophie. Do try
not to mention it to the authorities.'

I hold it up to the light. It's spotlessly clear, possibly flawless. It has dozens of carats. It's a monster.

'I'll chip off something for me, something for May,' I say.
'He'd have loved her, too.'

'Yes, I think so.'

And then we have to get home, my heart in my mouth the entire time.

Cal can't believe it. He stretches his long legs out on our moth-eaten sofa, nuzzling May the whole time.

'Oh my God,' he keeps saying. 'The Tate . . . and this . . .'

He glances at me. 'You know what this means?'

I smile back at him. 'We're going to be rich?'

'Argh,' he yells, and buries his face in his hand. 'Oh, no, no, no, no.'

'Your worst nightmare.'

'The worst thing that could possibly ever happen.'

I smile, and look at him, and he looks back at me.

'I just want to say,' I say. 'You and May – you are everything. Everything a girl could ever dream of.'

'And you to me, Cinders,' he says. 'But can we turn the central heating on now?'

'I don't think we have to,' I say. 'I think summer is finally here.'